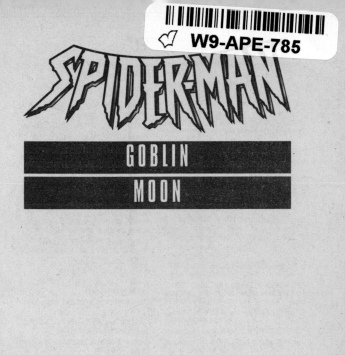

SPIDER-MAN

GOBLIN
MOON

W9-APE-785

MARVEL®

SPIDER-MAN®

GOBLIN
MOON

KURT BUSIEK
AND
NATHAN ARCHER

ILLUSTRATIONS BY ED HANNIGAN AND AL MILGROM

MARVEL®

BP BOOKS, INC.
NEW YORK

BERKLEY BOULEVARD BOOKS, NEW YORK

If you purchased this book without a cover, you should be aware that this book is stolen property. It was reported as "unsold and destroyed" to the publisher and neither the author nor the publisher has received any payment for this "stripped book."

This is a work of fiction. Names, characters, places, and incidents are either the product of the authors' imaginations or are used fictitiously, and any resemblance to actual persons, living or dead, business establishments, events, or locales is entirely coincidental.

Special thanks to Ginjer Buchanan, John Morgan, Ursula Ward, Mike Thomas, and Steve Behling.

SPIDER-MAN: GOBLIN MOON

A Berkley Boulevard Book
A BP Books, Inc. Book

PRINTING HISTORY
Boulevard/Putnam hardcover edition / June 1999
Berkley Boulevard paperback edition / July 2000

All rights reserved.
Copyright © 1999 Marvel Characters, Inc.
Edited by Steve Roman and Dwight Jon Zimmerman.
Cover design by Claude Goodwin.
Cover art by Bruce Jensen.
Book design by Michael Mendelsohn of MM Design 2000, Inc.
This book may not be reproduced in whole or in part,
by mimeograph or any other means, without permission.
For information address: BP Books, Inc.,
24 West 25th Street, New York, New York 10010.

The Penguin Putnam Inc. World Wide Web site address is
http://www.penguinputnam.com

Check out the Ace Science Fiction/Fantasy newsletter,
and much more, at Club PPI!

ISBN: 0-425-17403-4

BERKLEY BOULEVARD
Berkley Boulevard Books are published by The Berkley Publishing Group,
a division of Penguin Putnam Inc.,
375 Hudson Street, New York, New York 10014.
BERKLEY BOULEVARD and its logo
are trademarks belonging to Penguin Putnam Inc.

PRINTED IN THE UNITED STATES OF AMERICA

10 9 8 7 6 5 4 3 2

For
Super Medic,
the World's Mightiest Stuffed Lobster

"Medic Mirror on the wall,
who needs my help the most of all?"

ACKNOWLEDGMENTS

The authors would like to acknowledge the invaluable assistance of Keith "Muss 'Em Up" DeCandido, the support of their friends and family, and the work of Stan Lee and Steve Ditko, for creating both Spider-Man and the Green Goblin, and John Romita, Gil Kane, and Gerry Conway, in addition to Lee and Ditko, for the stories that made both characters so vivid and compelling.

They would also like to thank their mothers for not throwing out their comic books.

AUTHORS' NOTE

This story takes place shortly before the start of "The Gathering of Five" and "The Final Chapter" storylines, somewhere between *Amazing Spider-Man* #430/*Spectacular Spider-Man* #252, and *Amazing Spider-Man* #438/*Spectacular Spider-Man* #260.

Prologue

The music was soft and sweet, blending smoothly with the hum of conversation and the clatter of ice in liquor. A hundred elegantly clothed bodies milled beneath the gentle light of the penthouse chandeliers. A woman's sudden burst of laughter added a bright, feminine accent, and Norman Osborn smiled a thin, tight smile as he looked over the happy throng.

The sheep were gathered together at his bidding, bleating contentedly at one another, pleased he had chosen them for shearing. Everything was going smoothly.

Almost everything, at any rate. He caught sight of an empty champagne glass perched on the rim of a potted palm, and another on a windowsill. The tight little smile tightened further at the sight of this imperfection.

"Norman!" someone said, and Osborn turned, still smiling, to find himself face-to-face with Howard Thurston, CEO of International Substrate.

"Howie," Osborn said, transferring a half-full champagne glass to his left hand and reaching out to shake hands. The smile broadened, hearty and full. "Good to see you! I'm so glad you could make it."

"So am I," Thurston said. "Great party!" He held up his own champagne glass. "Quite a spread. And *this* stuff must have set you back a little!"

"Only the best for my guests," Osborn agreed. "The best food, the best champagne."

"And only the best guests," Thurston said, grinning. "Was that the mayor I saw over by the piano?"

Osborn glanced in the direction of the grand piano, but could not make out faces through the intervening crowd. "I believe so; he's certainly around here somewhere."

"Eager to mingle with his supporters and keep them happy, eh?" Thurston glanced around. "Well, if he's looking for money for his next campaign, it looks like you've done half his work for him—you must have every millionaire in New York here tonight!"

"Oh, I don't think so," Osborn said quietly. "I set the bar a good bit higher than *one* million."

Thurston laughed. He clapped Osborn on the arm. "Good one!"

Osborn's smile turned stiff and formal as he resisted the temptation to tell this tipsy buffoon that he hadn't been joking. Instead he said, "It's been good to see you, Howie, but I'm afraid there are some details I need to attend to. I do need to make sure that *everyone* is having a good time."

"Sure, sure!" He clapped Osborn on the sleeve again. "You go to it." He grinned and turned away.

Osborn also turned away, not grinning at all, and began making his way toward the kitchen of the rented penthouse.

As he moved smoothly between bodies wrapped in expensive silks and fine linens Osborn clenched his teeth in annoyance. Howie Thurston doubtless thought himself rich and powerful and important, and thought that he had been invited tonight in tribute to his importance. He thought he was here because Osborn considered him an equal worthy of acknowledgment.

Thurston was a fool. He had been invited only because he, through his money and connections, might be useful someday. Osborn gulped the last of his champagne and set the glass on a nearby table as he passed.

"Mr. Osborn!"

A woman's voice; Osborn turned.

"I don't know if you remember . . ." the plump woman in the cream-colored gown began, but Osborn cut her off.

"Of course I do," he said. "Anne Aarons! It's good to see you again." He bent and kissed her cheek, then noticed the attractive young woman Aarons had in tow. She was a petite thing in a low-cut evening dress of deep red satin, dark hair tied back demurely. "And this must be Rebecca," Osborn said. He took her hand and kissed her fingertips.

Rebecca was obviously startled by this old-fashioned affectation; Osborn, seeing her expression, quickly explained, "Forgive me; I spent several years in Europe, and I sometimes forget I'm back home."

"Oh, that's all right, Mr. Osborn!" Rebecca said quickly. "I think it's sweet."

"Ah, for someone as lovely as yourself to call me sweet, Ms. Aarons . . ."

"Becky. Please just call me Becky."

"And you must call me Norman," Osborn replied. "Anne, you never told me your daughter had grown into such a beauty!"

"I didn't want to brag," the elder Aarons said, smiling beatifically.

"Anne, Becky, I do hope I'll see more of you later, but right now there's something I really *must* attend to—you'll forgive me?"

"Of course."

Osborn kissed Becky's hand again, then released it and continued on his way toward the penthouse kitchen.

Behind him he could hear Becky murmuring, "You were right, Mother, he *is* charming!"

And her mother answered, "And he's alone in the world. You could do worse than getting to know him."

Osborn hid his anger at that. The hypocritical old biddy was trying to use her daughter to seduce favors from her betters, now that she was too deteriorated to do it herself. And she thought that *he,* Norman Osborn, could be tempted by a pretty face and a well-filled bodice! Did she think he would let her daughter weasel into his affections, so that she could steal away a chunk of his fortune?

It was just money, and he could always make more, but he would never yield any of it to such worthless and obvious baggage.

He reached the kitchen door and marched in as a tail-coated waiter dodged quickly out of his way. Once inside he looked about at the bustling efficiency of the staff, hurrying to keep the food and drink flowing.

Arthur Lewiston, vice president of public relations for Osborn Chemical, was standing by a counter overseeing the entire operation; Osborn made his way to Lewiston's side, took his elbow, and directed him toward the gleaming silver door of the kitchen's walk-in refrigerator.

Lewiston, startled as he was, knew better than to resist; he opened the refrigerator door and stepped inside, Osborn right behind him.

"What is it, Mr. Osborn?" he asked worriedly.

"Lewiston," Osborn growled, "why are there empty glasses everywhere out there? On the furniture, on the windowsills—those should be back here, out of sight of the guests!"

"Mr. Osborn, the staff is collecting the empties, but sometimes they get a little behind—I told them that it was more important to be sure everyone was being served . . ."

"They're *both* important!" Osborn interrupted. "I want everything perfect. I want this place to look clean and inviting *every second*. I want those glasses cleaned up. You hired these people, Lewiston—you couldn't find competent help, waiters who can collect empties efficiently?"

Lewiston was sweating, despite the cool of the refrigerator. "Ah . . . maybe I didn't emphasize it enough . . ." he stammered.

"Maybe you didn't." Osborn took the lapel of Lewiston's jacket between his thumb and forefinger. "Lewiston, do I have to do *everything* myself? Can't you even get something as simple as throwing a party right?"

"I'm doing my best, sir . . ."

"Well, it's *not good enough!*" He brushed Lewiston back with an irritable wave, releasing his jacket. "I want it done *right*. Now, you tell these morons you hired that I don't want to see a single empty glass left uncollected for more than fifteen seconds, and you make them understand that I *mean* it."

"Yes, sir."

"And if I need to come back here again and do it myself, you'll regret it."

"Yes, sir," Lewiston said. "I understand. I'll attend to it."

"See that you do."

Osborn glared at Lewiston for a second longer, then turned, straightened his tux, and strode calmly out of the refrigerator, smiling politely past the terrified hirelings who ducked out of his path.

Behind him Lewiston emerged more slowly, his face pale, and beckoned to the maitre d'. Osborn did not bother to look back; he left the kitchen and returned to his guests.

He was greeted by smiles and waves; as he made his way through the crowd he smiled and waved in return, acknowledging each person who called his name or a remark.

"Lovely party, Norman!"

"Good to see you again, Mr. Osborn!"

"Norman, your chef is a genius!"

He stepped out on the terrace. The crowd was much thinner here—the weather was unseasonably chilly and raw, keeping most of the guests inside.

The clouds that had hovered over the city earlier had broken, however, and a bright full moon shone down, its light sparkling from the glass facades of midtown's towers so brightly that the gaily colored party lights strung along the terrace seemed washed out and dim by comparison. Osborn stared up at that moon for a moment, then crossed to the railing. He gripped it in both hands and looked out at the city.

Traffic was heavy on Fifth Avenue, forty floors below, cutting a yellow river of headlights and taxicabs through the darkened office towers. The people on the sidewalks looked like scurrying insects—a cliche, but true all the same.

And that's what they *were,* Osborn told himself: nothing more than insects. Little people leading their miserable, meaningless little lives, hardly daring to ever look up at the world around them.

And most of the people at this party he was giving were no better. They were marginally more useful, or he wouldn't have allowed them to be there, and they undoubtedly thought of themselves as powerful and important, but they were fools and weaklings, every one of them.

They might think that because they were rich, because the little people deferred to them, because the *real* men like Osborn himself deigned to notice them, that they had some significance, some place in the world, that they knew something of how the world worked and what life was about—but Osborn knew better.

None of them understood. Not for a moment.

He understood.

He looked out at the city, at the streets and skyscrapers and hurrying people, and he knew that it was all there to be *used,* to be possessed, to be controlled—and that he, Norman Osborn, was there to use it, possess it, control it.

He *would* control it, and soon. His plans were already under way.

And not just the city. *Everything* was there for him to dominate—all the world, all the *universe.* He simply needed the will to take it, needed to defeat those who might resist him, and needed to never let up.

That was the real secret: Never let up, not for an instant. Never be satisfied. Never say, "Enough." Because no matter how much he had, how much he owned, how much he controlled . . .

There's always more.

And he intended to have it *all.*

Osborn released his grip on the railing; his fingers had left deep, irregular dents in the wrought iron. He turned back to the party.

He smiled.

Part One

One

irens still howled on Eleventh Avenue and red light splashed over the stone and scaffolding, but the police hadn't yet set foot inside the old IRT powerhouse that stood between 58th and 59th Streets. The building took up the entire block west from Eleventh Avenue to the Hudson River, and was now part of Con Edison's electrical grid for midtown Manhattan; it was built like a fortress, the doors few and easily secured. The Rat Pack had undoubtedly chosen it as their latest target with that near-impenetrability in mind.

The scaffolding that had surrounded the ground floor for more than a year, while the exterior was cleaned and repaired, added another complication for any direct assault.

Most importantly, though, the possibility of hostages kept the forces of Midtown North at bay. When the Rat Pack had first burst in, half an hour after midnight, they had herded most of Con Edison's night crew to an exit on West 58th Street—but no one was sure that *everyone* other than the intruders had been chased out of the building.

And no one outside knew just what the Rat Pack had planned. Charging in after them might get someone killed.

With that in mind, the city's defenders encircled the building and waited. Traffic on the lower end of the Henry Hudson Parkway was stopped or redirected for fear of snipers, while police deployed along the warehouses on West 58th Street, behind the row of tour buses stored along that block of West 59th, and under the scaffolding on Eleventh Avenue.

Meanwhile, inside the plant, half a dozen masked figures in olive-drab leather were moving quickly and efficiently along the floor of the power plant, each carrying two satchel charges to points predetermined to cause maximum damage to the immense turbines.

And eighty feet overhead, upside down on the ceiling, Spider-Man paced the leader of the bomb-carrying invaders. Moving smoothly and fluidly through the shadows, ducking around girders, he skittered as easily along the ancient ironwork as the men below crossed the concrete floor. Clinging by his fingertips and toes, his attention was entirely on his prey and not at all on his own precarious position.

Exactly how he could cling so easily to virtually any surface was a mystery, even to him—he simply knew he could, and had been able to ever since that day in high school, long ago, when he was bitten by a dying spider at a demonstration on the effects of radioactivity. Somehow that mishap had given him the proportional speed and strength of the spider, along with a spider's ability to stick to walls and ceilings, and a mysterious "spider-sense" that warned him of danger.

He'd never found any mention of a "spider-sense" in textbooks on arachnids, but he undeniably possessed this almost-supernatural ability, and made good use of it in his crime-fighting career. It was his spider-sense, combined with his amazing speed, that let him take on bigger, stronger, and more numerous foes and win—he would know when and where a blow was coming, when and where he could avoid an attack. Only a very few enemies, with special abilities of their own, could take him by surprise.

He wasn't bulletproof, and didn't wear armor; he relied on his spider-sense to help him *dodge* bullets. It was his primary defense.

And his greatest weapon, aside from his incredible spider-strength, was his web shooters. These were tiny high-pressure jets, mounted on each wrist and triggered by double-tapping buttons on his palms, that sprayed out streams of web fluid of his own invention. He had developed the formula while still a teenager, and put it to good use ever since.

His "webbing," which was stored in liquid form in little metal cartridges, hardened instantly on contact with air; by adjusting the spray he could make it into a long, ropy strand strong enough to hold a quarter of a ton, a simple adhesive, or a fine mesh suitable for wrapping and holding almost anything.

This webbing was not entirely stable. The same reaction with the air that hardened it continued, and after an hour or so it would crumble into a fine powder—harmless, but also useless. That was why he had never managed to sell it for industrial use. Despite his talents as a chemist, he now made a living as a crime photographer, specializing in photos of himself in action as Spider-Man.

He'd snapped a few quick photos from an office doorway as the Rat Pack entered the big room, then webbed his camera to a steel pillar, the auto-timer running and the motion sensor tracking him, before running up the wall, out of the invaders' line of sight.

They hadn't noticed him, of course, despite his red-and-blue costume; practically no one ever really looked up in places like this, which was why Spider-Man preferred ceilings. Hanging unnoticed overhead gave him time to observe the situation and think out his approach before the fun began. He generally tried to make it look, to anyone watching, as if he just burst in on the bad guys and bounced around at whim, bashing away; sometimes that really was what he did, but usually he preferred to plan out his attack. He was less likely to get hurt, and his opponents were less likely to escape, when he took a moment to figure out an effective approach before he threw himself into action.

These guys were pros, from the look of it, moving quietly and efficiently; the only sounds were trotting footsteps and the sirens and traffic noise outside. Nobody was calling last-minute questions or instructions.

But then, this was the Rat Pack, and they were supposed

to be very good at what they did. All the newspaper reports said so.

Spider-Man smiled grimly under his mask. *He* was good at what he did, too, and it was about time he'd caught up to these guys. He'd been after them for weeks.

The Rat Pack had first appeared a few years back. Initially they were scavengers, moving about the country, picking through the ruins after various disasters, stealing buried valuables, robbing corpses, salvaging abandoned weapons, and generally pilfering anything they could without a fight. The nature of the disaster didn't matter—floods, earthquakes, super hero battles, anything that left temporary chaos. They had run afoul of super heroes on occasion, had changed leaders, but had never been completely defeated.

They referred to each other by numbers instead of using names; their leader, whoever he might be at the moment, was always Number One. They used military tactics, careful planning, and whatever equipment they could get.

They had gradually gotten bolder, tackling less damaged targets but still mostly scavenging—until a few months ago, when they had begun a new pattern.

Now they stayed in New York City, where they would appear for a few days, striking frequently at one vital part of the city's infrastructure after another, looting each site and demanding ransom in exchange for not destroying it. Sometimes they carried out their threats; sometimes, either because of interference from police or super heroes, or for no apparent reason, they fled without doing any serious damage. After each series of raids they would vanish for weeks, but then reappear again in a new series.

So far, they had done a great deal of damage and caused New Yorkers massive frustration as their strikes snarled traffic, shut down the subways, cut off telephone service, or created other such nuisances, but they had collected very few of the ransoms demanded. Because they were continuing their raids despite this lack of success, Spider-Man suspected that they were playing at something beyond the obvious, that there was some as-yet-undetermined method to their apparent madness. They weren't stupid, going by their tactics; why would they stick to a strategy that clearly wasn't working well?

But just what they hoped to gain by closing bridges, tying up subway lines, or blacking out chunks of the city, he couldn't guess.

That meant he couldn't devise a long-term strategy of his own against the Rat Pack; he had to deal with their appearances on a case-by-case basis.

And in the present case, the first priority was obviously to get those explosives out of the way; this installation wasn't one of Con Ed's bigger establishments, but New York couldn't afford to lose even this plant's electrical output.

There were six men down there, carrying two explosive charges apiece—one bomb for each of the twelve big turbines. That was hardly even a challenge for an experienced web-slinger; he had no need to get fancy. He eyed the distances and angles quickly, estimated the lead man's speed—he had had years of practice at this sort of thing, and needed only a second or two to make his calculations.

And a moment later a red-and-blue figure swooped down out of the darkness on a forty-foot cord of webbing, yodeling a poor imitation of Tarzan's famous yell. The lead raider turned, startled, just in time to catch a bright red boot in the center of his chest.

The satchel charge in his hand went flying, and a strand of sticky webbing shot out, snagging it in midair.

"Hey, whatcha got?" Spidey called. "Can I see? Didja bring me one?" He reached the top of his arc and let himself go, landing lightly atop one of the huge turbines. His strange adhesion meant that he didn't need to worry about sliding off; his feet clung easily to the metal surface. He turned, the satchel charge in his hand, to look down at the Rat Packers. The leader was already rolling smoothly to his feet again, and the others were pulling weapons from their packs—AK-47s, by the look of them—and bringing them to bear on Spider-Man.

At a hand-gesture from their leader they spread out, the right- and left-most raiders going wide and drawing beads on Spider-Man from their respective positions. Clearly, they hoped to pin him down atop the turbine and catch him in a crossfire.

But aiming the guns meant dropping the charges they'd been carrying. Three of them still had their second charges slung on their belts, but the others had dropped both.

That was what Spider-Man had hoped for. They didn't know how fast he was, or how little guns concerned him. He slammed the satchel he held against a railing and said, "Aw, I think I broke it!" Then he fired a fresh stream of fluid at a steel beam overhead; by the time it connected with a wet "splut" sound he was snapping back the arm that held the web-line, hurling himself upward. He was already in midair, swinging down again, as he said, "But you've got more of them, and I just *know* you wanna share!"

The warm, stagnant air of the powerhouse, so different from the sharp fall air outside, rushed past him as he swooped down. Automatic rifles stuttered in three-round bursts, but another strand of web fired at an overhead crane let him change course in midair, dodging the bullets so quickly his spider-sense barely had time to tingle. He landed feet-first against a steel upright and ran quickly down its vertical surface; more webbing flashed out. A moment later two more satchels had been flung up onto the high catwalk along the north wall, above the offices and the crane track.

The Rat Pack's team leader finally spoke, shouting to be heard over the gunfire. He bellowed just three words: "Check your masks!"

Spidey didn't pause to think what that might mean; he was swinging from line to line, gathering up more of the explosive satchels, and kicking the gunmen as he sailed past. Glass shattered somewhere overhead as more bullets flew; he hoped Con Ed wouldn't be too upset about a few bulletholes and shot-out windows. He didn't think ordinary bullets were going to do any real damage to the solid metal casings of the turbines—those machines had been grinding away since 1904, and they'd been built to last.

He'd retrieved all the loose satchels now—nine of the twelve—and taken down two of the invaders. One was webbed to the floor; the other he hadn't been able to web yet, just kicked him in the belly and knocked the wind out of him.

The firing had stopped, he realized as he delivered the last of the nine satchels to the north catwalk; he turned and looked down.

The four men who were still upright were looking up at him, and he realized that there were protrusions on the fronts of their masks, which he hadn't really noticed before—some sort of air filters. They were wearing gas masks.

"That's silly," Spidey said to himself. He looked around at the turbine room—roughly seventy feet high at the sides and eighty at the center of the arched roof, at least eighty feet wide from the galleries on the north side to the interior wall on the south, and more than a hundred and fifty *yards* long. Did they think they were carrying enough gas to flood a room *this* size? They might be able to make a good-sized cloud, but he could hold his breath and swing down through it.

And yet they were, indeed, flinging gas canisters around. What *kind* of gas Spider-Man couldn't tell, but white clouds of vapor were hissing up on all sides.

Well, he told himself, he'd better put a stop to *that*. If the stuff was corrosive or long-lasting it might be a serious inconvenience for good ol' Con Ed. Besides, they didn't know how long he could hold his breath. It was time to put these people away.

He took a deep breath, grabbed his web-line, and launched himself out into the air.

One of the men had a knife out and was hacking at the webbing holding down his companion; Spidey decided that was the next target. He let go of his web-line and dropped lightly to the floor, his landing momentarily blowing away the thickening clouds of gas.

Even holding his breath and with his mask in place, Spidey could smell what was in those clouds—tear gas.

"I say, old chum, bit of a pea-souper tonight, eh wot?" he said, in an absolutely abominable fake British accent. "Good night to stay home and take a little nap!"

His fist connected with the knife-wielder's jaw, and the man went down—but his spider-sense tingled, and with inhuman speed and agility he turned and launched himself into a sideways handspring, inches ahead of a stream of bullets.

He landed on a patch of open floor, not far from a spurting gas canister, and again his spider-sense tingled. But why? His chest was beginning to feel tight, and his eyes were watering, but he could go much longer than this without a problem.

No need to retreat to fresh air yet. Instead he headed for the nearest Rat Packer, bounded lightly onto the man's shoulders, then reached down to grab his gas mask.

The green-clad invader collapsed under the unexpected weight, the mask coming off in Spidey's hands—but before he could don it, his spider-sense jangled for a split second before something slammed into his back, and a fierce jolt rammed through him.

He had felt that horrible sensation before—he had been hit with a taser, an electric "stun-gun" that was firing disabling but non-fatal voltage through him.

At least, it would have been disabling for a normal man; for someone with the proportionate speed and strength of a spider it shouldn't really have been much more than an annoyance. In fact, the shock was not enough by itself to do much more than slow him down momentarily.

That first impact had been startling, though, and as he

had arched his back in response he had inadvertently gasped, taking a good, deep breath of the tear gas that surrounded him.

The fabric of his mask did nothing to stop it; he felt it burning his throat and nostrils, and he began coughing uncontrollably. Combined with the taser bolt it was enough to stop him; he fell to the floor in a ball, choking. That was their plan all along, he realized; that was why they had used the gas. They were good, better than he had thought.

The gas mask fell from his hand, and was snatched away.

"All right, clear out," someone said. "This operation's blown. Seven, cut Eleven free; Five, you give Fifteen a hand." A radio crackled, and Spider-Man heard an electronic mumble but could make out none of the words.

He didn't waste time trying to stop anyone in his gassed state; he rolled away from the still-hissing cylinder, groping for clear air, trying to keep his hands steady enough to use his web shooters.

It took three shots before he managed to get a line securely anchored on an overhead girder; he was coughing too hard to aim properly. At last, though, he swung out of the cloud of noxious smoke into clearer air atop a turbine.

By then, as he saw at a glance, the Rat Pack had fled the main room into the maze of offices and storerooms along the West 58th Street side of the building.

He didn't follow them; his eyes and nose and throat were still burning, his back still aching, and besides, the building was surrounded by cops. There was nowhere for the Rat Pack to go; he could leave them for later. Instead of pursuing he stood up on the turbine and fired another web-line. He pulled himself up to the high catwalk, still coughing, and then up to the ceiling and out through a bullet-shattered skylight, until at last he knelt atop the power plant, mask pulled up to expose his mouth, coughing the last of the fumes from his lungs.

Around him, in addition to the normal sounds of New

York at night, he could hear sirens, shouting, and revving engines, but he was still too shaken to pay much attention.

Finally, though, he had his wits back—and at the crack of a pistol he snapped upright and ran westward along the rooftop, toward the sound.

There he saw that he had been wrong in his belief that the Rat Pack was trapped. The raiders were escaping—by water. Police had surrounded the power plant, but the terrorists had gone out a window, not onto the sidewalk but onto the scaffolding, one story up. From there they had run to the west end of the building and ridden a zipline to the roof over the Sanitation Department's West 59th Street pier—a zipline they had apparently set up earlier, but which neither Spider-Man nor the cops had noticed in the darkness.

A speedboat had been waiting in the gap between two garbage barges, and now they were halfway across the Hudson, on their way to New Jersey, far beyond the range of Spidey's web shooters. A cop had taken a shot at them from the shore, but to no real purpose.

No one in Manhattan was going to catch them now, and the police had not thought to call out their own boats in time.

"Rats," Spidey muttered.

He meant it as an expression of frustration, but he realized as he said it that these people *were* rats, after a fashion—they had named themselves after rats, and modeled some of their tactics on the sneaky little rodents. Rats were smart; they always had a way out.

And these rats had escaped.

Then he remembered that they might not *all* be gone— his webbing might have been tough enough to keep that one man pinned to the floor, and there were still those bombs to dispose of. He hurried back to the broken skylight and climbed back into the building.

The man was gone; the severed remnants of the webbing that had held him were still there on the floor. Half a dozen now-empty gas canisters still lay scattered on the concrete, as well; the cloud of tear gas had dissipated, but the place still stank of it.

And over by the door down to the south side of the plant were three olive-drab bundles, apparently dropped as the men were fleeing. Spidey stared at them.

The last three satchel charges. But why would the Rat Pack have dropped them? The plan to blow up the turbines had been stopped, but the Rat Pack never abandoned perfectly good weapons without a good reason.

And how had they planned to detonate those bombs, if they *had* managed to place them properly?

"Oh, my God," Spidey said, as he ran for the bombs. His spider-sense was quiet, which was the only reassurance he had that those things weren't going to blow up in his face in response to a radio signal.

It could be radio; it could be a timer; either way, he had to get them out of the building, away from people, as fast as possible.

He could hear voices—cops and Con Edison workers re-entering the building, probably. If he didn't get the explosives out *now,* whoever that was might die. He snatched up the three bombs and fired a web-line upward, half-expecting to hear them ticking.

They weren't—but then, electronic timers and radio triggers didn't tick.

The nine bombs on the catwalk had to be collected as well, of course, but a moment later he found himself clinging to the ceiling again as he smashed more glass out of the skylight so as to be able to fit a great mass of congealing webbing out into the open air—a mass of webbing that contained an even dozen satchel charges.

Once he was outside he ran westward, toward the river— and his spider-sense began to itch. By the time he reached the west end of the power plant's roof he felt as if robot ants in hob-nailed boots were doing six-legged polkas inside his skull; he didn't waste time on anything fancy, but simply bounded down from the roof to the edge of the Henry Hudson Parkway, where he heaved the huge ball of webbed bombs out over the water.

They went off in midair with a tremendous roar and a flash as bright as lightning; the shockwave knocked him back off his feet onto the pavement, and he heard windows shattering somewhere behind him.

But just windows. The lights never flickered; the power station was still on line and running smooth.

That was a victory of sorts. The Rat Pack had escaped, and his throat felt lined with broken glass where he had breathed that gas, but except for a few windows and a few dozen bulletholes the power plant was still intact. And he had a roll of pictures waiting inside that he might be able to sell to the *Daily Bugle;* the shots of himself and the fight might not come out, what with the clouds of gas in the way and how fast everything had moved, but at the very least he had pictures of the Rat Pack entering the room.

It wasn't what he'd hoped for when he had slipped into the building just twenty minutes earlier, but for now it would have to do.

TWO

The morning sun streamed in through the kitchen window so brightly that Mary Jane Parker's red hair seemed to be glowing like fire on a winter's night; Peter Parker paused for a moment in the doorway to marvel at it. She was seated at the table, with a bowl of corn flakes sitting half-eaten before her as she read the morning edition of the *Daily Bugle,* and she was so beautiful that he wondered again how an apparent loser like himself had ever wound up married to her.

She looked up from the paper and smiled at him. "You're in the news again, Tiger," she said.

"I am?" He crossed the room and peered over her shoulder, brushing aside a wisp of that crimson hair.

"No pictures of Spider-Man," Mary Jane remarked. "Just the Rat Pack."

"I took those before I webbed the camera in place," Peter replied. "None of the shots of me came out. I *did* set the motion sensor, but I was moving pretty fast, and the timing was off—not to mention there being tear gas all over the place. All I got was a few blurry glimpses of a boot or two."

"Jonah didn't want pictures of your boots?" She blinked at him, feigning wide-eyed innocence.

"I didn't even ask."

"Oh, you should have! They're such *cute* boots."

"I didn't know anyone but the Rat Pack had seen I was there," Peter said, looking at the paper and ignoring his wife's comment on his footwear.

"They didn't, for sure," Mary Jane said, pointing to a paragraph. "Maybe a couple of quick glimpses, it says here—one Con Ed manager is pretty sure he saw you jump from the roof to the Henry Hudson. But even if they hadn't seen you they found webbing all over the place, and where there's web, there's spider."

Peter frowned. "Maybe I should try to find a way to make the stuff dissolve faster."

Mary Jane lowered the paper. "So they won't know you've been there?" she said. "Like that's a big secret? Don't be silly. And why mess with success? You've made that goo the same way for years, and it's worked just fine. Are you afraid Con Ed will complain you've been littering?"

Peter grimaced. "They might," he said. "Spider-Man isn't the most popular guy in town."

"You saved their plant from being blown to bits, Tiger; that shift manager gives you credit right here in the paper, says he saw you fling the bomb into the Hudson. Good old Jonah says on the editorial page that you were probably working with the Rat Pack all along and the bomb missed the machinery by accident, but Con Ed's people aren't buying that. I think after seeing that explosion they'll cut you some slack on a couple of broken windows and some leftover web that dissolved before any cleanup crews could have arrived, anyway."

That all made sense, but Peter couldn't help finding other things to worry about.

"Okay, so Con Edison loves me," he said. "But I still think I should try to make faster-dissolving webbing. What if the Rat Pack got some of that webbing back to their home base intact, and got their chemists working on it right away . . ."

"The Rat Pack has chemists?"

Peter stopped and considered that. Mary Jane ate her cereal as she watched his face.

"They might," Peter said. "They seem to have everything else they need."

"And if they *do* have chemists?"

"Then they might be able to analyze my webs and find a way to make their own, or to dissolve mine on contact."

"In an hour or less? Could *you* do that?"

"Well, yeah, MJ," he said. "Of course I could, if I had enough intact samples to work from. It's just a matter of identifying the solvent base . . ."

"Peter Parker, Boy Chemist," she interrupted. "And if they figured this out, would dissolving the stuff be any more effective than cutting it?"

"Um . . ." He thought that over for a moment, then answered sheepishly, "No. Not really."

"So do you think the Rat Pack will really bother collecting and analyzing samples?"

"Um . . ."

"Has *any* super-villain done it yet? You've been up against plenty of genius-level wackos."

"Well . . ."

She smiled triumphantly up at him, then looked down at the spoon in her hand, then at the empty place across the table.

"Sit," she said, pointing at the empty chair with the spoon. "Eat. Pretend you live here."

Peter smiled; he had lived almost his entire life in this house. He had grown up here with his Aunt May and Uncle Ben, and had inherited the place after Aunt May died—but sometimes he felt as if his *real* life was swinging around New York in red-and-blue longjohns, and mundane details like breakfast cereal were intrusions.

Necessary intrusions, though—he had to eat. He fetched himself a bowl and spoon from the cabinet and started in on a serving of corn flakes.

A moment later he paused and said, "You know, about the webbing—I don't know *what* the Rat Pack would bother with, and what they wouldn't."

"Don't tell J. Jonah Jameson that," Mary Jane replied. "You'd destroy his faith in Spider-Man's secret involvement in every criminal scheme in New York."

"No, really," Peter insisted. "I don't know what they're doing, or how they're picking their targets. I mean, here's this bunch of highly trained crazies working together, with lots of fancy equipment and the brains to set up and carry out elaborate plans, and what are they doing with it? They always used to be roving scavengers, and okay, they've dropped that for now, but what *are* they doing? They're not robbing the Federal Reserve or looting the diamond district or going after any of the other big wads of money lying around the city; instead they're attacking the *city itself,* hitting stuff like subways and power stations, and then demanding ransoms. It's nuts."

"It is? Haven't they collected?"

"Oh, a couple of times, but mostly not. The mayor won't pay any ransoms. They only got paid when they went after private stuff, like that shipment of medicine they hijacked a few weeks back—and not always then."

"Maybe they're just setting up for some really big ransom, something where even the mayor has to give in."

"Maybe." Peter ate another spoonful of cereal, chewing thoughtfully. "At first I thought they were trying to run a really big-scale protection racket—you know, 'nice little city you got here, be a shame if something happened to it,' like that. I thought maybe they figured that would be something they could make permanent, where robbing the Federal Reserve is more of a one-shot. But if it's supposed to be extortion, they aren't very good at it."

"Well, maybe they aren't," Mary Jane suggested.

"But they ought to be," Peter insisted. "They're smart and organized. I can't believe they'd keep at something that doesn't work."

"They aren't really keeping at it, are they? I mean, they've been popping up for a couple of days, then disappearing for weeks at a time."

Peter nodded. "Yeah, I think they always attack at the full moon." He shook his head. "I don't know what they're doing in between."

"Maybe they have day jobs," Mary Jane suggested, "and the Rat Pack stuff is just, um . . . moonlighting?"

Peter mimed throwing his spoon at her. "I'll pretend you didn't say that."

"Well, don't *all* the crazies come out during the full moon?" Mary Jane asked.

"It seems like it," Peter admitted, "but these guys are smarter than that. I think they're doing it on purpose—I think they make their raids at the full moon because that's when the *other* crazies are more likely to be out, so the cops and everyone are busy, and there's less time and energy to deal with the Rat Pack."

"It comes out to the same thing," Mary Jane pointed out. She looked down at the newspaper again. "Whyever they're doing it, they're sure stirring things up. Jonah's in rare form on the editorial page, demanding something be done."

"He's not the only one," Peter said. "They've got a *lot* of people upset. Maybe that's got something to do with why they're doing this, instead of just robbing banks." He frowned thoughtfully.

"They're ticking off people *I* wouldn't want to mess with," Mary Jane said. "There's a quote here from our old friend Norman Osborn, and he's peeved."

"Osborn?" Peter leaned over and tugged at the paper to see what Osborn had said.

Norman Osborn was perhaps the one man Peter Parker, the amazing Spider-Man, feared and hated more than any other. Peter had still been in high school the first time he met Norman Osborn—though back then he hadn't known it was Osborn.

He had met and fought the Green Goblin, a madman with superhuman strength and an impressive array of nasty gadgets—a bat-shaped jet-powered personal flyer Osborn called a "goblin glider," a "bag of tricks" jammed full of bombs and traps shaped like pumpkins or bats or ghosts, a device in the glove of his costume that spat fiery sparks . . .

The arsenal was secondary, though—it was the man wielding it that truly made the Goblin a dangerous foe. The original Green Goblin was strong, fast, tricky, utterly ruthless, and relentlessly determined.

Others had worn the costume later, and used the gadgets, but the *true* Green Goblin was always millionaire businessman Norman Osborn, chief stockholder and CEO of Osborn Industries.

Spider-Man had learned that secret eventually, had learned also that Osborn's incredible intelligence and vitality—and probably his madness—came from a formula Osborn's former partner in Osborn Industries, a man named Mendel Stromm, had developed. Osborn was trying to mix the formula when it exploded. Spider-Man had found that much out long ago.

And Osborn, in turn, had learned Spider-Man's secrets. He knew that Peter Parker was Spider-Man, and had used that information to taunt him.

The Goblin didn't need money—Osborn was rich, after all. The Goblin had always been driven by a need for power, for control, for dominance over those around him. He had been especially determined to assert himself over Spider-Man, simply because it was Spider-Man who had resisted him.

And it had been in his mad quest to destroy Spider-Man that he had killed the girl Peter Parker loved—Gwen Stacy.

Peter still remembered the entire scene as vividly as if it had just happened—the sight of Gwen plummeting from the bridge, the hideous snap as her neck broke, the sight of Osborn standing there in his ridiculous ugly costume, grinning about it all as if it was all just a big joke.

It was no joke, and Spider-Man had made sure the Goblin knew that. Their fight had ended with the Goblin accidentally impaled on the steel nose of his own goblin glider.

He should have been dead. Everyone thought he *was* dead. No one could survive having sixty pounds of jet-powered steel rammed through his chest.

No one, that is, who hadn't been exposed to Stromm's formula. Osborn had awakened in the city morgue and found that his son Harry was already working to destroy any evidence linking respectable businessman Norman Osborn to the murderous Green Goblin.

Norman had needed time to heal, to recover, to plan; he had gone to Europe, letting all New York believe him dead. In his absence Harry Osborn had become the new Green Goblin—and had died in the process, leaving a widow and an infant son.

And then, eventually, Norman Osborn had returned, to plague Peter Parker anew. He had provided new funding for the financially shaky *Daily Bugle*, becoming co-owner of Peter's primary source of income. He had denounced Spider-Man as a menace. And he had publicly feigned friendship with Peter and Mary Jane—after all, they had been good friends of Harry's—while letting Peter know that their feud was not over, that the worst was yet to come.

The Green Goblin had returned as well—and had "died." Osborn had faked the Goblin's death and abandoned his costumed guise, at least for the moment. He was operating openly as a businessman, and any villainy was being done secretly, through intermediaries, not by flying around on a goblin glider throwing bombs.

Osborn had been quiet of late—which made Peter all the more nervous about him.

Now, though, Osborn was quoted in the paper, denouncing the Rat Pack. If he was making himself publicly visible again, that could not be good.

"Maybe if the Rat Pack gets him mad enough, we'll see the Green Goblin come out of retirement to go after them," Peter said. "I can't say *I'd* be upset by that—any time two of Spidey's enemies want to kill each other, instead of me . . ."

He didn't finish the sentence—partly because he didn't mean it. He didn't think the Rat Pack would stand a chance of killing the Goblin, if it came to that, and much as he wanted their raiding stopped, he had no desire to see the Rat Pack slaughtered.

On the other hand, if the Rat Pack somehow killed Osborn, either as the Goblin or as himself . . . but that wasn't going to happen. Peter had learned long ago that any man's death, even a madman's, was cause for sorrow, not celebration. But if there was any man Peter wouldn't regret seeing dead, Osborn came the closest, after all the pain he had inflicted, all the innocents he had killed. But there was no way the Rat Pack was going to do it.

If the Rat Pack annoyed Osborn enough, though, there was no telling what might happen.

Peter wondered, as he ate his corn flakes, just how annoyed Norman Osborn really was.

Peter Parker didn't see it, but three hours later, in a midtown hotel ballroom where Norman Osborn was the guest speaker at a Rotary luncheon, Osborn had something to say about just how annoyed he really was. He had finished his opening remarks and a few pro forma jokes that drew polite smiles rather than laughter when he looked down at the notes on the lectern in front of him, hesitated, and then pushed them aside.

"Ladies and gentlemen," he said, looking up again, "if you'll pardon me, I'd like to depart from my prepared remarks for a few moments."

The quiet buzz of conversation faded into expectant silence as the audience realized that this wasn't going to be the standard boring, meaningless speech. Glasses were set down on tables, bites of food quickly chewed and swallowed. Osborn looked out at a hundred well-fed, well-groomed faces, all of them awaiting his next word.

"We're all here today," Osborn said, speaking slowly and clearly, as if choosing his every word, "because we're active participants in New York City's business community. We live here and work here, and while we may have interests elsewhere in the world, New York is our home."

He swept his gaze across the room, past dark blue draperies, glittering chandeliers, white tablecloths, shining china, expensive suits, flattering dresses—all the outward signs of wealth.

"Like any home worth living in, New York depends on structures and amenities we hardly ever think about," he continued. "When we run water in the sink, or turn on a light, we don't think about the plumbing or the wiring. It's only when those systems break down that we notice them—when a pipe leaks, or a lightbulb burns out, or the phone doesn't work. On a larger scale, we only notice the city's systems—the subways and water mains and power lines—when something goes wrong, when something breaks down, when someone threatens them."

Everyone in the room was listening now—they knew exactly what Osborn was referring to. All of them were aware of the Rat Pack's depredations.

What they didn't know was what Norman Osborn might have to say on the subject.

"I don't know about you," Osborn said, "but I don't like to worry about the everyday details, so I have maintenance contracts for all my properties. There's a fellow who checks the heating systems regularly. There's someone who inspects the air conditioning. An exterminator takes a look around each building every few weeks to be sure I don't have any nasty little intruders. Instead of waiting for something to go wrong and then paying repair bills, I pay these people an annual fee, and if they find anything that looks as if it could become a problem they're supposed to fix it at no additional charge before it actually breaks.

"And the way I look at it, I have a service contract with the city—I pay my taxes and my utility bills, and in exchange the city is supposed to keep an eye on everything, and keep the city running. If someone tries to break something, the city government should stop that before it becomes a problem, not wait until it's actually been broken.

"And that's not happening. These quasi-military terrorists who call themselves the Rat Pack have been picking away at the city's infrastructure for *three months* now, and our police department has yet to apprehend a single one of them.

"If my exterminator took three months to dispose of termites eating away at the beams in my house, I'd fire him and find a new one—wouldn't you?"

There was a murmur of agreement. Osborn slammed a fist on the lectern and announced, "Well, our city has termites; and they're still chewing away! The police haven't caught them. The mayor hasn't stopped them. I can't fire anyone in the city government—at least, not until the next election—but I *can* tell them that I think they're falling down on the job, and not doing what we pay them for!"

He leaned forward over the lectern and looked out at his audience.

"I understand that this Rat Pack isn't just another bunch of petty thieves. I don't expect miracles. I know sometimes the exterminator can't get every single bug on the first try. But are our elected officials doing *anything* about this menace? Or are they just waiting for the Rat Pack to be satisfied with their take and go away quietly?"

He straightened up. "If one poison doesn't work on a particular infestation, you don't just keep putting down more of the same stuff—you try something else! But our mayor seems content to keep sending the police to tackle these high-tech bandits, and hasn't noticed that the boys in blue aren't getting the job done! We hear the sirens and see the lights, the cruisers go rushing about the city, but when all's said and done they're going back to Police Plaza with not a single prisoner in the back of those cars. These villains are *too much* for ordinary measures.

"It's time to try something new. I don't know what, I'm not an expert, but *something*. The Rat Pack dresses up like soldiers—why not call out the army to go after them? If they want to play soldier, we can play, too!

"But no, that's not *appropriate,* the mayor tells us. It

would be a bad precedent. As if letting outlaws run free is a *good* precedent!

"Or super heroes—New York's rotten with so-called super heroes. Why haven't *they* taken care of these skulking extortionists? Has the mayor asked the Avengers to take a few minutes out of their busy schedule saving the world and clean up a little mess in their own back yard? Has anyone asked Reed Richards of the Fantastic Four to apply some of his famous genius to dealing with this local problem of ours? And if not, *why not?*" He slammed a fist on the lectern and glared out at his listeners. "How can Hizzoner justify this outrageous complacency in the face of a very real, very obvious threat? Will he wait until a power plant is not merely threatened, but *leveled,* before he acts? Must commuters be not merely trapped for hours in stalled subway trains, but slaughtered, before he realizes something a little more than empty expressions of concern and business as usual might be called for?" He paused to wipe a handkerchief across his forehead.

"You tell 'em, Norman!" someone called.

"I *will* tell them," Osborn replied, grabbing the edges of the lectern. "I'll tell anyone who will listen! This rampant terrorism must cease! You all know I'm co-owner of the *Daily Bugle*—well, starting today, the *Bugle* will be devoting itself to a campaign demanding *action,* rather than empty promises and hollow assurances." He picked up a copy of that day's paper and waved it. "You'll see in today's edition that we've covered the Rat Pack's latest outrage, their abortive attack on the old IRT power plant. You'll see that we have interviews with people who were there on the scene, talking about what they saw—and none of them mentioned talking to the police." He shook the paper violently. "*Why not?* These people were there, they might have seen something—why haven't the police questioned them in detail, tracked down every possible lead to the identity and whereabouts of the members of the Rat Pack?"

He smacked the front page with the back of one hand.

"Spider-Man was there last night—at least one man saw him, and a dozen found his webbing inside the plant. Why hasn't *he* done anything to stop the Rat Pack? Why hasn't he told the police what he knows? My partner and publisher of the *Bugle,* Mr. J. Jonah Jameson, believes Spider-Man may even be working *with* the Rat Pack—has anyone investigated *that* possibility? This hooded menace is roaming our streets as free as a bird, while the honest people of this city huddle behind closed doors, afraid of the guns and bombs of terrorists—maybe he *is* working with them. Has anyone even *asked?*"

He dropped the newspaper on a nearby chair and leaned over the lectern again.

"Which side is Spider-Man on?" he demanded. "What's *he* doing about these scavengers? Why hasn't he come forward with what he knows about the Rat Pack?" He pounded a fist on the lectern. "Where is Spider-Man *right now,* and what is he planning?"

He glared out at his audience, as if awaiting an answer.

At that moment Peter Parker was stepping off the elevator at the editorial offices of the *Daily Bugle,* but he had scarcely cleared the elevator door when Betty Brant snagged him by the elbow and turned him around.

"Just who I was looking for," she said. "Jonah said to grab the first photographer I found, and you're always my first choice, Peter, so come on."

"Come on where?" Peter asked, as he allowed himself to be herded back onto the elevator.

"A storm drain near Battery Park," she replied. "The cops have a homicide victim. You've got your camera? And it's loaded?"

"Of course!" Peter let himself be dragged into an elevator, and while Betty pushed the button marked "L" he quickly checked to be sure that yes, his camera did indeed have film in it, and functioning batteries.

A few minutes later, after wading through the midday

crowds on the sidewalks and making their way down into the Grand Central Station subway, they boarded the last car of a southbound 5 train and found a pair of just-vacated seats.

"So who's this we're going to look at?" Peter asked, as they sat down. "You got a description?"

She nodded. "Part of one. The man who found the body called us right after he called the cops. I promised him ten bucks. *He's* probably a wino, but he swore that the victim wasn't."

Peter shivered. "A reporter's life is such a cheerful thing, huh, Betty? Dead bodies and winos."

"Oh, it's not so bad, Peter," she said. "I like it. It beats the heck out of being a secretary—at least I get out of the office more."

"You didn't like being a secretary?" He looked at her sideways.

"I *hated* it," she said, with surprising vehemence.

"It didn't show," Peter said.

For a moment she didn't reply as the subway train pulled into the 33rd Street station. The doors slid open; a handful of people boarded, and then the doors closed and the train rolled on.

"Maybe it wasn't just the job," she said. "Maybe it's who I was back then—scared and mousy, doing what I was told . . ." She shook her head. "I never wanted that job. I only took it because of my mother, and I'm glad that's all over." She looked at Peter and said, "I'll bet you don't miss those days, either. I sure never got the impression you enjoyed your high school career."

"It wasn't so bad," Peter said uncomfortably.

"Oh, come on," Betty said. "Flash Thompson used to rag on you *constantly.* You were practically a textbook example of a nerd."

Peter could hardly deny that—but there had been compensations.

Not that he could tell Betty that. Explaining that it had

been at a high school physics demonstration that he had been bitten by a radioactive spider and acquired super-strength and the ability to stick to walls—well, he wasn't going to tell her that.

And if his social life had mostly been the pits before he started dating Betty, his classes weren't bad—he had loved chemistry and physics. After all, he had learned enough in high school chemistry and his own after-hours research to create the web-fluid he still used.

Uncle Ben and Aunt May had still been alive, too—at least, until that burglar murdered Uncle Ben, and Peter realized that he had to use his abilities as Spider-Man to stop criminals like that from hurting innocent people.

He had done a lot of good as Spider-Man, and that had made the razzing he got in school seem pretty unimportant by comparison.

He had had his failures, of course, but they seemed minor compared to some of what came later. Being Spider-Man had been serious business ever since Uncle Ben died, but back then it was also *fun*. Some of the fun had gone out of it since then—especially since Gwen Stacy died as he tried to rescue her from the Green Goblin.

Gwen was dead—and the Goblin, Norman Osborn, who he had believed for years had died as well, was still alive.

Gwen was long dead, Osborn's son Harry was dead, Aunt May was dead—so *many* of his friends had died! And Osborn was alive and free.

"It wasn't so bad," he repeated.

Betty stared at him, puzzled, then shrugged.

They left the subway at Bowling Green and found Betty's informant waiting where he had said he would be, on the northeast corner of Broadway and Bridge Street—and if he wasn't a wino, he did a good imitation; he wore a ragged overcoat, fingerless gloves, and a four-day growth of graying beard. He took his ten dollars and pointed them in the right direction.

It wasn't hard to find the right storm drain, down between the Coast Guard building and the Staten Island Ferry terminal—it was the one surrounded by cops and yellow crime-scene tape, a few yards from the waiting ambulance.

Peter went to work immediately, snapping pictures of the blanket-covered shape that lay on the stretcher two paramedics were carrying; no one paid much attention to him. Reporters and photographers were all too familiar.

While Peter's camera clicked, Betty found the detective in charge and began asking questions.

Peter could see through the viewfinder that Betty's informant had had at least one thing right—this corpse had not been just a wino. The dead man's shoes were expensive Italian leather, polished to a shine that had somehow survived the stay in the storm drain, and his curly brown hair was trimmed and styled, if somewhat mussed. Everything in between the shoes and hair was covered by the paramedics' yellow blanket, but Peter, having seen his share of gore over the years, didn't mind missing the details of a shooting.

When the body was loaded into the ambulance and the doors were closed the obvious part of Peter's job was done, and he turned his attention to the conversation between Betty and the detective.

". . . Charenton?" Betty was saying. "I know that name from somewhere, don't I? The mayor's office?"

"Not exactly," the detective said. "You've heard the name, though. Paul Charenton was the Public Advocate of the City of New York—he had his *own* office at City Hall." He cleared his throat. "I'm not sure of this, ma'am, so don't quote me, but I believe he's the highest-ranking city official to ever be murdered in New York."

"Then it's definitely murder?" Betty asked, holding out her pocket recorder.

The detective sighed. "There are unmistakable bullet holes in his shirt and chest, complete with powder burns, but no gun anywhere in sight—our forensics boys are still down that storm drain, seeing what they can find, but they swear there's no gun. No gun means no suicide, and people don't get shot and stuffed in storm drains by accident. It's not official, you understand, and I'm just giving my own opinion here, but I think we can safely say that Mr. Paul Charenton was indeed murdered by person or persons unknown."

"You said he was a high-ranking city official," Betty asked. "Do you think the Rat Pack might be behind this killing, as part of their terror campaign against the city?"

"I can't rule it out," the detective said, "but I have no evidence to support it, either. There was no ransom demand; we didn't even know Mr. Charenton was missing. That's not the pattern they've followed up until now."

Peter didn't listen to the rest of the conversation; instead he watched as the ambulance pulled away. The driver didn't bother with lights or siren; after all, Charenton was on the way to the morgue, not a hospital.

Might the Rat Pack have done this? He didn't see why—as the detective had said, no money was involved—but then, he didn't know why the Rat Pack was continuing their raids when they hadn't been collecting many ransoms in the first place.

They *might* have done this—and if so, then something deeper and more complicated than mere ransom demands was going on here, something he didn't understand yet.

And it was something that Spider-Man might want to look into.

Three

The Members' Lounge of the Century Club was quiet the following morning, the thick walls shutting out the noise from the street below. Dust danced gently in the sunlight from the big south-facing windows. Only half a dozen men were present, most of them minding their own business as they sat in the red leather armchairs, reading books and newspapers.

Two of them, however, sat face to face by one of the windows, conversing softly.

"I heard that speech you gave, Norman," one of them said, leaning forward intently, his bald spot catching the light from the window.

"Of course you did, Mr. Mayor," Norman Osborn replied, sitting back comfortably in his leather chair. "That was the *point*."

"If I might be blunt, Norman, you know, I didn't like it much . . ."

"You weren't supposed to," Osborn interrupted.

The mayor ignored this reply and continued. "You talking about how I'm letting down the side, not keeping my end of the bargain with the taxpayers—that *hurts*, Norman. I've tried to be good to you since you got back—why are you busting my chops about this? It's not like these paramilitary yahoos, these Rat Pack jerks, are going after any of *your* stuff—we're all in it together, and we're doing the best we can. This city's come through hell a dozen times, Norman, you know that—we've had Galactus walking around the rooftops, that whatsisname from Atlantis, Namor, invading us, we've had super-villains throwing skyscrapers around like a bunch of kindergarteners having a food fight. These Rat Pack guys, they're strictly small-time, really, and we'll get them sooner or later. You know that, I know that. So why are you giving me such a hard time?"

"Because you *deserve* a hard time," Osborn growled. "You talk as if it were just another garbage strike or something, you call them small-time—haven't you noticed that they're deliberately targeting the city's weakest points, to do the maximum damage to ordinary people? Mr. Mayor, you know I don't expect your police to ticket Galactus for jaywalking the next time he shows up, I know he's out of your league, but these terrorists are *exactly* the sort of problem the city needs to be able to handle!"

As Osborn made this speech the mayor watched his face, looking for some clue to the man's *real* motivation.

Osborn was a puzzle to him. The man had this real split personality—he came on at first as everybody's best buddy, happy to meet you and eager to please, lavish with his money, but then when something went wrong this cold, hard, downright *vicious* side showed through, and the man turned real ruthless.

That was hardly unusual, of course—there were hundreds of people like that in any politician's life. The whole electorate was like that at times.

Osborn, though, took it to an extreme. He could swing back and forth between Mr. Nice Guy and hard-nose jerk in a single sentence.

And when other people pulled the good-cop-bad-cop-all-in-one-head routine, Hizzoner could just about always figure out *why*. He could see that they were nice and friendly when things were going well, and that the mean streak showed when they were scared or angry about something.

But Osborn didn't quite fit. Oh, sure, he *said* he was angry about the Rat Pack, but the mayor didn't buy it. His eyes didn't light up when he talked about it. He wasn't scared of the Rat Pack; he didn't even seem really *mad* at the Rat Pack. You didn't get anywhere in elective politics, certainly not to the top post in the world's greatest city, without learning to read a person's body language, and Osborn's body language wasn't showing frightened or angry.

If he didn't know better, the mayor would have thought Osborn was looking greedy.

Why would the Rat Pack's raids make anyone *greedy?* Did Osborn want a piece of the action?

That didn't make sense. The Rat Pack was a bunch of penny-ante chiselers who'd steal the coins off a dead man's eyes. They'd literally stolen gold teeth from corpses after that Onslaught disaster. Their current extortion scheme was barely paying enough to buy them all a good dinner. They were thoroughly small-time, and Osborn was worth millions.

About two hundred million, the mayor estimated, just personally, not counting his larger influence.

And the Rat Pack weren't touching any of Osborn's holdings—so far as anyone knew.

Of course, who knew just what Osborn's holdings were? The man had a history as tangled as a plate of spaghetti. That crazy partner who went bad on him and then disappeared, the whole mess about someone making up the Green Goblin's dead body to look like Osborn—that had fooled almost *everybody* for a while, and it was still a mystery why Osborn hadn't come back from Europe sooner to clean up the mess. And then Norman's son Harry had gotten himself killed, and there were half a dozen run-ins with costumed types, and the whole business with bailing out the *Daily Bugle*—Hizzoner knew he didn't know the half of it.

But what he did know didn't show any reason why Osborn should be acting like this.

Osborn paused in his speech, and the mayor began, "Now, Norman . . ."

"Let me finish!"

The mayor had thought he *was* finished. He threw up his hands. "Okay, okay! You got something to get off your chest, spit it out!"

Osborn leaned forward and jabbed an accusing finger at

the mayor. "I don't expect you to get out there and face down cosmic menaces," he said, "but this Rat Pack—they're just men with stolen guns and fancy equipment, and they're making fools of you and your staff, and the entire NYPD. They're endangering the lives of the people of this city! If they take out the power system, or flood the subways, hundreds of innocent people could die."

"Yeah, and that would be a tragedy, and we're doing everything we can to prevent it, but c'mon, Norman, you're taking this personally . . ."

"Of course I am!" Osborn shouted, shattering the peace of the lounge and startling the handful of other men present. "Thousands of employees of Osborn Industries live and work in New York, and if the Rat Pack isn't stopped some of them may be *dying* in New York, and I won't stand for it! Those employees are my people; it's my duty to see that they're safe in their homes and my offices and factories, and I take that duty very seriously. And it's *your* duty, as mayor, to see that they're safe! Right now, as long as the Rat Pack's free to do as they please, it doesn't look to me as if New York's doing a very good job of keeping *anybody* safe!"

The mayor stared at him for a minute.

That explanation was the purest load of bull-pucky he'd ever heard. Sure, there were guys out there running companies who really truly cared about their employees, but the idea that Norman Osborn was one of them was less believable than a linebacker in drag.

Osborn was after something—but so far, the mayor didn't know what.

"Look, Norman, I can see you're really upset about this," the mayor said, "and maybe you've got a point, maybe we didn't take these guys as seriously as we should have at first, maybe we thought Spider-Man or the Avengers would take care of them for us, but I swear, we're *trying,* we're doing everything we know how."

"Well, it's *not enough!*" Osborn said, slamming a fist

on the arm of his chair. "Osborn Industries pumps millions of dollars a year into this city's economy, and you're putting that investment at risk every minute you let the Rat Pack remain at large. There are other cities that would take the concerns of the business community more seriously. Are you aware of just how much my companies contribute here?"

The mayor remembered well just how many zeroes had been on Norman Osborn's last check to the party's campaign fund. "Oh, believe me, Norman, I'm aware of it . . ."

And the mention of contributions made something click. He thought he knew what Osborn wanted—the same thing *any* big political contributor wanted: A say in how the government was run.

Ordinarily that would have meant naming Osborn as the figurehead chairman of a committee to investigate the problem, but somehow he didn't think Osborn would settle for figurehead status. He had to be after a position with some real authority to it.

And there was even an opening.

"I wouldn't have guessed it from your actions," Osborn said coldly.

"Oh, that hurts, Norman." The mayor clutched at his heart dramatically. "Look, I see you're upset, and I don't *want* you to be upset. I want you on my side on this one. You know what they say, you want something done right, do it yourself, right? So you aren't happy with the job I'm doing, running the city? Then you give me a hand with it!"

Osborn stared silently at the mayor for a moment, suppressing a smile. Everything was going as he had planned. He asked, "What did you have in mind?"

"You understand this advance word is entirely unofficial," Deputy Mayor Flaherty said, spreading his hands as he addressed the gathered reporters and others in the *Daily*

Bugle's city room. "The mayor won't be making the formal announcement until tomorrow's press conference, but due to the special relationship this newspaper has with Mr. Osborn . . ."

"Get on with it," J. Jonah Jameson growled from his position two steps outside his office door. "Just what is it Hizzoner wants us to know about my partner?"

"Mr. Jameson, you sound angry," Flaherty said. "I assure you, it's good news . . ."

"He *always* sounds angry," Betty Brant interrupted. She was seated on her desk—not behind it, but perched on one corner. "Don't mind Jonah." She threw her employer a quick smile, then turned her attention back to Flaherty.

Peter Parker was standing just behind Betty; the working day was ending and they had been chatting, talking shop as they prepared to head home, when Flaherty had arrived and called for everyone's attention for an announcement from the Office of the Mayor. Peter said nothing, but watched Flaherty closely. Anything connected with Norman Osborn was cause for worry, and an announcement from the mayor's office had the potential to be very bad news indeed.

"I'm sure you're all aware of the ongoing terrorist crisis facing the city . . ."

Jonah snorted, interrupting the deputy mayor. "This is a *newspaper,* Flaherty," he said. "Of course we know."

"Yes, of course you do," Flaherty continued, undaunted. "And I'm sure by now you all know that Paul Charenton, Public Advocate for the City of New York, was found murdered yesterday near the Battery, shot dead, leaving the people of this city without the direct link to city government that they've come to rely on in the few years since the office was created. There's even reason to believe that the Rat Pack killed Mr. Charenton as part of their deliberate campaign to disrupt normal life in New York . . ."

"What's *ever* been normal about life in New York?" Charley Snow called.

Flaherty paused long enough to smile, acknowledging the chuckles Snow's jibe elicited.

"As normal as it ever gets, then," he said. "And here's a tidbit of hard news for you reporters—the preliminary forensics report from the NYPD indicates that the bullets that killed Mr. Charenton match bullets fired at the Con Ed plant on Eleventh Avenue two nights ago. This Rat Pack is a gang of killers, and must be stopped."

Peter found himself nodding at that, his mouth tightening. The Rat Pack *was* implicated in Charenton's murder, then. Something more complex than simple extortion was going on, no question about it.

They hadn't struck again after Charenton's murder—or after the power plant incident; Peter wasn't sure just which had actually happened first. That fit with their recent pattern of a few days of frequent attacks, followed by about three weeks of inactivity. Presumably they wouldn't strike again until the approach of the next full moon.

"Our mayor recognizes the urgency of keeping the city government operating normally, in defiance of these attacks," Flaherty continued. "We must show these people that they aren't hurting us. Leaving the position of Public Advocate untenanted until the next election, weeks from now, or for even a few *days* in the current crisis, is simply unacceptable. Therefore, the mayor has invoked his emergency powers to make a temporary appointment, filling the office."

Peter had a sudden ghastly suspicion he knew what was coming.

"The mayor has asked Mr. Norman Osborn, president and CEO of Osborn Industries and co-owner of the *Daily Bugle,* to assume the duties of the Public Advocate until a special election can be held. Mr. Osborn has put aside many of his own interests and accepted."

Peter frowned. Why had Osborn taken the job? Had he *wanted* it? If he had, why? The Public Advocate was a sort of ombudsman, the office any New Yorker called about problems with the city government—why would *Osborn,* of all people, want such a position? He didn't care about people; he only cared about power.

"We like to think this appointment is the best move possible for the public good," Flaherty said. "Mr. Osborn has repeatedly demonstrated his concern for the welfare of the citizens of New York, and the mayor can't think of a better man for the job." He smiled a broad, insincere politician's smile. "And frankly, my friends, neither can I."

"I can think of about four million, right off the top of my head," Peter muttered. Flaherty, if he heard, ignored the remark, but Betty threw a warning look over her shoulder, and Peter shut up.

Ben Urich called, "Mr. Flaherty, I take it the mayor doesn't see any possible conflict of interest in appointing half-owner of a newspaper to this position?"

"I wouldn't know about that, Ben," Flaherty said, still smiling. "It'll be a good question to ask at the press conference tomorrow."

"And of course, you'll mention it to Hizzoner tonight, won't you, so he'll have time to come up with an answer?"

Flaherty's grin widened. "Of course. Just as you'll have time to think up other questions." Then he straightened up, tugged his lapels into place, and said, "I've made my announcement, ladies and gentlemen, and any questions you may have will have to wait for the press conference, so my job's done here. I expect I'll see some of you again tomorrow." He turned toward the city room door.

Ben Urich followed.

"Flaherty," he called as they approached the elevators, "let me buy you a beer."

Flaherty didn't even pretend to hesitate. "You're on," he said.

Half an hour later Flaherty sat at a bar a block away, a half-finished mug of Shotz in his hand, with Ben Urich seated on one side and Charley Snow on the other.

"There's no hidden motive, boys," Flaherty said. "It's all out in the open."

"Oh, sure," Ben said. "A businessman with no previous experience in government or consumer affairs is obviously the *perfect* public advocate!"

"Right," Charley chimed in. "He doesn't have any nasty preconceptions getting in his way. *I* believe that, don't you, Ben?"

"Hey, I never said it wasn't politics as usual," Flaherty said, holding up a hand. "I just said there wasn't any deep secret about it. I mean, off the record, it's pretty obvious, isn't it?"

"Ol' Norman's been pretty vocal about not being satisfied with how the mayor's been handling the Rat Pack, if that's what you mean," Charley said.

"Of course it's what I mean," Flaherty acknowledged. "What better way could there possibly be to shut him up? He can't very well complain about the city neglecting public safety when he's the city official in charge of public safety, can he?" He gulped the last of his beer.

"I guess not," Ben said. "So that's really all there is to it?"

"Absolutely," Flaherty said, thumping the empty mug down on the bar.

"So just what does *Osborn* get out of it?" Charley asked. "He's never been an altruist. Even if he really isn't the Green Goblin, he's not exactly Mr. Warmth."

"He gets a chance to boss around the entire city government, and show 'em how their jobs *should* be done, maybe," Ben suggested.

"That'd fit," Charley admitted, running a finger along the bar. "I'd still have thought he'd consider it beneath him." He looked at Flaherty. "You think that's all that's motivating him? The urge to teach people their jobs?"

Flaherty shrugged as he turned away from the bar and picked up his coat. "On that," he said, "your guess is as good as mine."

Four

Spider-Man loped easily along the vertical facade of the warehouse, untroubled that he was at right angles to the human world. At the corner he paused. Across a narrow alley was Josie's Bar, a notorious hangout for hired muscle and petty hoods of every sort—relatively quiet just now, as it was early in the day for serious drinking. To the right a broad expanse of mostly empty pavement separated warehouse and bar from the Hudson River, and from a couple of rusty freighters. A few steel drums, heavy chains, and assorted other dockside clutter added visual interest to the scenery; a pair of loading cranes were standing unused by the nearer freighter's stern. Half a dozen large crates were stacked by that freighter's gangplank—and as Spider-Man approached, an explosion blew the top one open, showering splinters and excelsior in all directions and sending a ball of smoke billowing upward. White plastic bags tumbled from the ruined crate.

Spidey had come down to the docks on a hunch, nothing more; it was simply one part of the city where a friendly neighborhood Spider-Man might find something to do to work off some of his frustrations.

Going by that explosion, it appeared that hunch was about to pay off. Spider-Man paused and looked at the scene ahead and to the right, behind the crates, where half a dozen men were holding a loud discussion. Several of them were gesturing at the smoldering remains of the blasted crate, and the plastic packets dangling from it.

Ordinary dockworkers didn't wear skintight purple-and-blue battlesuits, but someone in that group did.

The professional assassin who called himself Boomerang regularly wore purple and blue, in more or less the pattern this man displayed. If that was Boomerang, then Spidey had found the trouble he was looking for. He hurried closer, eager for a better look.

The tall, rather thin man in purple and blue stood by the gangplank of a freighter, shouting at a cluster of surly-looking fellows in jeans, work shirts, and watchcaps; when he got close enough for a decent look, Spider-Man knew beyond question that this was Boomerang. If the costume itself wasn't enough to settle it, the gleaming white boomerangs stuck to it with Velcro clinched it.

And as Spidey watched, Boomerang plucked one of those boomerangs off his costume and tossed it in a hard overhand throw that sent it whistling in a long, complex path. It skimmed over the men's heads before smashing into the next crate in the stack and blowing that one open, as well. More white plastic bags spilled out.

The men all ducked, first when the boomerang buzzed them, and then again when it went off and showered them with smoking splinters.

That purple-and-blue outfit was garish, even by super-villain standards, but Spidey knew that Boomerang was no pushover—he was strong and fast and tricky, and those white boomerangs concealed various deadly gimmicks, not just bombs. His shiny blue boots had jets built into them that allowed him to fly short distances—that was a pretty useful option to have available.

"Besides," Spidey muttered to himself, as he glanced at his own red-gloved, web-patterned hands, "who am I to criticize anyone's fashion sense?"

Fred Myers, Australian-born former major-league pitcher, had taken up the Boomerang costume and identity to stand out from the ordinary run of hit men and hired muscle and to emphasize his throwing skills; he hadn't been trying to impress anyone as a sharp dresser.

He stood out, all right. It was hard to miss him, and Spidey knew he was still wanted by the cops—not to mention that blowing up crates had to violate a law or two, even if it turned out that all that was in those plastic bags was sugar. Which Spidey doubted.

Taking Boomerang down and delivering him to the nearest precinct house would clearly be a good thing to do.

Marching over there and asking him to surrender wasn't going to work, of course. The idea was to accomplish something, rid the city of a criminal or two, not to get himself killed, so stealth was called for; Spider-Man clambered quickly up to the warehouse roof.

He didn't think anyone had spotted him yet, but he couldn't be sure, which made speed as important as stealth; he wasted no time in firing a long stream of carefully aimed web-fluid at a convenient crane, as close as he could to directly over Boomerang's head.

Cranes, he thought, were a wonderful thing; he was very glad that no one had yet found a better way of offloading freighters. One of these days Henry Pym or Reed Richards or someone was going to sell the shippers anti-gravity platforms they could use to lift crates and bales, and not only would it put a lot of crane operators out of work, it would complicate Spider-Man's life no end.

For now, though, that big yellow arm a hundred feet in the air was just what he needed; he climbed quickly up his web-line, swinging off the warehouse roof as he did.

A moment later, dangling almost directly above the freighter's gangplank, he lowered himself gradually back down. Boomerang was still talking, not quite so loudly now, and Spidey wanted to hear what he was saying—after all, Boomerang didn't generally work alone; he hired his services out. It would be good to find out who he was working for before giving him a boot to the head.

". . . you know what's good for you," Boomerang said, waving a boomerang threateningly at his listeners. Spidey cursed his luck in not hearing more than that.

"Look," one of the men said, "I don't want any trouble with you, but if we just hand over the stuff without a fight, we'll never get another job like this!"

"And if I blow your head off, you won't get any more jobs at all," Boomerang replied. His Australian accent had faded slightly since their last meeting, Spidey noticed.

He also noticed one of the other men was looking up and had spotted him. That man elbowed the one who had answered Boomerang, and pointed. The spokesman looked up and saw Spidey, as well.

Spider-Man waved cheerfully.

"Hey, is he with you?" the spokesman asked Boomerang, pointing.

"What are you . . ." Boomerang began. Then he glanced up, and saw Spidey.

"You!" he bellowed.

"Me," Spidey agreed, waving. "Me Spidey, you Fred. How ya doin', Fred?"

"Don't call me that!" Boomerang roared, pulling a razor-edged boomerang from his chest and hurling it.

Spider-Man had been expecting that and dodged the throw easily, but his web-line was sliced through and he dropped fifteen feet to the ground.

Fifteen feet, for a man with the proportional speed and strength of a spider, was no problem at all; he landed in a crouch as Boomerang caught the returning razorang in a Kevlar glove.

"But, Mr. Myers," he said, "aren't we old friends? I thought sure by now we'd be on a first-name basis!" He did a forward roll, came upright a few feet from Boomerang's face, and held out his right hand.

"I mean, really, do I complain when you call me Spidey?" he said.

He was standing so close that Boomerang had no room to throw anything, and the assassin wasn't stupid enough to pit mere fists against Spider-Man. He stepped back, muttering insults under his breath, and triggered his boot-jets, to get himself some distance and the advantage of the air.

Spidey had been waiting for that—he closed the hand he'd held out to shake, middle fingers pressing the hidden button in his palm, and a line of sticky web shot out and snagged one of those shiny blue boots as they swept upward.

"Don't rush off!" Spidey called. "I'll be good, Boomy! No more name jokes!" Then, as soon as the web-fluid had gelled, Spidey gave the line a good, hard jerk, effectively yanking Boomerang's feet out from under him—while he was about eight feet off the ground.

The men by the gangplank applauded.

Boomerang spun backward and fell out of the sky onto the hard asphalt pavement, but his athletic skills hadn't deserted him; he landed rolling, and struggled to get to his feet, the razorang still in his hand.

He had forgotten, however, that the webbing was still attached; Spidey gave the line another tug, and Boomerang sprawled sideways, cursing. This time, rather than trying to right himself, he twisted around and threw the razorang at Spidey again.

Spider-Man ducked, but again his web-line parted. He fired another, this time aiming for Boomerang's face—no matter how good his throwing arm might be, Myers couldn't aim if he couldn't see.

Boomerang sprang upright, bellowing and clawing at the webbing that covered his eyes. Spider-Man decided the time had come to end this charade quickly; he stepped forward, fist cocked—and Boomerang fired his boot-jets again, launching himself upward.

"That trick *never* works!" Spidey called, as he fired more webbing. He was going through his supply of web-fluid a little faster than he liked, but there was no time to worry about that just now.

Boomerang had gotten a better launch this time; the web-line didn't bring him smashing down again, but did pull him off-course. Spidey hung on, firing more web, and a moment later he found himself spinning Boomerang around at the end of a fifteen-foot tether of tangled webbing.

He knew what to do now, of course, and at the right moment he snapped off the web shooters in both hands and let go, sending Boomerang flying, completely out of control, toward the wall of the warehouse.

Or rather, Spidey had intended to slam him into the warehouse, but his timing had been off by just a fraction of a second.

"Oops," he said, as Boomerang smashed through the plate-glass front window of Josie's Bar. Shards sprayed in all directions, and voices shouting in surprise and protest could be heard over the racket.

Spider-Man shrugged. "Oh, well, no one's perfect," he said. "Let's call that one ball four." He bounded toward the shattered window. "Hey, Boomy, you can take a walk— first base is in a jail cell!"

He jumped easily through the gaping hole in the glass and landed atop a table inside the bar. He crouched there, looking around.

A brown-haired woman in a low-cut dress stood behind the bar, staring at him; a dozen assorted patrons were seated here and there; and Boomerang lay motionless on the floor by the table.

"Spider-Man!" the woman shouted.

"That'd be me," Spidey replied.

"You smashed my window!"

That, Spider-Man thought, would probably mean this person was Josie. "He smashed your window," he replied, pointing at Boomerang. "Sure, he only did it because I threw him at it, but still . . ."

"Who's gonna pay for it?" Josie demanded, in a voice trained by years of shouting over drunken brawls.

"Ah—your insurance company, I hope," Spider-Man said. "Excuse me a minute. Got a little business to finish up here." He jumped down from the table, suddenly worried—Boomerang still wasn't moving.

Myers was breathing steadily, and a quick check found

a strong, even heartbeat, but he was out cold. Spidey hoped he didn't have a concussion.

Concussion or not, he might wake up at any time, so Spidey quickly wrapped a ring of webbing around him, trapping his arms at his sides.

Boomerang obviously wasn't going to be naming his employer any time soon, though. Spidey frowned under his mask. He looked up.

"Call the cops to come get this guy, would you?" He turned his attention to the bar's patrons, who were watching him intently. At the word "cops" a couple of them looked clearly uneasy, and one man rose to head for the door.

It occurred to Spidey that these people were not necessarily upstanding, law-abiding citizens. He couldn't very well ask Boomerang who had hired him, not while he was unconscious, but he could ask the rest of these people, and some of them might even know something.

And some of them might know something about the Rat Pack, as well. Those apparently pointless raids were always at the back of his mind of late, giving everything he did an edge of frustration.

"Hey, what's your hurry?" Spidey asked the man who had stood up.

"No hurry," the man said nervously, quickly sitting back down.

"Good! Because hey, I have *really* been looking for someone to play 'Twenty Questions' with, and *you* guys just got elected. All of you." He jumped back on the table. "Anyone have a problem with that?"

That elicited a few growls and grumbles, but no one made any intelligible protest.

"Good!" Spidey said. "Now, the way *I* play the game, is that I give you a subject, and *you* guys tell me everything you know about it. Got it?"

"And what happens if we don't?" a big bruiser demanded, pushing back his chair.

"Oh, then we play a *different* game," Spidey said, as he jumped up to the ceiling, stuck there, and scampered over to hang directly above the big man's head. He reached down and grabbed the back of the man's collar and lifted. "Then we play catch," he said.

"Okay! Okay!" the big man said, squirming. "I was just askin'!"

Spidey dropped him, and looked around. "Today's subject," he said, "is the Rat Pack. Who wants to go first?"

No one wanted to go first, so he picked someone.

By the time he finished a quick interrogation he could hear sirens approaching. No one in Josie's had admitted to knowing what the Rat Pack was really up to. They did admit that the current Number One had been seen and heard recruiting recently, adding to the Rat Pack's numbers, but he hadn't been blabbing a lot of details. Someone was apparently financing the Rat Pack's expansion and telling them what to do, but none of Spidey's informants knew who this employer was—or at any rate, none would admit it.

"The Kingpin?" Spidey asked one burly but reasonably cooperative man.

"I dunno, I swear," the man replied. "The guy I knew didn't say. I don't think he knew himself. He said Number One got money and orders and did what they said, but I dunno if *anyone* knew who was giving the orders."

It was probably true—but it might not be. If he pounded on a few more thugs . . .

But how would he *find* more thugs?

And besides, he had a date—he was supposed to meet Mary Jane and a few friends at the Daily Grind, a little cafe just off the campus of Empire State University, in . . . he glanced at the clock over the bar.

In five minutes. All the way across town.

"Oboy," he said. Any more thug-bashing would have to wait until later. He bounded out through the ruins of Josie's front window.

Three police cruisers were pulling up; rather than spend time answering the cops' questions, he left, scurrying up the warehouse wall.

Five minutes later he was not at the Daily Grind; he was instead hurrying through the city in his own unique fashion, the wind whipping at him as he went. He would fire a web-line upward, attach it to an overhanging cornice or other fancywork, then swing down, like Tarzan on a vine. At the end of each arc, as he was slowing to a stop and about to reverse direction, he would attach a new line somewhere ahead, let go of the old, and swing on.

It was an odd way to travel, and dizzying for anyone who wasn't used to it, but he had been getting around the city in this fashion for years. In the summer the breeze helped keep him cool, even in his bodysuit and mask; in the winter the wind was much less pleasant, but exertion kept him from freezing. Right now, in early fall, when the weather was just turning brisk, it was invigorating.

The big advantage of web-swinging, he thought as he swooped down toward the sidewalk and then swept upward again, clearing the heads of hurrying pedestrians by a yard or so, was that there wasn't any traffic twenty feet up. Even the other super heroes didn't generally use that altitude— the ones who could fly mostly went clear over the rooftops. Oh, a few of the rest were swingers or climbers—Daredevil, for example—but not enough that Spidey had to worry about running into them. Just concentrating on getting the webs solidly anchored in the right spots so he didn't go slamming into the side of a building was tricky enough without having to dodge moving obstacles.

Twenty minutes later he was in street clothes, hurrying into the Daily Grind. Mary Jane, Betty Brant, and Flash Thompson were at a table for four, coffee cups already in front of them.

"Glad you could make it, Pete!" Flash called.

"Sorry I'm late," Peter said, as he took the one remaining empty seat at the table. "Traffic was bad." He didn't mention that he had been swinging over that traffic, rather than fighting his way through it.

"Isn't it always?" Betty asked. "Oh, it varies with the time of day, but people talk as if one day is completely different from another, and it always seemed to me that it's pretty constant."

"Oh, I don't know . . ." Mary Jane replied.

They talked about nothing in particular, as friends will, for the better part of an hour. While other topics came up, the subject kept drifting back to the city around them—traffic, street repair, and so on.

And eventually Betty asked Flash, "Did you hear about Norman Osborn?"

"What about him this time?" Flash asked. "Is he terrorizing people again, or funding orphanages? I never know what to expect from that guy; even if he's not really the Green Goblin, and I'm still not convinced either way, he gives me the creeps."

"The mayor's named him to replace some city official who got murdered," Peter said.

"The public advocate," Betty said. "You know, the office you call if you need the city to fix something and you don't know which department it is, or if you want to complain about something the city did."

Flash shuddered. "Bet once people get to know him they'll make a lot fewer calls with ol' Norm running things there. He's a scary guy. I wouldn't ask him to go to bat for me." He shrugged. "Maybe the mayor's trying to cut the budget for the advocate's office."

"He's just trying to make Mr. Osborn happy," Betty said. "Osborn's a powerful man, and he's raised a stink over these Rat Pack terrorists."

"Well, he isn't anyone *I* want in city government," Peter said.

"Yeah," Flash agreed. "Poor Harry was okay—most of the time, anyway—but his father's a world-class creep."

"Poor Harry," Betty said.

The memory of their dead friend cast a pall over the discussion, and after a moment's uncomfortable silence Betty glanced at her watch and said, "Oh, look at the time! I have to go."

"We should get rolling, too," Mary Jane said, and the party broke up.

After leaving the shop Peter and Mary Jane ambled side by side down the sidewalk, toward the Astor Place station to get the Lexington Avenue line uptown. The evening air was cool and almost pleasant, the city's omnipresent distinctive stench of grit and auto exhaust relatively faint.

"You were pretty quiet in there," Peter remarked.

"Just basking in your brilliance, Tiger," Mary Jane said with a smile. Then she turned serious. "I had a long day of classes," she said. "And it makes me nervous whenever Norman Osborn's in the news."

"Me, too," Peter said. He looked up at one of the buildings they were passing, automatically noting that the cornice would be suitable for web-swinging. "You know, what I don't understand is why Osborn took the job."

"Run that one by me again, would you, Tiger?"

"I mean, I see why the mayor would offer the job, to shut him up," Peter explained, "but I don't see why Osborn *accepted* it. God knows he doesn't need the money, and we both know he's not the kind to want to spend his time dealing with the everyday problems of ordinary citizens. Why'd he take it? What does he get out of it? Where's it taking him?"

"Well, after all the fuss he's made about the city not doing enough about the Rat Pack, maybe he felt he couldn't turn down the offer without losing face," Mary Jane suggested. "Or maybe he's thinking about how the public advocate job can lead to the mayor's office."

"He's already *got* access to the mayor's office," Peter protested. "I mean, I'm sure Hizzoner takes Osborn's calls—he's a big shot."

"No, Peter, that's not what I mean," Mary Jane said. "I

mean, the public advocate is next in line to the mayor in the city hierarchy. We were going over this in my poli sci class just today—Professor Thrushbotham didn't know about Norman Osborn, but he read about Charenton's murder, so he was explaining about the public advocate's office. The job was only invented in 1993, when the city charter was revised, so people tend to think of it as not all that important, if they ever heard of it at all, but really, the public advocate has access to everything in the city government, and he's next in line if the mayor dies."

"Next in line how?" Peter asked uneasily, slowing his pace and looking intently at his wife.

Mary Jane shoved him playfully. "You need it in words of one syllable? If the mayor dies, the public advocate takes over as the new mayor."

They were nearing the stair to the subway, but Peter stopped on the sidewalk and caught Mary Jane by the arm. He looked her in the eye.

"Wait a minute," he said. "You mean that if the mayor dies tomorrow, *Norman Osborn* becomes *mayor of New York?*"

"You got it, Tiger."

Peter stared at her for a long moment. Pieces of the puzzle were beginning to come together.

Norman Osborn was next in line to be mayor of New York City because he had been appointed public advocate. He had been appointed to the job because he had spoken out so strongly against the Rat Pack's recent activities—activities that didn't have any obvious and believable goal, activities financed and ordered by some anonymous power.

Peter couldn't be sure, of course—it was all just guesswork and suspicion, with no evidence behind any of it—but maybe, just maybe, this was exactly what the Rat Pack had been hired to bring about.

Maybe Norman Osborn had staged this whole thing to get himself into the mayor's office—not as a guest, but as the mayor!

ome on, Jonah," Peter said, perching himself on the corner of Jameson's desk. "I need the money, and while I know you don't care about that, someone's gotta cover this reception!"

The reception in question was one that Norman Osborn and the mayor were giving that night at the Plaza Hotel to "provide an opportunity for the people of New York to meet their new public advocate."

Going by the guest list, "the people of New York" apparently consisted entirely of millionaires and celebrities.

Peter Parker was not a millionaire, and was a celebrity only in his Spider-Man guise, but he urgently wanted to attend as himself, not a wall-crawling super hero. He wanted to see if he could figure out any more about just what Norman Osborn was up to. He wanted to look for any sign that Osborn really was behind the Rat Pack's raids.

Plain old Peter Parker couldn't get into an affair like this as an invited guest, but a press pass would serve his purposes just as well.

"And someone *will* cover it," J. Jonah Jameson growled, chewing on the stub of a cigar as he read the sheet of copy in his hands and refused to look at Peter. "It won't be a blasted crime photographer, though. It'll be someone from the society page who might actually know which people are worth photographing."

"Hey, *I* know who's worth photographing at these things!" Peter protested. "Anyone wearing diamonds, or with a flower in his lapel."

"Oh, that's just wonderful, Parker," Jameson said, putting down the paper. "You go by that standard and we'll be running pictures of the waiters!"

"Okay," Peter said amiably. "Anyone with a flower in his lapel who Osborn or the mayor will talk to."

"Waiters vote."

"So anyone *Osborn* will talk to."

"Ah, he's probably going to run for office, too, just so we'll run your pictures of waiters on the front page."

"Now, now," Peter said, waggling an admonitory finger. "Is that any way to talk about your partner? C'mon, Jonah, I'll just *ask* Mr. Osborn who's important and who isn't, and *he'll* know, for sure!"

"Fine! Fine!" Jameson flung the cigar stub at the wastebasket; it teetered on the rim before dropping in. "You go, then, Parker—get out of my face and go. I'll send Friedman, and you can tag along, and I'll buy the best shots, whoever takes 'em."

"We both get press credentials?"

"How else would you get in? Pick 'em up at the desk. They'll be there."

"Thanks, Jonah!" Peter said, as he slid off the desk. "You won't regret this."

"I already do, Parker."

Peter threw him a jaunty wave as he hurried out the door of the office; Jameson watched him go, wishing he hadn't tossed the cigar—there wasn't enough left to be worth relighting, but just chewing on it was better than nothing.

"Blasted kid," he muttered, as he turned his attention back to the papers on his desk. "And the worst of it is, he probably *will* get better pictures than Friedman."

He never could figure Parker out. Sometimes the kid brought in clear, sharp pictures of the most amazing things; other times he couldn't seem to snap anything but blurry shots of elbows and webbing, with faces or entire heads— or entire *people*—cut off. It was as if half the time he just clicked the shutter at random, without bothering to aim.

Sometimes Parker was all over the place, getting underfoot, poking in where he wasn't wanted; other times he'd disappear for days at a time. Sometimes he'd up and leave right in the middle of something, for no apparent reason.

If there was trouble, though, it seemed as if Parker was always there. It was as if he had an extra sense that drew him to disasters.

And personally—sometimes the kid was a total wimp, but sometimes he'd stand up to anyone.

J. Jonah Jameson preferred people he could figure out; Peter Parker was a constant irritation to him.

But for all his contradictions, when he hit with something, he tended to hit big. He'd been so determined to attend that fool reception—maybe he knew something.

Maybe that confounded web-slinging glory hound would be there, and Parker knew it. It was a mystery to Jonah how Parker managed to find Spider-Man so often, but he was always glad to take advantage of the resulting pictures.

Much as he hated the wall-crawler, Jonah had to admit his picture sold papers.

That evening Peter Parker wore his best suit, but still felt as out of place in the Plaza ballroom as a slug on a Persian carpet. He suspected that most of the invited attendees at the reception had spent more on their socks than he had on his entire outfit.

Of course, the press tag around his neck and the camera in his hand excused his appearance, and meant that instead of eyeing him with distaste the guests merely ignored him. No one stopped him as he moved through the crowd, snapping pictures of familiar faces—and making sure he had a few good, clear shots of waiters, just to keep Jonah happy, secure in his pose that he thought his employees were all morons.

Norman Osborn and the mayor were standing side by side at the door, greeting new arrivals—Friedman of the society page, along with a couple of photographers from rival papers, was snapping pictures of the more prestigious guests as Osborn shook their hands. That left Peter free to roam.

He had come here tonight to get a fresh look at Norman

Osborn, to see if he could find any evidence, any *hint,* that Osborn might have somehow arranged his appointment as public advocate as a stepping-stone to the mayor's office. If Osborn was indeed connected with the Rat Pack he might slip up somehow, might say something suspicious—or he might not; as Peter knew only too well, Osborn's ability to conceal the truth was phenomenal.

There might be others here, though, whose self-control was less perfect. Osborn had probably used go-betweens, assistants who had found the Rat Pack for him and who carried his orders to the Rats, and those assistants might well be here tonight. One of *them* might slip, even if Osborn himself didn't.

Peter watched Osborn greeting the arriving guests, and tried to see whether anyone got more than the usual share of attention. There were few obvious stand-outs, but Osborn did talk for a moment with one woman.

"Who's that talking to Norman Osborn?" Peter asked a passing waiter.

"I'm afraid I don't know, sir," the waiter said without pausing, but a white-haired woman behind him had heard the exchange.

"That's Abby somebody," she offered. "She works in the public advocate's office. Probably trying to get to know her new boss."

"Thanks," Peter said.

That seemed harmless enough—but if Osborn had planned this whole thing he might have had people inside the public advocate's office all along. Peter edged nearer and snapped a few quick shots of "Abby somebody."

Friedman noticed and said, "Don't bother with her, Parker. She's nobody. You're wasting film."

"Oh," Peter said, lowering the camera.

"I heard that," Osborn said, turning. "Ms. Lamron is not 'nobody.' She's a valued part of my staff."

"Sorry, sir," Friedman said. "No offense meant. I'm sure

she's an asset to the city, but I don't think her picture's what the public looks for in the paper."

"You take all the pictures you want, Parker," Osborn said, ignoring Friedman. He smiled and added, "While you still have the chance."

Peter grimaced as he snapped a quick shot of Osborn himself; he knew a veiled threat when he heard one.

"While he has the chance, sir?" Friedman asked, as he snapped a shot of the mayor and a statuesque blonde in a low-cut gown.

"Oh, I don't think our friend Parker is going to be around here forever with that camera of his." Osborn smiled—or at least bared his teeth. "I'm sure you've got other things to do besides take pictures, don't you, Parker?" Osborn continued, momentarily stepping away from the receiving line.

"I don't think I know what you mean, Mr. Osborn," Peter murmured.

"Oh, of course you do, Peter, m'boy!" Osborn said. "I've met that pretty little wife of yours." He clapped a hand on Peter's shoulder.

Peter suppressed a shudder. He hated to hear any mention of Mary Jane from this man. Mary Jane was the best part of his life, the light and joy of his existence, while Osborn was a walking nightmare, everything he dreaded—a powerful and implacable enemy who knew all his secrets.

"And of course, both of you were such good friends of my own boy, Harry . . ." A pained and slightly puzzled expression flickered across Osborn's face for an instant, vanishing so quickly Peter wasn't sure he hadn't imagined it. "I'm sure you know how I feel about you both."

Peter knew, all right. He felt his stomach knot.

"As public advocate," Osborn said, "I represent all the people of New York, but I want you to know, Parker, that I take a very *special* interest in you, and when I've had time to settle in you can expect to see some real changes in how things are done around here—changes that will affect *you,* and everyone around you."

Peter tore his gaze away from Osborn's face and real-ized that a dozen other people were staring at them, taking in this entire conversation—and not one of them, he knew, recognized Osborn's threats for what they were. They all just heard a businessman-turned-politician spouting the usual hot air to a constituent.

He knew what Osborn was saying, though—and he had to reply; he couldn't let this monster gloat so blatantly.

"I kind of liked things the way they were," Peter said. "You know, a couple of years ago it seemed like the city was a pretty pleasant place." He did not say aloud, *when you were believed dead.*

Another puzzled look flitted across Osborn's face. "I . . . I don't really remember that," he said.

That wasn't the reaction Peter had expected. He had thought Osborn would have a snappy comeback. Heartened, he said, "I thought for a while—after the Green Goblin died, say—that things were pretty quiet, and that it was kind of nice. Too bad they didn't stay that way."

"The . . ." Osborn's smile, already wilting, vanished com-pletely; he looked lost and confused. "The Green Goblin?" To Peter's astonishment, beads of sweat appeared on Os-born's forehead, and he stepped back slightly, blinking.

"Sure. You remember. For a while we thought *you* were the Green Goblin."

"I . . ." Osborn swallowed. "I don't remember that. Don't say that name—it gives me the creeps."

"You mean the Gree . . . oh. Sorry." Peter watched closely, baffled, as Osborn flinched at the unfinished name.

It didn't look like an act. It looked genuine.

For a moment Peter stared uncomprehendingly at Os-born's apparent discomfiture; then something clicked. He remembered how once, years before, well before Gwen's death, Osborn's madness had temporarily taken on a new form—partial amnesia. Osborn had forgotten his entire se-cret life as the Green Goblin, as well as all the secrets he had learned as the Goblin, such as that Peter Parker and

Spider-Man were the same man. While the amnesia lasted—not long enough!—the mere mention of the Green Goblin had been painful and unsettling for him.

Had the amnesia returned?

That was almost too good to be true.

But if the amnesia was back, and Osborn no longer remembered his other self, could he still be the one behind the Rat Pack's raids? Had he arranged Paul Charenton's murder? The amnesiac Osborn had truly been the law-abiding, if somewhat ruthless, businessman Osborn always pretended to be; he was no criminal mastermind of any sort. He wouldn't have arranged Charenton's murder.

So maybe it was all just a coincidence after all; maybe someone else was the Rat Pack's mysterious employer, and there was nothing devious or illicit in Osborn's appointment to his new office.

Or maybe this new amnesia was real, but different—maybe Osborn had developed a third personality, a criminal mastermind other than the Green Goblin.

Or maybe he was faking.

But if he was faking, he was good at it—the sweat on his brow was unmistakably real.

Of course, Osborn *was* good at deceiving people . . .

It was Peter's turn to be confused. He needed to get away for a moment, to think without seeing that hated face smiling at him.

"Listen," he said, "it's been a pleasure talking to you, Mr. Osborn, but I need to circulate, take some more pictures." He gestured at the crowd.

"Of course, of course!" Osborn said, recovering swiftly. He slapped Peter on the shoulder. "You go to it, Parker. Take your photos, do your job. You've got your priorities. But hey, someday we'll get together for a *real* talk, man to man, won't we?"

"You bet, Mr. Osborn," Peter said, throwing him a mock salute.

A real talk, all right, Peter promised himself—spider and goblin, letting their fists do the talking. Someday.

They stepped apart, backing away from each other before turning away; then someone else demanded Osborn's attention. "Mr. Osborn, you may not remember me . . ."

"No, I'm afraid I don't," Osborn said, turning to shake the speaker's hand. "The memory isn't what it once was, you know." He laughed, a quiet, controlled laugh nothing like the Green Goblin's insane cackle.

The other man smiled. "We met years ago, at your psychiatrist's office . . ."

Then Peter could no longer make out the words. He frowned, and lifted his camera.

Was Norman Osborn, alias the Green Goblin, conspiring to take over the city, or wasn't he? Had he risked thousands of innocent lives by hiring the Rat Pack, and had he had Paul Charenton murdered—or perhaps even done it himself!—all to give him a shot at his new job? Peter knew he was capable of it all—but had he actually done it?

Or was he genuinely innocent and amnesiac, and the crimes all someone else's doing?

Peter didn't know.

And what was worse, he had no idea how to find out.

Furthermore, no matter which was true, he had no idea how to stop the Rat Pack. If he knew that Osborn was behind it all he might at least have a clue where to start—but if Osborn *wasn't* the mastermind, if the amnesia was real, then he would not only be wasting his time prying into Osborn's affairs, he'd be risking giving Osborn the sort of shock that might restore his memory and bring the Green Goblin back.

For the rest of the reception he drifted in and out of Osborn's vicinity, listening and watching for any sign, any clue to Osborn's true intentions.

He saw none, and he returned home that night more confused and frustrated than ever.

Part Two

Six

The scene was a sidewalk in midtown Manhattan, where a hulking figure in a skin-tight banded green costume loomed over a crouching Spider-Man, fists clenched, face twisted in a furious grimace. The costume included a long tail, as thick as a man's arm, that was swinging around toward Spider-Man's head, having already knocked a chunk out of the solid limestone facade of a building behind the green-clad villain.

Anyone familiar with Spider-Man's career would instantly recognize the wall-crawler's attacker as the Scorpion—as Mary Jane Parker did.

She held the newly developed photo by one corner and stared at it with mild distaste while her husband cheerfully explained: ". . . so he swung that tail of his at my head, but I just ducked under it and shot a web right in his face. He let out this really great scream—I bet you could hear it for a dozen blocks—and charged at me again." Peter tossed the next photo on the desk and looked expectantly at Mary Jane.

"Let me guess," Mary Jane said. "You said he threw the manhole cover at you—so the open hole was right in front of him?"

"You got it, Red." Peter grinned broadly. "He'd forgotten all about it. When his foot hit it he yelled again, but it was too late."

"He fell in?"

"Not completely *in,* exactly, but he fell *over,* anyway, and whacked his head on the pavement, which rattled him enough to let me get a few good punches in. After that it was easy to web him up until the cops got there. Pretty cool, huh?" He held up the final photo in the series. "And look at the pictures!" He flipped back to an earlier shot. "See this one? That close-up of his face, that's when I dodged and he charged right up to where I'd hidden the camera—I judged it exactly right! Man, when I heard the shutter click at just the right time . . . and look at this one, back here." He shuffled through the pictures quickly. "And see this one, where he got me in the face with his tail? I knew it was coming, and I rolled with it, it didn't hurt a bit, but this *picture* is great—Jonah's gonna love it. It'll go right in the 'make Spidey look stupid' file. And for everyone else, I've got the Scorpion stepping in a manhole, making *him* look stupid. Not bad, huh?"

He looked at her expectantly.

She shrugged. "I'd say it's up to your usual standard, Tiger."

Peter didn't bother to conceal his disappointment at her lack of enthusiasm. "You aren't impressed?"

She reached up, threw her arms around his neck, and pulled him down for a kiss. He was startled, but enthusiastic.

When she released him a moment later and he had caught his breath she said, "*That* was impressive, Tiger. Dropping the Scorpion down a manhole is just business as usual for Spider-Man."

"The Scorpion's no lightweight!" Peter protested.

"And neither are you," Mary Jane said.

"But . . . hey, just whose side are you on here?"

"Yours, Tiger, never doubt it." She reached up to rumple his hair. "But you've been whomping on the bad guys for a long time, and never more than the last couple of weeks. You've brought in the Scorpion, Boomerang, the Grizzly, Lightmaster, and the Kangaroo. It's a little hard to stay excited."

"The thrill is gone, huh?" Peter asked, smiling.

"Oh, I wouldn't say *that*," Mary Jane said, grinning back, "but I'd agree the novelty has worn off."

"Well, I still take pride in my work. I mean, nobody *asked* me to stop the Scorpion from robbing banks."

"And nobody asked you to throw Boomerang through a plate-glass window, or hang those muggers from a street-lamp, or any of the others. Peter, don't you think you're pushing a little hard lately?"

"What, I shouldn't fight the bad guys?"

"Of course you should—but you don't need to kill yourself doing it. Look, your whole cheek's one big bruise."

"The Scorpion's pretty quick with that tail," Peter admitted.

"The Scorpion isn't who you really want to punch out, though, is he, Tiger?"

"Who says I want to punch anyone?" Peter protested. "I don't mind if they surrender without a fight."

"I say you want to punch someone. And I know who it is, too."

"Oh? Madame MJ knows all, sees all—so tell me, Wise One, who is it I actually want to hit?"

"Norman Osborn, of course."

"Of course," Peter said. He hesitated, then shrugged. "Okay, you're right, I'd like to paste him one and see him safely behind bars, instead of walking around free and riding herd on half the city government. Maybe someday soon I'll get to do it. For now, though, all I'd get for punching him is an assault charge, and there are these other guys running loose who I *can* hit, and do some good doing it." He smiled. "And doing good for us, not just for the city." He held up the camera he'd set on top of a bookcase and wiped the last bit of webbing off it. "I've been getting some good pictures, and Jonah's been buying them. You saw that shot of ol' Scorpy running out of the bank, and the close-up. And the one I got of him stepping in the manhole. J.J.J. ought to come across with some nice money for these—and we *already* have enough to pay that nasty ESU bookstore bill you brought home last month. Shucks, there's enough in the bank to buy a romantic little dinner at *L'Ours*

Merveilleux, if madame would be interested." He bowed, the camera still in his hand.

Mary Jane squealed. "You *bet* I'd be interested!"

"Then it's a date," Peter said with a bow. "See? There *is* some good coming out of my web-slinging. Maybe I can't nail Osborn yet, but we're heading in the right direction, and I'll get him eventually."

"I hope so, Tiger." She glanced up at the clock. "Oopsy, I've got a class coming up. Gotta get a move on."

"Hey, I'll join you as far as Lexington Avenue." He lifted the camera. "I've got some pictures to deliver."

Forty minutes later Peter walked into the *Bugle* city room, whistling cheerfully, a stack of freshly printed photos in his hand.

"Peter!" Betty Brant called. "What on earth happened to your face?"

Peter stopped dead, trying to think what she could be talking about; he had a momentary nightmarish thought that he'd left his Spider-Man mask on, but he knew that couldn't be the case. The world didn't have that slightly milky glint his white plastic eyepieces produced, and there was no cloth over his nose or mouth.

"I don't know," he said. "What *did* happen to my face? Am I suddenly gorgeous?"

"You're suddenly black and blue," Betty retorted. "You've got a bruise the size of Staten Island on your cheek!"

"I do?" He reached up and touched his injured face. He had completely forgotten that; the Scorpion had landed one blow right on him with that tail of his. He had been too distracted by endangered bystanders to heed his spider-sense in time. "Oh, that," he said. "Hey, being a crime photographer has its risks—you can walk into things while lining up a shot."

"Is *that* what happened?"

"More or less," he said. He held up the sheaf of photos. "It was worth it, though—got fresh pics of Spidey taking down the Scorpion."

"Let's have a look at them," Joe Robertson called—he had overheard the exchange.

Peter happily handed over the pictures. "Jonah's gonna like these," he said. "There's one of the Scorpion smacking Spidey a good one. And if he picks the right shots he can make it look like the Scorpion tripped and knocked himself out, and Spidey didn't actually do anything."

"Is that what happened?" Robbie asked, as he flipped through the photos.

"Nope. Spidey set him up."

"That's what we'll run, then."

Peter shrugged. "It's your call, Robbie; I just take the pictures."

"And walk into walls doing it," Robbie said, looking up from the photos and gesturing at Peter's cheek. "You should be more careful, Pete—this isn't the first time you've come in here with cuts and bruises."

"It wasn't a *wall*," Peter corrected him. "It was more like a tree trunk." The Scorpion's tail definitely resembled a tree more than a wall. "And no one ever promised me a rose garden, Robbie—I'd have to be an idiot not to know my work is dangerous."

"*Are* you an idiot?"

Peter grimaced. "I guess I deserved that. No, I'm not an idiot—and I do try to be careful out there, honest. I'm not any fonder of getting beat up than you are."

"You could have fooled me. I've seen you when you get caught up in something, Pete—did you even *notice* when you got that bruise?"

Peter laughed. "This one, yeah. Sometimes I haven't, I admit it, but I felt *this* one just fine." He touched it carefully. "It probably looks worse than it is just because it's so spread out. You don't need to worry about me, Robbie; I can take care of myself."

"Apparently," Robbie said. "What I can't figure out is

how you do it." He tapped the sheaf of photos on the desk, straightening them. "You've been bringing me these shots for years, and half the time it looks as if you were right in the middle of one of these super-hero brawls—either that, or hanging off a rooftop by your toes. I can't figure out why you weren't killed years ago. No other photographer we have ever gets the angles you do."

"A zoom lens is an amazing thing, Robbie." Peter gestured at the batch of pictures he had just delivered. "So, what's the verdict?"

"We can use two, maybe three of these," Robbie said, pulling out the ones he had chosen—the shot of the Scorpion running from the bank, one of Spider-Man leaping over the Scorpion's swinging tail, and one of the Scorpion falling forward across the open manhole. They were exactly the three Peter had expected him to buy.

Jonah would have taken the one of the Scorpion's tail hitting Spider-Man in the face, but Robbie didn't like to cater to his boss's obsession that way—and Peter didn't really mind. Except for making Spider-Man look stupid, it wasn't really a good shot.

It was a shame, though, that the last one, of the Scorpion stepping in the manhole, had been taken from behind by the camera on automatic; the expression on the Scorpion's face as he fell had been priceless, and no one but Peter had seen it, or would ever see it.

"Any chance of a bonus?" Peter asked.

Robbie shook his head. " 'Fraid not. Just the usual terms. You've been bringing us so many pictures lately my discretionary funds are just about gone." He pulled a paper from one of his desk drawers, quickly filled in the date and some basic information, then signed it and turned it for Peter to countersign—the standard agreement assigning rights to the pictures to the *Bugle,* and guaranteeing payment.

"Thanks, Robbie," Peter said as he handed back the pen.

He started to turn away—but just then the door of Jameson's office opened.

"Parker!" Jonah called. "I thought I heard your voice out here, distracting my staff."

"Good to see you, too, Jonah," Peter called back. "I was just leaving, so everyone should be back at work in a moment or two."

"Not so fast. I've got someone in here who wants a word with you."

"You do?" Peter blinked in surprise. He felt faintly uneasy—was that the twinge of his spider-sense, or just an ordinary discomfort at the unknown?

"Yes, I do," Jameson said. "Now get in here, don't keep us waiting."

Puzzled, Peter circled Robbie's desk and stepped into Jonah's office.

Sure enough, someone was waiting there for him—someone in an expensive dark suit, with wiry red hair trimmed short above chiseled features and a narrow chin.

Norman Osborn.

His spider-sense was jangling faintly at Osborn's mere presence.

"Peter!" Osborn said, rising from his chair and smiling broadly. He held out a hand for Peter to shake; Peter managed to fumble with his pockets to avoid taking it. "Good to see you! I've just been talking to Jonah about you."

Peter threw Jonah a quick glance. He seemed irked about something—he was scowling, his shoulders hunched. Jameson was just about always irritable, but this looked like a little more than his usual annoyance.

The normal, expected thing would be to say something like, "Good things, I hope," to Osborn, but Peter couldn't bring himself to make polite chit-chat with this man. "About what?" he asked bluntly.

He didn't like this at all. Ever since Osborn had bought half-ownership of the *Daily Bugle* Peter had been afraid that his major source of income, selling pictures to Robbie and Jonah, might vanish—Osborn hated him, and while the labor laws might protect an employee from being fired without a good reason, Peter wasn't an employee. He was a freelancer, and had no such legal protection. The *Bugle* could stop buying his pictures at any time, without warning, without any reason, and he would have no recourse. Osborn could have him thrown out of work in an instant.

The real surprise, Peter thought, was that he hadn't done it sooner.

It looked as if the time had come, though. That would explain Jonah's annoyance—he wouldn't be eager to give up a source of newsworthy photos.

"About your work here," Osborn replied.

Peter felt his stomach tighten. Here it comes, he thought. And he'd been feeling so good a couple of hours ago, telling Mary Jane how much money they had in the bank . . .

"You've been bringing in some very remarkable photos lately," Osborn said. "More than any of our other freelancers. It's really quite astonishing, some of the pictures you've taken for us."

Peter blinked again. *That* didn't sound like the preliminaries to telling him to leave and not come back. In fact, it sounded downright complimentary. He was suddenly as confused as wary.

"You've been doing a *great* job, Peter," Osborn said. "I know that if Harry were still alive he'd be proud to have you as his friend—you've been doing some *outstanding* work. And all for our standard freelancer fees. You deserve better than that, my boy."

Peter didn't dare open his mouth for fear he would gape like an idiot. This sounded *very* much as if Osborn was about to do something *nice* for him—a bonus, perhaps.

That didn't make any sense—unless his amnesia really *had* returned, and he had forgotten that he was the Green Goblin, forgotten that Peter was Spider-Man. In the days since the reception Peter had convinced himself the amnesia was an act, something Osborn had done just to throw him off-guard—but maybe it was more than that.

"I think it's time you got what you deserve, Mr. Parker, and what's best for the *Bugle*," Osborn said. "So Jonah and I have decided to make you an offer we don't think you'll want to pass up."

"What is it?" Peter managed to ask.

Osborn smiled broadly at him.

"We're prepared to offer you a full-time job as a staff photographer, with full benefits—health insurance for you and your wife, a dental plan, a generous travel allowance, vested pension, everything. Instead of this part-time piece-work you'll be working for us every day, on salary . . ."

Peter's jaw dropped, despite his best efforts to keep his composure.

And then Osborn finished triumphantly, ". . . in our European office."

Seven

Peter stared blankly at Osborn for a long moment, then stammered, "Eur . . . Europe?"

"That's right," Osborn said, smiling. "Europe. It's obvious you deserve to be on the staff, not freelancing, but here in New York we're full up with talent. There's no suitable opening—if we put you on salary we'd have to fire Friedman, and he's got those two daughters in college."

"Ah," Peter said, since some sort of response seemed to be called for.

"At first I thought we were stuck," Osborn continued, "that we couldn't find a position that would do your talents justice, but then I realized that we could use a good lensman in the European office. Our photo staff there is weak, really needs some fresh blood—we mostly rely on the local freelancers, and a lot of them are just paparazzi who sell to whoever bids highest, which means we either pay too much or we don't get the pictures we want. Having another good staff photographer out there would be just what we need to get away from dealing with those weasels."

"But . . ." Peter was momentarily staggered, unable to frame even the simplest question. At last he gathered his wits sufficiently to ask, "Where in Europe?"

"Oh, you'd be based in Paris," Osborn replied. "That's where we've always had our main office over there. You'd get around, though—we'd send you wherever the news is. London, Rome, Berlin, Brussels, Geneva, wherever there's a story. If it's someplace dangerous, like Bosnia or Symkaria, there'd be hazard pay. And of course, all your expenses would be covered no matter where you went."

"Paris?" Peter's voice cracked. "*Paris?* The one in France?"

Osborn smiled. "Oh, we know it's an expensive city, so we'd be paying top dollar—I won't name an exact salary until I've run the numbers, but don't worry, it'll be good money and full benefits, with double pay for August—French labor laws, you know."

"But . . ." Peter stammered, "I . . . I mean . . . Mary Jane . . ."

"Ah, that lovely wife of yours! Of course we'd find something suitable for her—and she's worked as a model, hasn't she? Plenty of modeling work in Paris once she's finished her education."

"But she hasn't . . ."

"I know, I know—she's working on a degree at ESU, isn't she? Don't worry. I have connections over there, through the European branch of Osborn Industries. She can continue her classes. I'm sure I can arrange for her to transfer her credits to the University of Paris—or maybe the Sorbonne, but I can't promise that until we've sent her transcript over there for evaluation."

Peter struggled to regain his composure, but blurted out, "But . . . why? Why are you doing this?"

Osborn smiled.

"I told you, Parker," he said. "You're perfect for the job. You're young and eager and you're good at what you do. You could be very valuable to the *Bugle* someday, even in an executive position, if you get the kind of challenges and opportunities you need now. We'd expect you to stay over there for a long time, provide some stability."

Jonah made a muffled noise at that, and Peter threw him a glance.

" 'Stability' is not the first word I think of when I look at Parker," Jonah said.

"Well, what *chance* has he had for stability?" Osborn asked, turning to Jameson. "Orphaned young, working his way through college . . ."

"You could get plenty of more stable photographers," Peter said.

"Yes, we probably could," Osborn agreed, "but would they be as good as you are? Besides, I have faith in my son's judgment, and he considered you his best friend, Parker. He saw something in you, something trustworthy. I respect that—and I'd like to see it become something more. If you were good enough for my Harry, you're good enough for me and for my newspaper."

"*Half* yours," Jonah muttered.

Osborn ignored Jameson. "So, Parker, what do you say? Should we book your flight?"

"I . . . I don't know," Peter said.

"Oh, come on, Parker," Osborn said. "It's a dream come true, and you know it. It's ideal for you. Why aren't you grabbing it?"

"It's just . . . just so sudden, Mr. Osborn. It sounds too good to be true."

"It *is* true, though, and it's just what I say it is—no hooks or catches."

Peter looked at him for a moment more, and saw none of the hatred and evil he had come to expect from Osborn, but only a friendly smile. He knew that smile could be false, that Osborn could be a master of deception when he chose, but it didn't *look* false—it looked just as genuine as when Osborn had first had amnesia, and had forgotten his hatred, had forgotten his identity as the Green Goblin, and had known Peter simply as a good friend to his son Harry.

Confused, Peter turned to Jonah, who had settled behind his desk, looking disgruntled.

"Jonah, is this for real?"

Jonah frowned. "Darn right it is, Parker," he said. "Don't think it's *my* idea, though—Norman thought this one up all by himself. I've told him that you're more use here—Paris isn't crawling with super heroes the way New York is, and you can't just follow that blasted wall-crawler around the way you do here. I've told him that the European job should go to someone older. I told him you're a hometown boy, lived your whole life in New York. But he's right when he says that's the only staff position open." He coughed. "And much as I hate to admit it, you're good enough to be on staff."

Good enough, Peter thought, but that didn't mean Jonah *wanted* him on the staff, in Europe or anywhere else.

Osborn wanted him to take the job.

Why?

Peter couldn't help being suspicious any time Norman Osborn suggested *anything;* he tried to think of reasons that would explain the offer.

One possibility was that it was just as Osborn said—he was doing Peter a favor because Peter was a good photographer who had been Harry's friend. His amnesia had returned, and he no longer remembered that Peter was Spider-Man, no longer hated Peter Parker.

Another, more sinister possibility was that he was setting Peter up for one of his sadistic, vicious plans, that he would somehow use this European job offer to hurt Peter or the people Peter cared about. Just how that would work Peter had no idea, but he wouldn't put it past Osborn to have something like this in mind.

And a third possibility, the one that seemed most likely, was that Osborn wanted him out of the way, thousands of miles away from New York, so that he could continue his plan to take over the city without having to worry about any interruptions from everybody's favorite human arachnid.

If Osborn's amnesia was genuine, then the first possibility was the most likely. If the amnesia was as phony as Peter suspected it to be, then that possibility was completely out—and despite Osborn's convincing performance at the reception, he couldn't quite believe in the returned amnesia; it was too convenient, too easy.

The second possibility seemed unlikely for a very simple reason: Osborn liked to *see* his victims suffer, with his own two eyes, and he had just taken a position as public advocate that would keep him in New York. He could hardly watch his plans unfolding in Europe.

The third possibility . . . that seemed very likely. It would fit right in with Osborn's twisted thinking. If Peter took the job he would be leaving New York undefended, would be turning tail and running, and Osborn could gloat over his foe's cowardice as he carried through his schemes. It could well be that he had deliberately wormed his way into the public advocate's office because he intended to remove the mayor—probably by assassination. If that happened while Peter was in Europe, if Osborn became the mayor . . .

That was unthinkable.

If Peter *didn't* take the job, Osborn could watch Peter suffer, could revel in the knowledge that he had forced Peter to throw away a chance at a happy, comfortable existence. He would win either way—and no, having Spider-Man in New York wouldn't really be any sort of loss for Osborn; arrogant as he was, he was undoubtedly supremely confident that he could handle anything Peter could do to him, that Spider-Man wouldn't be able to prevent him from doing as he pleased.

Peter hoped that confidence was misplaced, but he knew that Osborn believed himself invincible, despite his occasional past defeats at Spider-Man's hands.

So if Osborn's amnesia was real, Peter knew he should take the job; if the amnesia was faked, he *couldn't*. He couldn't leave New York when Osborn was so close to usurping total control of the city government; there was no one else in New York ready to stop him, no one else who knew how dangerous Osborn was, almost no one else who believed that Osborn had really been the Green Goblin.

After all, everyone knew the Goblin was dead, impaled by his own glider, and Norman Osborn was very clearly still alive, so Norman Osborn *couldn't* be the Goblin. That the Goblin had had Osborn's face under his mask was assumed to be yet another of his insane tricks—after all, the Goblin had apparently had other identities through the years.

Peter knew that Osborn was the Green Goblin, the original, the deadliest of all the criminals who had ever worn any sort of goblin disguise, that the chemicals that had given him his superhuman strength, that had driven him mad, had somehow allowed him to survive his impalement—but he couldn't convince anyone who hadn't been directly involved.

After all, who would the cops or the Avengers or anyone else be more likely to believe: a respected multimillionaire industrialist, or a masked wall-crawling vigilante? An important public figure, or an obscure crime photographer?

That was an easy choice, and one Peter could hardly blame anyone for making.

So Spider-Man had to battle Osborn alone—and he had to be in New York to do it . . .

. . . *if* Osborn and the Rat Pack were really planning to remove the mayor and take over the city.

But if Norman Osborn had forgotten his other identity, forgotten that Peter was Spider-Man, become no more than he appeared, then he was almost harmless, and turning down this job in Europe would be perhaps the stupidest thing Peter had ever done.

Paris with Mary Jane. Traveling all over Europe. Money, benefits, a steady job.

How could he turn that down? He looked at Osborn again, saw that charming, friendly smile.

"Well, Peter? You'll take it, won't you?"

Peter started to open his mouth. He was looking Osborn right in the eye, and that eye was clear and just oozing sincerity . . .

But then something slipped, and just for an instant Peter saw past that genial smile into the depths of madness. There was a light in Osborn's eyes—a light of triumph, of victory. And the corners of his mouth twisted slightly, turning the smile into a leer, a cruel grin. It wasn't much of a shift, and maybe no one else would have seen it—but it was no longer Norman Osborn's face Peter saw, but another.

Peter knew that face. That was the face of the Green Goblin.

Then it was gone and the smile was back, and Osborn was holding out a hand.

"Put 'er there, Parker, and we'll consider it done."

Peter stepped back.

"I can't, Mr. Osborn," he said. He glanced at Jonah; he couldn't speak freely with Jonah here and the *Bugle* staff just the other side of a slightly open door. He had to keep up the pretense.

He knew now, though, that the amnesia was a fraud, that the job offer was a trick, probably intended to get him out of New York while Osborn took possession of the city and turned Peter's home into . . . into something hostile. Peter didn't know the details of what Osborn had planned, but he knew it could only be bad.

"Whyever *not,* boy?" Osborn looked convincingly surprised and hurt.

Peter hesitated. "Well, I'm not saying *no,* Mr. Osborn, but it's so sudden. I need some time to think it over, to talk things over with my wife. It'd be a pretty big change for us both, after all."

"She'll *love* it in Paris," Osborn said. "Just you wait and see."

Peter shrugged. "I still need to ask her, not tell her, Mr. Osborn."

"If you insist," Osborn said. "But you keep in mind, Peter Parker, that I can't hold this job offer open for you forever; we need to settle this in the next few days. If you won't take the job, we'll find someone who will, and I don't think it'll be hard."

"I'm sure it won't," Peter agreed. "I'll let you know by Monday at the latest, I promise."

"Sooner would be better," Jonah grumbled. "You're being a fool, Parker."

"I probably am," Peter agreed miserably. "I'll let you know as soon as I can." He looked at Osborn, then at Jameson. "Thanks for the offer, whatever happens," he said. "I appreciate it, Jonah."

And he did appreciate it—whatever Osborn's reasons, Jonah surely wasn't involved in them. Jonah had admitted that Peter deserved a position on the *Bugle* staff, and Peter knew that admission had to be sincere.

Coming from J. Jonah Jameson, that was high praise, and he felt honored.

But he couldn't let that affect his decision. He had responsibilities here in New York.

He turned and left the office, almost walking into the door before he remembered to open it.

He was thinking hard—not about the job itself, not about leaving New York, but about why Osborn had made the offer.

And one more thought. Osborn was too canny to make the slip he had earlier. So had Peter imagined it, or had Osborn done it on purpose?

And if so, why?

Did he just want Peter out of the country? Or did he want him gone while *knowing* that it was a surrender, an admission of failure?

Peter shook his head. How could you make sense of a guy like Osborn? How could anyone?

Eight

Peter sat crammed into a corner of an outbound E train, lost in his own thoughts and oblivious to the other commuters jammed in around him.

He was remembering.

He remembered meeting Norman Osborn for the first time—Harry's father, a wealthy businessman, who seemed eager to meet and befriend all of Harry's friends, but who quickly showed a darker side, shouting at Harry, belittling him, whenever Harry failed to live up to his impossible standards.

And he remembered meeting the Green Goblin—the maniacal monster jetting about on his bizarre little "goblin glider," throwing funny little pumpkin bombs that were anything but a joke.

The "glider" wasn't a glider at all, of course—it was jet-powered, a steel contraption shaped halfway between a rocket and a bat, and the Goblin had stood with one foot strapped on each wing, riding it like a unicyclist.

Building that thing, and the Green Goblin's other gimmicks, had taken mechanical and chemical brilliance, even though the plans for them had been stolen. And using them had required superhuman strength and agility—which the Goblin unquestionably had.

Peter remembered the shock he had felt when he pulled off the Goblin's mask and saw the face of poor Harry's bullying father—he had expected to see a stranger, or some known criminal, not a well-respected man like Osborn. But that had been nothing to what came after.

Osborn had learned *his* identity, as well—he knew that Peter Parker was Spider-Man. And he had used that knowledge to torment Peter. Osborn lived in a world where nothing mattered but power and possessions, where competition was the be-all and end-all of human interaction, and his greatest joy was to demonstrate his own power, his own superiority, by harming anyone who dared defy him.

Spider-Man had dared to defy him, and Peter Parker was Spider-Man, so Norman Osborn, as the Green Goblin, had set out to make life miserable for anyone and everyone associated with Peter Parker.

That had climaxed with the Goblin's kidnapping of Gwen Stacy, the woman Peter had loved, and who had loved Peter—he and Mary Jane were only friends back then; it had been Gwen he loved and hoped to marry.

And it had been Gwen that the Green Goblin flung to her death from atop the Brooklyn Bridge.

That had been one of the moments when Peter Parker's entire life changed, when his whole understanding of the world around him shifted.

There had been important events in his life before, certainly—the death of his parents, the spider-bite that gave him his strange powers, and so on—but only one other moment had wrenched his entire reality around the way Gwen's death did. That had been when he caught the man who had killed his Uncle Ben, and realized that it was the same petty thief he had let escape earlier.

That was when he had come to understand that with great power comes great responsibility, that as Spider-Man it was his duty to stop criminals from harming innocents, simply because he *could*. That was when he had truly realized that not only do actions have consequences, but *inaction* can have consequences just as severe. That was the moment when he really became Spider-Man.

But the moment Gwen died had changed everything again; that was when he had come to understand that sometimes taking action isn't enough, that things can go wrong, that sometimes the best intentions don't matter, that the world is a cold, hard place where sometimes the good guys lose.

His childhood had died when Uncle Ben died, but his innocence had died with Gwen. Ever since that day atop the bridge his world had been a darker, grimmer place.

And it was the Green Goblin who did that to him.

It was Norman Osborn.

But he had pursued Osborn, trapped him, defeated him, and finally watched as he was impaled by his own out-of-control goblin glider. The pointed nose of that malicious machine, driven by the full power of that amazingly compact jet engine, had punched through the Goblin's chest, smashing sternum and ribs and heart.

Any ordinary man would have died. Peter had thought Osborn *did* die—certainly he had been unconscious, not breathing, his heart stopped. Peter had thought that Gwen's death was avenged, that Osborn had paid for his crimes and was gone for good—not that that could bring Gwen back, or restore what Peter himself had lost.

But the chemical formula that had transformed a businessman into a monster, that had given Norman Osborn his superhuman strength and driven him mad, was more powerful than anyone had realized. Osborn's mortal wounds had healed. He had woken up in the morgue and escaped, taken shelter in Europe while he recovered.

Everyone knew the Green Goblin was dead—dozens of people had seen the body; a doctor had issued a death certificate. Osborn and his helpers had covered his tracks after he awoke; as far as the world knew, the Green Goblin was dead.

But Norman Osborn was still alive, and after years of healing, of rebuilding, of plotting and planning, he had at last returned to New York, seeking revenge.

And obviously, since he was alive, and the Goblin was dead, Norman Osborn was not, had never been, the Green Goblin. So he had said, and so most people believed.

But Peter Parker knew better. Osborn might not wear that hideous costume any more, he might not ride around on a goblin glider pulling gadgets from his bag of tricks, he might have suppressed his insane laughter, but he was still, underneath it all, the monster who killed Gwen, who wrecked the lives of everyone around him and blamed it all on his victims' own weakness.

He had reappeared after years of hiding in Europe, and his reappearance had been an endless nightmare for Peter. Years of emotional healing had been undone, the mental scabs ripped away, as he saw his worst enemy standing there proclaiming innocence of any wrongdoing. Images Peter had thought buried were dragged to the surface— Gwen's terror-stricken face as she fell, the Goblin's leer as he let her.

And even while Osborn had been playing the wronged innocent in public, in private he had made it plain to Peter that their struggle was not over, that he still intended to destroy Peter. He had killed others—even Ben Reilly, who'd been closer to a brother to Peter than anyone else he'd ever known. Osborn had beaten Peter a dozen times, and gloated that the worst was yet to come.

And now he was claiming not to remember any of that. He was treating Peter as a friend, offering him favors— but it was all a trap, all just more maneuvers designed to torture him. It had to be. The job in Europe was surely just a plum dangled in front of Peter's face, knowing full well that Peter wouldn't dare take it—or that if he did, that in doing so he was betraying himself and the memories of Gwen and Uncle Ben by leaving New York undefended.

Peter realized he was trembling at the very thought. He looked up, and realized that the train was passing through the 67th Avenue station—Forest Hills was the next stop. He was almost home.

He found his way out of the subway lost in a fog of bad memories, his stomach roiled by thoughts of Norman Osborn; he barely saw his surroundings as he made his way home.

When he walked up the street he saw that the house was dark, and he realized that Mary Jane was still in class, and wouldn't be back for at least an hour. He should have thought of that, he told himself.

And ordinarily, he *would* have thought of it, and he would have spent an hour or two web-slinging in Manhattan, looking for some sign of the Rat Pack, or failing that, for some other wrongdoer he could clobber. His little meeting with Osborn had shaken him; he hadn't given any thought to anything but getting home.

He could still suit up and work off some energy—going back to Manhattan would take too long, but Queens wasn't exactly crime-free. He couldn't expect to find the Rat Pack or Dr. Doom holding up a liquor store in Flushing, but *somebody* might be, and Spider-Man had always been an equal opportunity hero—no mugging or holdup was beneath his notice.

But right now, Peter admitted to himself that he simply didn't feel like it. It was too early for burglars or most other thieves, and swinging around aimlessly looking for litterbugs and jaywalkers seemed stupid.

There was a real super-villain out there, apparently plotting to take over the city, and Peter had a pretty good idea who it was and more or less where he was. He couldn't interest himself in mere muggers when someone like Norman Osborn was out there scheming.

Norman Osborn, Public Advocate—*there* was a horror! Just a heartbeat away from becoming mayor.

And Peter, having had time to think on the subway train, no longer had any doubt at all that sometime soon, if no one stopped Osborn, that the mayor's heartbeat would stop. That had to be why Norman had taken the job in the first place.

He didn't think Osborn would kill the mayor himself; Osborn surely knew there were still people out there who hadn't entirely accepted his lie that he had never been the Green Goblin. He would want to have an absolutely ironclad alibi. And he probably wouldn't have the mayor killed within the next day or two, either. He had already waited a couple of weeks—it would be too suspicious if the mayor died so soon after Osborn's appointment to office.

But sometime in the month between now and the election, Peter was sure the mayor would die.

It might look like an accident, or a suicide; it might be an obvious assassination, carried out by the Rat Pack; it might be an execution-style job, like the murder of Paul Charenton. Any of those would be well within Norman's capabilities.

The mayor had guards, of course—in fact, since the Rat Pack's raids began, once the mayor had refused a few of their ransom demands, he had been guarded as heavily as the president, with cops and various security people accompanying him everywhere he went. The concrete barriers were in place around City Hall again, to keep car bombs away from the building, and the fences were up, limiting access on foot.

That wouldn't be enough, Peter knew; the finest guards in the world couldn't hope to stop every sniper or hired super-villain.

Spider-Man, with his spider-sense, might be able to prevent the murder—if he devoted virtually every waking hour to guarding the mayor.

And of course, that was assuming he didn't go to Europe as the *Bugle*'s new staff photographer.

So he couldn't go. That was obvious.

He couldn't go.

Peter realized that while he had been thinking this through he had reached his own front door, and that he was standing there staring blankly at the doorknob. He grimaced. He was in no shape to go out hunting crooks even had he wanted to; he was far too distracted. He'd probably forget to shoot the next strand of web, or not even notice a holdup until a panicky thug took a shot at him.

He fished his key out of his pocket, opened the door, and slipped inside.

He was sitting in the living room, still thinking hard, when Mary Jane arrived ninety minutes later.

"Hey, Tiger," she said, as she dropped her notebook on an endtable. "You're looking pensive—what's up?"

"I saw Norman Osborn today," Peter said. "At the *Bugle*."

"Not a surprise," Mary Jane said. "He's half-owner, he has an office there—sometimes you're gonna run into him. Sometimes you *have* run into him. So how come this time you're in a funk about it?"

"I didn't just run into him in the hall this time," Peter explained. "He called me into Jonah's office, and we talked there."

"Wow, that must have been fun," she said. "Bet the hatred was seething so thick even Jonah could see it—not that *he* has any great love for our pal Norm these days."

Peter shook his head. "Osborn's feigning amnesia," he said. "You remember, he had amnesia once, and forgot who I was, and who he was?"

"I remember," she said. "It's back?"

"He's faking it," Peter said. "I'm sure of it."

"So he's pretending he doesn't hate you and want to ruin your life?" She flopped onto a sofa. "Okay, I give up—how is this a bad thing? And if it's *not* a bad thing, why's he doing it?"

"I don't know," Peter said. "Not for sure. I guess he's trying to lull me into a false sense of security."

"Judging by your face, it's not working."

"No," Peter agreed.

For a moment they sat silently, Peter still lost in thought, Mary Jane waiting for him to snap out of it.

When he didn't, after a moment she asked, "So what did he want to talk about?"

"He offered me a job," Peter said.

Mary Jane blinked and sat up straight. "A job?" she asked. "What, at Osborn Industries?"

Peter shook his head. "Working for the *Bugle*," he said. "In Europe."

"Working for the *Bugle* would be . . . wait a minute. In *Europe?*"

"Mostly based in Paris, he said. But there'd be a lot of travel."

Mary Jane stared at her husband as he sat on the couch, mindlessly tracing circles on the fabric of the arm with one finger.

"I think you'd better tell me all about it, Petey," she said.

Hesitantly at first, but picking up speed, Peter told her the whole story.

"Osborn's taunting me," he said at last. "He knows I can't take the job, not while he's staying here in New York. He's just dangling it to tease me."

He waited for Mary Jane's response, the quick comforting agreement he expected, the assurance that he was doing the right thing, but it didn't come. Instead an awkward, uncomfortable silence grew.

Peter looked at Mary Jane.

"Paris," she said, staring back at him, unseeing. "The Sorbonne. Money. Medical insurance."

Peter blinked. "But I can't go," he said.

"I know, but . . . you're *sure* he's faking the amnesia? There isn't the least little chance it's genuine?"

"I'm sure," Peter said.

"You don't . . . I mean, Petey, there's no chance at all that you're letting the fact that this is *Norman Osborn* cloud your judgment? You're sure? Because this . . . this would be *so* cool. Are you *absolutely sure* that you aren't making a mistake? You know how Norman gets to you sometimes—you have every reason in the world to hate him, Peter, and yes, he really *is* a treacherous, murderous liar, I know that almost as well as you do, but isn't there *any* chance that this whole amnesia thing is for real?"

He stared at her helplessly.

"I'm sure," he said. "But MJ, even if I weren't sure, how could I leave New York now, with the Rat Pack on the loose? Even if they aren't taking their orders from Osborn—and I think they probably are—they're still a threat."

"Spider-Man isn't the *only* super hero in New York," she protested.

"But I'm the one who's most involved in this," he replied. "Look, you've known all along who I am . . ."

"Of course I know," she interrupted. "That's not it. I know why you're Spider-Man. I know you have to do what you can to help people, that if it comes down to choosing between you and me being a little better off and Spider-Man saving innocent lives that it's going to be Spidey to the rescue every time —I know that, and I approve of it completely, Petey. It's one reason I love you—I mean, how could I *not* love someone who does the things you do, putting yourself at risk to help others, putting their concerns above your own safety, and your own happiness? It's *noble* of you. The whole Spider-Man thing, all that responsibility that comes with your powers, that's *fine*—you can help people, so you do, and that's wonderful. But Peter, there are innocent people in danger in Europe, too. There's crime there. There are super-villains there. You wouldn't be giving up the tights and web shooters."

"But I have responsibilities *here*. The Rat Pack is in New York. Norman Osborn is in New York."

"The Avengers are in New York," Mary Jane retorted. "The Fantastic Four are in New York."

"But they won't stop *Osborn*."

"Are you really sure he *needs* stopping? Maybe the amnesia really *is* back . . ."

"It isn't."

"Maybe he's pretending it's back because he wants to put his past behind him and really be the philanthropist he pretends to be, then!"

Peter sighed with exasperation. "MJ, this is *Norman Osborn* we're talking about!"

"Exactly!" Mary Jane replied. "He's the man you hate more than anyone else in the world. Are you *absolutely sure* you aren't letting that affect your thinking, Peter? Are you turning down this job because Spider-Man is needed in New York, or just because it's Norman Osborn who's offering it?"

He stared at her in frustration. "It's because Osborn is offering it that I know I'm needed here!"

"So if Jonah had offered it, and you hadn't known that Osborn arranged it, you'd take it?"

Peter hesitated, then said, "No—not with Osborn in the public advocate's office."

"You're sure?"

"You keep *asking* me that!" Peter exploded. "Yes, MJ, I really am sure! Osborn is faking his amnesia, and I'm turning down the job because I'm needed here in New York, where I know what's going on, more than I'm needed in Paris, where I barely even speak the language and don't know one subway stop from the next!"

"If you turn down this job, you may lose the freelance work you do for the *Bugle,* too, you know—you'd be giving Norman an excuse to cut you off."

"Does he even *need* an excuse?" He frowned. "I think he likes being able to dangle things in front of me, then snatch them away. If I *did* accept the Paris job he'd probably find a way to ruin it for us!"

"But maybe not—maybe it would be worth it to him to have you out of New York."

"That's exactly what I'm afraid of!"

She stared at him, her hands on her hips.

"Tiger, maybe *you* should do some dangling," she said. "You don't need to give Osborn your decision right away, do you? Can't you keep him hanging for a while? Maybe you'll find some way to get rid of the Rat Pack, or maybe . . . I don't know. Anything could happen. Osborn could drop dead of a heart attack. Can't you put it off?"

"I can put it off for a while, I suppose, but if Osborn

asks me straight out for a decision, take it or leave it, I'll have to leave it. You see that, don't you?"

"I don't *want* to see it," Mary Jane replied, but without any force behind her words.

"I know you don't—but you have to, honey. I can't stand by and let innocents suffer, whether it's bystanders during the Rat Pack's next raid, or the mayor when Osborn tries to murder him. I've let too many bad things happen."

"Like your Uncle Ben's murder," Mary Jane said.

"Like Uncle Ben's murder," Peter agreed. "You know all about that. You know I need to make up for just standing by when that burglar escaped—I can't let someone else's Uncle Ben die like that."

"You can't stop *everything* bad that happens, Peter. You can't wipe out crime all by yourself."

"But I have to do what I *can*—and I can do it better here in New York than I could in Paris, and right now New York needs me more, with Osborn where he is."

"But how do you know there isn't some mastermind plotting to take over Paris even as we speak? And he wouldn't know how to deal with Spider-Man, where Osborn . . ."

She stopped without finishing the sentence.

"Where Osborn knows exactly how to stop me?" Peter said bitterly. "Is that what you were going to say?"

"I wasn't going to say it, Tiger, but I might have been thinking it." She shrugged. "Can't blame a girl for thinking, can you?"

"I guess not," he mumbled, "but I don't have to like what you're thinking, do I? Besides, I'll get Osborn eventually. Somehow."

"Of course you will—but when? Maybe a stay in Europe would give you a chance to make plans, give you a new perspective, help you come up with something he doesn't expect."

"There isn't *time* for that," Peter protested. "If he really is planning to murder the mayor to put himself in power, he'll have to do it before the election."

"And how are you going to stop him?"

"I don't *know!*" Peter shouted. Then he caught himself. "I don't know *yet.*" He took a deep breath. "I need some fresh air," he said. "I need to think."

"I take it you aren't talking about a romantic walk around the Unisphere?"

"Walking wasn't what I had in mind," he admitted. "But if you'd rather . . ."

"Nope. Go for it, Tiger—sling those webs. I'll bet we both could use a little time alone to think." She smiled wryly. "I've been talking too much myself. But think about this while you're swinging around out there, Tiger—is it Norman that's making you turn this down, or is it Spider-Man? If there's a threat out there you have to be ready for it. But if there's no threat, and you're *creating* one, inventing one in your own mind because this chance is too good to be true—then what? What happens the next time a lucky break comes along? Do you turn away from that one, too?"

Peter hesitated, unable to reply immediately.

"I can't answer any of that," Mary Jane said. "Only you can—and I'm sure you need to think about it. But remember, Tiger, the promise you made to your Uncle Ben's memory was a vow of responsibility, not a vow of poverty."

He leaned forward and kissed her. "I know," he said. "And thanks for reminding me. I love you." Then he hurried upstairs, unbuttoning his shirt.

A moment later a shadowy figure in red and blue slipped out the back bedroom window and fired a line of webbing at the nearby oak tree.

At first Spider-Man didn't think about the job offer, or Norman Osborn, or even where he was going—he simply swung through the night, moving away from the house by old familiar habit. The moon overhead was bright and round, almost full, and combined with the perpetual glow of the city gave him plenty of light to find his way, even in areas where no street lamps functioned.

It was October, Indian summer had settled in, and the air was warm and fresh. In weather like this even the city, that vast web of concrete and asphalt, smelled of damp earth, an odor that seeped through Spider-Man's mask.

For twenty minutes he moved almost randomly through the streets of Queens, steering toward the areas with taller buildings—and darker alleys. He was well west of Forest Hills when he spotted what he was after.

A beat-up Chevy was stopped in front of a liquor store— but the engine was still running. A man in a leather jacket entirely unnecessary in the present weather was walking from the car into the shop; he looked nervous, and his hand was fumbling inside the jacket.

Spider-Man swung down and stuck to the cornice above the store's front window, just below the neon sign reading HAL'S LIQUOR. Hanging upside-down, he peered inside.

As he had expected, the man in the jacket was looking about uneasily, waiting until there were no other customers. An elderly, white-haired gentleman with a very red nose was at the checkout, paying for a bottle of something.

Spider-Man dropped, spinning in midair, and landed crouched in the doorway, just behind the old man as he stepped outside. The man in the leather jacket was just pulling a gun out of his armpit, his attention now focused entirely on the clerk behind the counter.

When the string of still-damp webbing yanked the gun from his hand he yelped in surprise, then stared down at his empty hand.

"Got a permit?" Spidey asked from the door, dangling the gun from one finger like a yo-yo. "If not, there's this little thing called the Sullivan Act . . ."

The would-be holdup artist turned, finally aware of Spidey's presence; his jaw dropped open in shock. Then he turned the other way and started running.

No back door was visible; the thief was simply panicking. A line of webbing shot out and snagged his heel, and he fell flat on the floor. The impact stunned him.

"Wow," the man at the counter said. "I mean . . . wow. Thanks."

"Hope he didn't break anything," Spidey said, addressing the cashier. "You might want to call the cops to come pick him up on that Sullivan violation. Since he didn't have time to take anything a robbery charge might not stick." As he spoke he leaped into the store and quickly, expertly webbed the semi-conscious robber to the floor.

That done, he turned. "And if you'll excuse me, I believe there's a getaway driver out there being oblivious— I've been listening for the engine, and he's still idling. Gotta go explain to him that he should have been paying more attention." He shook his head. "You just can't get a good driver these days."

Just then an engine roared, and tires squealed, as the getaway driver *did* realize something had gone wrong.

"Oh, good," Spider-Man said. "Exercise!"

With that he bounded out to the street.

In open country, or on any decent highway, he would never have been able to catch up to the Chevy—but this was a back street in Queens. There were traffic lights, and traffic, and other impediments.

Still, it was an entertaining chase for perhaps three blocks; when the driver lost his nerve and skidded to a stop at a red light simply because there was heavy traffic in the other direction and charging through would require a skilled Hollywood stuntman, Spidey was able to drop himself onto the roof of the car.

His uncanny ability to stick to any surface kept him secure as the driver spotted a break in traffic and floored the accelerator, whipping around the corner to the right, onto the larger thoroughfare. Even as the panicky would-be thief pounded on his horn and swerved through city traffic at about forty miles an hour, Spidey crawled forward and thrust his head down in front of the windshield.

"Peek-a-boo," he said—a line that was hardly original, that he'd used a hundred times, but still effective.

The driver screamed—Spidey could hear it even over the roar of engines and the cacophony of car horns. He slammed on the brakes, and the car fishtailed, missing a truck in the next lane by inches before swerving up onto the curb and smacking into a trash can. It came to a rubber-smoking stop a foot short of ramming a lamppost, the engine stalled out.

"Sheesh," Spidey said, swinging his head around to the half-open driver's side window. "I was just trying to be *friendly,* you know. Seems to me that's pretty reckless driving you were doing there."

"Aaaaugh," the driver replied.

"Say, is this your car? What year is it?"

"Arrgh."

"I notice you aren't using the key. Is hotwiring the fashionable thing now? I hadn't heard."

"Gaaah."

"What's that? It's *not* your car? Oh, what a shame—that's grand theft auto, isn't it? Naughty, naughty." He had to maneuver carefully to get his hand through the window and positioned properly; he hoped the driver wouldn't be clever enough to close the glass on his wrist.

But then, if he were clever, he'd hardly have been helping his buddy hold up a liquor store. The driver didn't reach for the window crank; instead he tried to bat away Spidey's hand as if it were an approaching insect.

All that did, when Spidey pressed the button on his web shooter, was get the man's left hand securely webbed to the side of his head.

Sirens were approaching—police sirens. Someone in one of the passing cars had probably used a cell phone to call 911, Spider-Man thought.

He tidied up the webbing a little, then straightened up, kneeling on the roof of the car. He could see the approaching lights of a police car; they would handle this.

He fired a web-line at the corner of a nearby building, and a moment later he was airborne, swinging away.

He had stopped a robbery and apprehended two criminals, and he tried to tell himself, as he swung away, that he should be feeling at least a little satisfaction over that. A liquor store's receipts were safe, and someone would presumably be getting his car back, and no shots were fired—wasn't that a good night's work?

Whether it was or not, it wasn't satisfying. He still felt frustrated and angry. He knew that he was right about turning down the European job and staying in New York—he *knew* it—but Mary Jane wasn't happy with it, and that meant that *he* wasn't happy with it.

And besides, what if she were right? What if what he knew—knew deep in his bones, with a deep, cold certainty—said more about his own pessimism and obsession than it said about Osborn's plans?

Could he live his life that way, constantly worrying about Osborn, seeing Osborn's hand in everything, good or bad, that came along? Could he ask Mary Jane to live like that?

He wished he had someone to take out his frustrations on, someone who could give him a real fight, not just petty crooks. He felt about ready for a tussle with good old Dr. Octopus, or the Rhino, or even something like Stegron the Dinosaur Man—someone he could hit with his full strength. Just tripping that goon back in the liquor store might have left him with a broken jaw or cracked wrist if he landed wrong, and Spider-Man hadn't laid a glove on him.

He wanted to really *hit* someone.

And of course, he knew exactly *who* he wanted to hit. But he couldn't even do *that*—Osborn was a respectable businessman and an important city official, so far as the rest of the world was concerned.

If only everyone knew what a monster Osborn was . . . if only there were some way Spider-Man could *show* them all that Osborn was a murderous thug.

He couldn't show them anything by taking out a pair of stickup men out here in Queens, though.

If only he could be sure just what Osborn was really up to—*was* he after the mayor's office? Was he really the man behind the Rat Pack's raids?

He frowned under his mask.

He wasn't going to find any evidence against Osborn out here, but maybe, just maybe, he might find something if he looked in the right place.

The offices of Osborn Industries, for instance. Osborn was careful, but he could slip up—there might be files, there might be some link to the Rat Pack . . .

It was worth a look, anyway.

Nine

Norman Osborn had at least half a dozen offices scattered around the city, but the one that seemed most likely to harbor guilty secrets was in the Osborn Industries chemical plant in the Astoria section of Queens, near the East River and Hell Gate, which had once been the company's central office and home base for the Green Goblin. It was there that Osborn had robbed and broken Mendel Stromm, and taken the goblin formula. Although all the administrative functions had been moved to newer quarters in Manhattan, the company's research labs were still there—and Peter Parker suspected it was still where Osborn kept his deepest secrets.

Reaching it took less than twenty minutes; Spider-Man swung his way along where there were suitable buildings, and hitched rides atop buses on the difficult stretches.

At last he sprang atop the base of a broken lamppost at the back of the plant and stared up at the place.

The entire building was surrounded by a high chain-link fence topped by razor wire, but that was no problem; he could leap over something like that with room to spare. The plant itself was six stories high; the original structure appeared to be at least fifty years old, but it had obviously been completely remodeled more than once in that time. Areas that had once been windows had been filled in with concrete, new windows had been cut, concrete stair towers had been added to the exterior. At one time the facade had been glass and red brick; now there was more concrete than brick.

Despite its patchwork nature, it managed somehow to not be particularly ugly in appearance—many of the changes had actually been improvements. Smell was another matter; the place stank of solvents. Spider-Man wondered whether it was violating any EPA rules.

It almost certainly was, he thought, but Osborn would know who to threaten, bribe, or flatter to ensure that nothing was done about those violations.

Spider-Man paused before swinging over the fence, looking for danger, listening, giving his spider-sense time to react. This was, after all, Osborn's stronghold, much more than his midtown office, and there were undoubtedly secrets here Osborn wouldn't want discovered. There would be security guards and alarms everywhere.

But those secrets were exactly why Spider-Man was here, and he could not detect any immediate threat.

He leaped to the facade of a neighboring building, anchored a web-line to a cornice, then launched himself over the fence. He let go of the web once he had cleared the razor wire, intending to drop down to the narrow strip of asphalt behind the fence, but at the last instant he fired a strand of webbing up to the overhanging eaves of the plant and caught himself in midair—as he had approached the pavement between the fence and the building his spider-sense had warned him off.

He still couldn't see anything, but he realized there were probably sensors of some kind—electric eyes or pressure sensors—all through that paved area, ready to spot any intruder, and those had triggered his spider-sense. That meant ground level was clearly not his best way in.

Instead he landed on the side of the building, twenty feet up. The glass and concrete here were sheer, unbroken by any ledge, sill, or niche, but that was no problem for someone who could stick to any surface.

He hung there for a moment, considering his next move.

Crawling down and getting in on the ground floor would almost certainly mean facing a battery of alarms, and he could hardly expect Osborn to have left windows open— the window his left hand was sticking to didn't look as if it *could* open. That left two possibilities: going up to the roof and finding a way in, or *making* a way in through the wall.

He could almost certainly punch through a window—they might well be bulletproof, given Osborn's history, but they probably weren't spider-proof, not if he put his back into it. That, however, might draw unwanted attention—a broken window would be visible to anyone passing by, such as, for example, a police prowl car on patrol, or a roaming security guard. And falling fragments might set off those alarms his spider-sense had warned him of, down at ground level, or the windows themselves might all be equipped with alarms.

That left the roof. He scurried up the side of the building, moving hands and feet with an odd, inhuman rocking motion that he had mastered, seemingly by instinct, years ago when he first acquired his arachnid abilities. This movement let him peel each hand or foot free, then set it securely in its next position.

A moment later he thrust his head above the low parapet and looked at the roof.

"Figures," he muttered to himself.

The roof was cluttered with antennas, vent pipes, and various instruments, and anywhere that nothing so utilitarian intruded, the space was divided up by coils of razor wire; there was no open area more than a yard across anywhere. No one would be able to land, say, a helicopter or a quinjet on this place without doing some damage.

In fact, even a friendly neighborhood Spider-Man would have trouble making his way through that maze.

Osborn was clearly a man who wanted his privacy.

"Why, if I didn't know better," Spider-Man mumbled under his mask, "I might even say he was paranoid."

But that was not entirely fair—after all, someone *was* up here trying to break in. Was it still paranoia if you really *did* have enemies after your secrets?

Spider-Man peered over the tangle, looking for a route he could follow, and found one: drainage channels. Surely those would be safe, if somewhat narrow. He swung up over the parapet and started to set foot in the nearest gutter.

His spider-sense tingled, and he froze, his foot still in midair.

Pressure sensors, he thought. It had to be. Electronic eyes or infrared would be set off by rainstorms or pigeons, but a pressure sensor set to register something of human weight—say, anything over sixty pounds—would work just fine.

So, he told himself, he wouldn't put that much weight on the sensors. Instead he stuck himself, both hands and feet, to a nearby heavy-duty vent pipe.

The black-painted surface was polished and slick, and anyone else would have slid down it, but his clinging ability did not fail him. He swung himself around it carefully.

From that vent he was able to stretch out to the next, and then to an equipment box, and so on, making his way across the roof, looking for an entrance to the rooms below.

There was no entrance to be found.

In which case, he told himself, he would just have to make one. Clinging to the side of a large steel box containing softly humming machinery, he reached around the corner and gripped the lower edge of that side of the box. Then he heaved, with all his superhuman strength, and peeled the steel away as if he were opening a TV dinner.

As he had hoped, that exposed a blower pumping out warm air. It was easy for him to wiggle under it and slip into the wide vertical airshaft beneath.

The shaft was completely dark; he could see nothing at all once he was inside. The sides he felt through his thin, porous gloves were not plain sheet metal, but some sort of slick, highly polished plastic coating, so smooth that he actually slid a few inches before he was able to attach himself.

Once he had stopped he felt around, using all his senses to get an idea of where he found himself.

He was head-down in a shaft that was at least seven or

eight feet across and round, so that he could not brace himself across it or wedge himself into a corner; the only thing that kept him from plummeting down into the dark was his spiderlike ability to stick to walls.

He grimaced to himself beneath his mask. The official explanation for the plastic, if anyone had ever asked, was probably to keep the chemical fumes from corroding the vents, but he had a strong suspicion that it was really to keep intruders like himself from using the ventilation system to move around the building. Any ordinary burglar, or for that matter even most other non-flying super heroes, would have slid straight down the shaft to . . . to somewhere. He had no idea what was at the bottom, and he didn't think he wanted to find out.

He clambered slowly down the shaft, amazed at how hard it was to keep from sliding—he had never before encountered a surface so slick; by comparison, Teflon felt like glue. He didn't hurry; not only was it a difficult climb, but he wanted to give his eyes time to adjust to the darkness. He peered intently down into the blackness beneath, and gradually made out lighter spots.

Faint light was seeping in from half a dozen openings below him, all at the same height—horizontal vents, presumably. He approached the nearest and felt the outline of the seam where it joined the main shaft.

It was a normal rectangular vent, its sides ordinary galvanized steel—and it was only about a foot wide and six inches high. Ant-Man or the Wasp could have crawled through it, but *he* couldn't.

"Nobody ever has these problems in the movies," he muttered. "In Hollywood all the ductwork's big enough to fit the Hulk." Which, he realized, was probably why Osborn had made sure that these vents weren't—good ol' Norm probably invested in more movies than he watched, but such a cliché wouldn't have escaped him. With a sigh, Spider-Man began working his way around the shaft, checking the other vents.

All six were the same size. He couldn't fit into any of them.

He could, however, enlarge an opening. Smashing an air duct would mean that Osborn would know someone had been here, but it seemed to be the only way in.

Bracing his feet as well as he could against the almost frictionless side of the shaft, he shoved both hands into the nearest duct and forced them apart.

For a moment the frame resisted even his incredible strength, but then with a squeal of tearing metal the vent split open, the sides of the shaft's opening crumpling; the plastic coating around the opening shattered with a sound like pouring corn flakes.

Spidey didn't wait to admire his handiwork; he slid quickly through the hole, head first, and found himself squeezed into the gap between a concrete floor above him and a drywall ceiling below. In the dim glow that leaked in from somewhere he could make out wires and plumbing, but no details that would tell him where he was.

He braced his back against the concrete, hands and feet on the drywall, ready to push—and he waited.

His spider-sense did not react.

Whatever was below the ceiling beneath him was therefore not immediately deadly. He pushed, drywall crunched, and he tumbled through into an empty corridor in a shower of plaster dust and paint chips.

He landed rolling and sprang to his feet, ready to defend himself against whatever he found, and discovered himself face to face with a bulletin board.

The corridor itself was unlit except for security lights at the corners, but that was enough for Spidey to read, "Will whoever removed the blue goggles from 445-B please return them? They are my personal property and have sentimental value." That was tacked over a safety notice on the treatment of chemical burns. Next to it was the printed schedule for the Osborn Industries softball league, with several amendations written in in pen—apparently one team had forfeited several games, resulting in some rearrangements.

There were no messages for the Rat Pack there, no announcements of the Green Goblin's next target, nothing out of the ordinary at all; if Spider-Man wanted to find something tying Osborn solidly to the Rat Pack, or even the Goblin, he would have to look further. He turned and studied the corridor.

The floor was scuffed gray tile; the walls were green tile from the floor to waist height, and painted white above that. The whole place smelled slightly of carbon tetrachloride or something very like it, reminding Spidey of his days in high school chem lab.

The passage ran at least twenty yards in either direction, with half a dozen widely-spaced doors along either side; all the doors were closed and dark. At each end another corridor crossed this one, forming a T, and at each intersection one modest light shone from the ceiling. He was near the center, standing amid a mess of dust and broken drywall.

And of course, he had no idea where any guilty secrets might be hidden. It was a big building.

"Gotta start somewhere," he said, choosing one of the nearer doors at random.

It was locked, but that couldn't stop someone with the proportional strength of a spider. He twisted the knob until something snapped, and the door opened.

The room inside—446, according to the number on the door—was a small lab, with a black workbench down one side, a ventilation hood set into the opposite wall, and a spotlessly tidy desk in the corner. It didn't look promising. There was a file cabinet, and Spidey eyed it for a moment, but then he shrugged and turned away.

"If I try to go through every file in the whole building I'll be here until New Year's," he muttered.

This was obviously just an ordinary chemist's office—

or lab, or both. He wanted Osborn's personal area; that was where anything incriminating would be.

There had to be a building directory somewhere—down in the lobby, most likely, or maybe beside the elevators. He took a step down the corridor—then froze.

He had just heard the soft whir of an elevator door opening, and his spider-sense had kicked in.

A night watchman making his rounds, probably—or perhaps company security, looking for an intruder; breaking that lock might have set off an alarm somewhere, even if his entrance through the ventilation system hadn't. He bounded quickly to the wall, and then ran diagonally upward onto the ceiling, where he clung flat to the drywall with hands and feet.

Nobody looked at the ceiling at first. He might go completely unnoticed up here. He waited.

And then the first figure came around the corner, shining an incredibly bright flashlight down the corridor.

This was no mere night watchman. At first Spider-Man thought he might be looking at a robot, but then he realized it was a man in elaborate high-tech armor.

He wore a gleaming black helmet and electronic eyepieces midway between goggles and binoculars; above either shoulder complicated handles thrust up from a large padded backpack. His chest was covered with ribbed black plastic, and silvery metal plates covered each shoulder. His hands were encased in shiny black gauntlets, and he held a massive black gadget that Spidey couldn't identify, but that was pretty obviously a weapon—it had hand-grips and a tubular part that looked like the business end. The flashlight was mounted atop this sinister device.

If this was a security guard, Osborn had gone a little overboard—the typical New York rent-a-cop did not wear armor or carry what looked like a disintegrator beam. Spidey hung as motionlessly as he could—and he had his arachnid namesake's ability to be utterly still—as the new arrival shone his light along first one side of the corridor, then the other, checking for open doors.

"Central, this is Rogers," the man said—Spidey couldn't see a microphone, but he assumed there must be one. "At the corner now. Corridor B looks . . . it's Spider-Man! He's on the ceiling!" He raised the weapon and pointed it at the wall crawler.

Spider-Man did not wait for the inevitable; he let go, first with his hands, then with his feet, and dropped off the ceiling into a handspring and roll that sent him sailing, feet first, toward the armored man's chest.

The man dropped flat, as if his legs had folded up on him, and Spider-Man soared over his head.

He hadn't expected that, but he had years of practice in dealing with the unexpected; he recovered instantly and ricocheted off the wall of the cross-corridor, kicking himself upward to land on the ceiling again.

And from this new vantage point he could see that the armored man wasn't alone. Three other similarly armored men were positioned in a triangle down to the left, in front of the elevators. The farthest was facing the other way, guarding against any attack from the other end of the corridor, and Spidey could see a red-and-white company logo on his massive backpack—SECURITEAM, it read. Another line of white print was too small to read from this distance.

"Oh, you've brought friends!" Spidey exclaimed. "How jolly!"

"Spider-Man!" one of the group by the elevator called. "We've been authorized to use lethal force if you don't surrender!"

The man who had dropped and rolled was on his feet again; he and two of the others now had their weapons trained on the wall-crawler, while the fourth man, after a single quick glance, was still watching the other direction.

"Hey, you!" Spidey called, waving. "I'm over here! Your friends found me!"

The fourth man didn't turn, and Spidey let the waving hand dangle, thumb ready on his palm.

"It's just me, you know," he said. "There's no one over that way."

"We can't take your word for that, web-spinner, and you know it," the team spokesman called. "He's following procedure—if you did bring help, we don't want them sneaking up on us. Now, are you going to come peacefully?"

"Well, that depends, I guess," Spider-Man said, cocking his head. "What happens if I do?"

"We'll escort you out of the building and let Mr. Osborn argue with the insurance company about who pays to fix the damage you've caused. That's all—no cops, no charges. Come on, don't make this hard."

"Oh, *that's* no fun!" Spidey's hand moved, and webbing shot out, entangling the nearest man's weapon; the other two responded by firing their weapons at the same instant that Spider-Man released his hold on the ceiling.

Spider-Man had expected energy bursts, or rockets, or perhaps high-explosive bullets, and had assumed the ceiling would be blown to bits; he had anticipated fire and smoke and loud noise and a shower of dust that would add to the confusion and give him cover. Instead the weapons *hissed,* and something spattered against the ceiling with a sound like heavy rain on a tin roof. There was no muzzle flash.

"What on earth?" He rolled when he hit the floor, then bounced up and sprang onto a wall. There he paused long enough to look at the ceiling.

Little blue lumps were stuck everywhere, as if an entire school full of kids had stuck wads of used blueberry chewing gum on it.

And the firing had ceased almost immediately; no one was shooting at him now. "You call *that* lethal force?" he asked. "What *was* that stuff?"

"Fast-acting sedative that'll soak right through clothing and skin," the man with the webbed gun replied. "Our job is to keep this building secure, Spider-Man, not shoot it up ourselves." He seemed completely undisturbed by the fact that his hands and weapon were a single sticky mass of grayish webbing. "One more chance—surrender now, before someone gets hurt!"

"Hey, tougher guys than *you* have tried to hurt me!" Spidey replied.

The webbed man sighed. "Option three," he said.

The wall-crawler's spider-sense went berserk; he dodged, leaping off the wall, not knowing what he was dodging until he heard the whistle of a lash inches from his ear.

The lash also *crackled,* he noticed, and bluish light flickered across the dim hallway; he guessed it was some sort of high-voltage taser. He pinwheeled down the hallway, and as he did he saw that both of the two men who had fired at him before were now wielding electrified metal whips. He had been distracted by the blue gunk on the ceiling and talking to the team leader, and hadn't even seen them switch weapons.

These guys, he decided, were pretty good.

That was when a fifth man in SecuriTeam armor stepped out of a door just inches away, snapping another whip at him.

Okay, he told himself, they're *very* good, getting that guy into position without him noticing a thing. It was time to stop messing around and take these guys down, so he could look around the building a little. He stopped tumbling long enough to fire a web-line and swing it behind him, intending to entangle the newcomer's lash.

Instead the lash sliced through the webbing.

"Uh-oh," Spidey said.

That was not good at all.

These guys were just hired muscle, but they were legal hired muscle. They were amazingly polite about trying to stop him, and clearly didn't go out of their way to hurt anyone. All the same, there were limits to just how nice he could afford to be, and he had now reached them.

"Nighty-night," he said, bouncing off a wall to get an unexpected angle and nailing the SecuriTeam man squarely on the jaw with a red-gloved fist.

The man went down—but there was another behind him, and with a hiss a new stream of sedative capsules sprayed at Spider-Man. He dodged quickly, bounced, and came back at this newest threat.

More armored figures were approaching—suddenly the corridor seemed to be filled with them. Some held the sedative guns, some the taser whips, and others had weapons Spidey hadn't yet seen in use. Some were wearing gas masks.

This was getting out of hand.

Something flashed past him with a whine like an angry hornet, its sudden glare startling him, and another lash swung at him, missing by only an inch or two. His spider-sense was now permanently in overdrive and therefore almost useless. If he was going to win this fight he had to take some of these people down *quickly,* to cut the numbers against him. He leaped wildly, spotted a target, and kicked.

His foot hit a ridged plastic chestplate—and he felt the electric tingle right through the sole of his boot. That armor wasn't just for looks.

As he rebounded a lash finally connected, across the back of one shoulder, and he spasmed, his back arching, as electric current burned through him. He spun away, looking for room to recover.

"He's still standing," an awed voice said.

"Hold it," someone called. "Stand back, everyone."

Instantly, the assault stopped—these guys had discipline. The man whose gun he had webbed stepped forward—and Spidey noticed that the webbing had already been cut away from the weapon, leaving just a few dangling strands; these guys were *good.*

"Okay, Spider-Man," the team leader said. "You still want to fight, we'll fight—but our job isn't to kill you or take you down, it's to protect the building and everyone in it, and if we go on like this we could do some real damage. Whatever you came here for, you aren't gonna get it. Now, why don't you just cut your losses and surrender?"

Spidey looked around himself as his spider-sense tingle faded away.

He had wound up in the room the fifth guard had entered through—a large, shadowy lab of some sort, with a variety of computers and file cabinets scattered among the flasks and beakers, and a wall of windows overlooking the factory floor of the chemical plant from four stories up. The factory had security lights on, and the windows provided him with enough light to see his foes clearly—there were, by a quick count, eight active SecuriTeam members in this one room, and at least a couple more still in the corridors, not counting the two he had managed to knock down so far.

The team leader was right. He thought he *might* be able to beat these guys—he was starting to get a feel for their tactics—but what good would it do? He wasn't going to find anything useful here, and if no one had called the cops yet, someone would soon.

"Do I get a cookie if I surrender?" he asked.

The team leader's mouth twitched in a quickly suppressed smile. "That could be arranged," he said.

"Chocolate chip?"

"Don't push it."

"Awww . . ."

"You have until I count three to surrender, wall-crawler, or we open fire."

"Don't bother," Spidey said, straightening from his wary crouch atop a lab table. "I'll take the cookie and go."

He could sense the team relaxing slightly, but the weapons didn't move. They were still pointed at him.

"Good," the leader said. "Now, if you . . ."

He stopped in midsentence, listening to something Spidey couldn't hear. Not for the first time, Spider-Man wished that he'd somehow acquired the proportional hearing of, say, a rabbit, or a hunting dog—spiders weren't much in that department. A message was presumably coming over the radio built into the team leader's helmet, but Spidey couldn't make out a thing.

"It seems we aren't going to just escort you out of the building after all," the leader said.

"Hey, no changing the rules!" Spidey said. "I still get a cookie, right?"

"It's not up to me any more," the leader said. "Mr. Osborn's on his way up."

Spidey forgot about the cookie.

If he was going to learn anything useful here tonight, this was the best chance he would get. Here, at an unplanned meeting where Spider-Man was in his costume rather than street clothes, Osborn might let something slip, might say or do something that would demonstrate once and for all that the amnesia was faked, that the Paris job was a setup.

It was only a few seconds before he heard footsteps approaching. He tensed.

Norman Osborn walked in, pausing at the door for a fraction of a second to flip a switch and flood the room with fluorescent light. His gray silk suit was perfect, every crinkly red hair neatly in place. He stopped a foot or two from the door and stared silently at Spider-Man for a few seconds.

He ignored SecuriTeam as completely as if they weren't there at all.

"So, Spider-Man," he said at last, "here you are again, breaking and entering like a common burglar."

"Burglars are still common with all the security you've got here?" He gestured at the SecuriTeam. "Wow, Normie, this must be one tough neighborhood!"

"Very funny," Osborn said. No trace of a smile showed

on his features. "No, it was a figure of speech—only an obsessed freak like you could get this far."

"Yeah, you've turned this place into a fortress, haven't you, Norm? Alarms and booby traps everywhere, and all these guys dressed up like a high-tech SWAT team. I guess there must be hundreds of people out there just *desperate* to break into a chemical plant and fall in a vat of something toxic, and that's why you need it all, right? It couldn't possibly be that you have anything to *hide,* could it, Norm? Maybe evidence of a few criminal conspiracies?"

Osborn replied icily, "I am an honest businessman, you wall-crawling scoundrel—it's you and the others who slander me who are the criminals! I can only assume you're jealous of my power and prestige, that even with your freakish abilities you can't begin to equal me. I suppose that's why you abuse me, tell lies about me, accuse me of crimes. What nonsense! I am *above* crime, Spider-Man."

"Oh, of course. And you have these guys with their fancy armor and weapons . . . why, exactly?" He gestured at the black-clad guards.

Osborn glanced at the guards behind him as if just now noticing their existence—though Spider-Man was certain he had been keenly aware of them all along. Osborn wouldn't waste time justifying himself to Spider-Man, but he had a front to maintain around his employees.

"SecuriTeam?" he said. "I hired them because they're the *best,* Spider-Man. They're not criminals. They didn't hurt you. They *could* have, but they didn't, because unlike *you,* you web-slinging freak, they respect the rule of law."

"I'll say they could hurt me," Spider-Man agreed. "I think these guys could give the Avengers a hard time! They'd probably leave your standard-issue burglar just a wet spot on the pavement."

"The best," Osborn agreed.

"So they must be expensive, then. You know, I haven't noticed them patrolling any of the other factories in the area, so why are they *here,* if you're just an honest businessman with nothing to hide? You like throwing the stock-holders' money away?"

Osborn seemed to swell with anger. "They're here because people like you keep *hounding* me!" he bellowed. "You, the Molten Man—who knows what super-powered lunatic is going to break in here next?"

Spider-Man put an index finger to his chin, tapping thoughtfully. "I suppose Doc Strange might know," he suggested. "Or maybe the Mad Thinker—he's big on probabilities and predictions."

"I don't *care* who it's going to be next," Osborn shouted. "I just want whichever of you menaces might take it into his head to intrude kept *out*!"

"Oooh, temper, temper!" Spidey said, wagging an admonitory finger.

Osborn stopped shouting and snapped his mouth shut. Spider-Man watched, impressed despite himself, as Osborn swiftly erased every visible sign of anger from his face in an awesome display of self-control.

"Enough joking, Spider-Man," he said. "I've called the police, and they'll be here any minute. I intend to see you rot behind bars."

"Oh, what fun is that?"

Osborn stared at him silently for a moment, then, without taking his eyes off Spider-Man, said, "Briggs, get your team out of here."

"Sir, I'd advise against it . . ." the SecuriTeam leader began, glancing warily at the web-slinger.

"Your warning is noted and appreciated," Osborn said. "Now get out. I can take care of myself; I'm not frightened by this so-called super hero."

Reluctantly, Briggs signaled to the others, and the room gradually emptied of black-armored guards. A moment later Spider-Man and Osborn stood alone, face to face, between two of the lab benches.

"You're almost right, wall-crawler," Osborn said. "Sending you to jail *would* be fun—but not *enough* fun. So it's not what I'm going to do. Instead, you're going to escape before the cops get here. I'll file a complaint, and you'll be a wanted man, and it'll make your life just that much harder—and you won't be able to do a thing about it, will you?"

"I've been a fugitive before," Spidey said, trying not to let any hint of dismay into his voice. He *had* been a fugitive before, and he hadn't enjoyed it at all. He had a good working relationship with parts of the NYPD at the moment, though, and he hated to lose it. "It's no big deal," he lied.

"No," Osborn agreed. "It's no big deal. It's just one more *little* thing. It's the little things that add up and eat you alive, and you know it."

"Hey, I don't sweat the small stuff," Spidey said. "You should know that."

Osborn grinned a wide, toothy, thoroughly nasty grin. "You're lying, punk. Everything I do to you just shows how much stronger than you I am, how much I'm the better man, and it's gnawing away at you. You wouldn't *be* here if it weren't. You broke in here looking for some way you could bring me down, some way you could get the upper hand—but there *isn't* any. I'm in control, and I'm going to *stay* there, and I'm going to watch you suffer just from *knowing* it."

"Whoa, that's quite an attitude problem you've got there, Norm, that whole *schadenfreude* thing. I'd have a talk with your therapist if I were you." Spidey wished he felt half as cocky as he sounded—and he could see he wasn't fooling Osborn any more than he was fooling himself.

"You think I don't know you?" Osborn said. "I know you better than you know yourself. It's just the two of us in here now, Spider-Man—just you and me, man to man, no guards, no cops, no fancy weapons unless you want to count those silly web shooters of yours. If you're really so tough, if you really don't care what your life would be like, then go ahead and hit me. Give me your best shot.

You've got your freak strength—you ought to be able to kill me, right? Someone as strong as you are ought to be able to kill an ordinary human being with one punch, snap his neck like a twig—or maybe I should say *her* neck."

Spider-Man flinched as if he was the one who had been punched, as if Osborn had just kicked him in the gut, at the reference to Gwen's death.

And the reference was clearly deliberate—but that meant Osborn remembered what had happened to Gwen. He did still remember his time as the Green Goblin.

"But you—you're not . . ." Spider-Man began, choking out the words.

"Not an ordinary man?" Osborn interrupted. "Of course I'm not. But still, I'm here, unarmed, unprepared—couldn't you beat me to death if you tried? How could I stop you?"

"I . . ." Spidey clenched his fists, but did not move toward Osborn.

"You won't kill me," Osborn said. "You won't kill me because you're weak, you're soft. You don't want to spend the rest of your life branded a murderer, hounded by the police and your fellow heroes. And because you don't want to think of yourself as a killer. You think you're *better* than that—when you're really just *weaker* than that."

"I did it once . . ."

"You expect me to believe you *planned* that? That you knew the glider would hit me?"

Any possible lingering doubt that Osborn's amnesia had been faked vanished with that question—this man clearly knew that he had been the Green Goblin. Spidey took a step forward, fist ready.

"And maybe you literally *can't* kill me," Osborn said. "After all, if sixty pounds of jet-powered steel rammed through my chest didn't kill me, can *anything* you could do finish me off?"

"Maybe I don't need to *kill* you," Spidey said, taking another step.

"And I don't need to kill *you,* either—though someday

I might do it all the same, when it suits me. I don't need to kill you, because I already control you, Spider-Man. If you hit me, whether you kill me or not, you're a criminal. I'm a high-ranking official of the City of New York—had you forgotten? I'm the public advocate. Lay a hand on me and the police will hunt you down, will make your life a misery—even more of a misery than it already is."

Spider-Man stopped.

"You can't touch me, Spider-Man," Osborn said. "But I can touch *you*. Any time I want to, any way I want to. Remember that."

Slowly, Spider-Man's fists opened. He stood staring silently at Osborn.

"Get out of here, Spider-Man. You've had your fun. Now go." He pointed to a door at the back of the room. "That opens on a stairway down to the factory floor, and the loading dock's open. You don't need to smash anything or hit anyone. Just get out. Admit you can't face me and go."

Spidey stared at him, seething—but Osborn held all the cards here. SecuriTeam was almost certainly still close at hand, ready to close in and smother Spidey with numbers and high-tech weapons—and that was assuming that Osborn wasn't up to the job himself.

And he was right—hitting him would mark Spidey as a criminal, and would gain nothing. He couldn't take Osborn down as easily as that. There were problems a fist in the face couldn't solve.

He leaped to the doorframe.

He half-expected a trap, but the door was unlocked, and the promised staircase was there, just as Osborn had said it would be.

He was halfway across the factory's main floor, swinging above a vat of solvent, when he heard a sound behind him and turned to see that Osborn had opened one of the windows in that fourth-floor lab.

Osborn leaned out and shouted after him, "You should have taken the European job, boy!"

Ten

Spider-Man swung from one building to the next without conscious thought, letting habit, training, and spider-sense guide him. He made his way across Queens without paying much attention to where he was going.

He had taken worse physical abuse at least a hundred times in the past; SecuriTeam had hardly touched him, and Osborn had never laid a hand on him. Emotionally, though, he felt as if he had just gone toe-to-toe with the Hulk; Osborn had rubbed Spidey's nose in his impotence, his utter helplessness against his most hated foe.

There were other enemies he couldn't put away for good—Wilson Fisk, better known as the Kingpin, for one. The others, though, generally treated him as a worthy opponent, someone to be dealt with when the need arose but not pointlessly antagonized. And all of them were known to other crime fighters—if not the cops, then Daredevil, or the Fantastic Four, or whoever—as criminals.

Norman Osborn was his own personal devil. No one else would help him against Osborn. And Osborn took delight in tormenting him.

He was wrung out, emotionally exhausted. He did not go looking for trouble, for someone to hit, this time; all he wanted was to go home and shut out the world for a while, talk to Mary Jane for a little reassurance, try to get back a little of his lost peace of mind.

The house in Forest Hills was dark; he slipped in through the old familiar back window into the bedroom, and stripped off his costume.

Mary Jane lay in their bed, unmoving, sound asleep. He stared down at her for a moment, at the fine web her red hair made on the pillow in the bright moonlight.

He wanted to talk to her, tell her that now he *knew* for certain that the amnesia was faked and the job was a setup, that he wasn't imagining anything—but he couldn't bring himself to wake her up. She looked so peaceful lying there, so calm.

Instead he put away his costume, brushed his teeth, and tucked himself in beside her.

Despite his late return he awoke early the next day, while the last trace of dawn still lingered in the eastern sky. He slipped out of bed without waking Mary Jane— she must have been exhausted, he thought as he dressed. This whole Osborn matter was probably weighing on her almost as heavily as on him, and she had her classes to worry about as well.

Her first class today wasn't until the early afternoon, so there was no reason to rouse her.

Getting some rest had helped his own peace of mind; as he sat at the table eating a quick breakfast he went over the facts in his head.

Last night Osborn hadn't really told him anything he hadn't already known, on some level; Norman had simply confirmed a few things, removed a few doubts. The amnesia was faked; the job was a trick. Osborn was probably behind the Rat Pack's actions, but Peter still had no proof—in fact, he didn't even have any real evidence, just his own theorizing.

But he did know that the *Bugle* had offered the European job to get Spider-Man out of the way—Osborn had practically said so last night. That meant he had to turn it down.

And, he thought, he might as well get it over with, not let it drag on any longer than absolutely necessary. Mary Jane had been unhappy about the prospect of turning it down, but he knew she would understand, and would accept it once it was done, so the sooner it was done, the better.

With that in mind he finished eating and headed out the door.

The subway ride downtown was uneventful, and he arrived at the *Daily Bugle* without incident. There was no sign of Norman Osborn in the lobby or the elevator, but Peter kept expecting to turn a corner or open a door and see that hated face waiting for him, pointed chin high and mocking eyes bright.

In the city room he waved a greeting to Betty Brant and Ben Urich, then knocked on Jameson's door.

"Come in," Jonah growled. It occurred to Peter that ordinarily, Jonah really only had two ways of speaking—growling and bellowing. For most people those were reserved for moments of extreme emotion, and normal communication was done in a conversational tone, but for Jonah it was the reverse—he growled and bellowed as a matter of course, and any other tone meant that something had jarred him out of his normal habits.

Peter wondered just how Jameson had ever become what he was. Had he had such a strange childhood that he thought his gruff manner was normal? Or had he developed it in adulthood as a protective shell?

He opened the door and stepped into Jameson's office, where Jonah was standing by his desk, glowering at a thin sheaf of computer print-out. Peter waited, not wanting to interrupt Jonah's work.

The silence grew for a few seconds; then Jonah slapped the papers down on his desk and bellowed, "Well, Parker? What is it?"

"It's about that job offer, Mr. Jameson," he said. "The one in Europe."

"Oh, that. I suppose that pretty little wife of yours begged you to go to Paris, and you want us to go ahead and book your flight?"

"Uh . . . no, sir. I came to let you know that I'm turning it down. I appreciate the offer very much, Jonah, but

New York is my home, it's where my roots are, and I just wouldn't fit in in Paris."

Jameson stared at him silently for a moment, working his mouth as if preparing to spit out something distasteful.

"You're a fool, Parker," he said at last. "Was this your wife's idea?"

"No, sir. It's *my* decision. Mary Jane doesn't even know I'm here."

"I don't understand it," Jameson said.

"What, why I'm turning it down? Because I . . ."

"No, not that," Jameson interrupted. "What I don't understand, Parker, is how a spineless wimp like you can get some of those pictures you bring in. You don't have the guts to grab at a chance for a real career even when it's shoved in your face."

"It's not a matter of *guts* . . ." Peter began.

"Of course it is," Jameson interrupted. "What else could it be? You've got your safe little rut here in New York, and you don't have the nerve to climb out of it even when we're hitting you over the head with the ladder. Well, you had your chance, Parker."

"It's not that . . ."

"Don't argue with me. Of course that's it." He picked up a paper from his desk, and waved Peter toward the door. "As long as you're staying in New York, Parker, go take some pictures and stop bothering me. I have a paper to get out, and nobody's paying me to stand here talking to *you*."

Peter hesitated a moment longer, wanting to protest the unfair accusation of cowardice, then shrugged and turned away. *He* knew the truth, even if J.J.J. didn't. Staying here was the real act of courage. He had to stop Osborn.

Now that he knew the amnesia was faked, that Osborn remembered perfectly well that Peter Parker was Spider-Man, and that he himself had been the Green Goblin, it seemed likely that Osborn intended to assassinate the mayor—not personally, but through hirelings, most probably the Rat Pack. He would have to do it soon, before the upcoming election—there were other candidates for public advocate, and Osborn hadn't even declared that he was running.

Until the election, though, he was public advocate, and that meant he would become mayor if and when the mayor died. Peter guessed he would then declare a state of emergency in response to the assassination.

And that would give him the authority to do almost anything he wanted to the City of New York. He could terrorize almost at will. Peter wasn't sure exactly what Osborn had in mind once he was securely ensconced in the mayor's office, but it couldn't be good.

So it was Spider-Man's job to make sure that Osborn never got that far. Until now Osborn would have held off, in case Peter took the Paris job, and simply because the longer the gap between his appointment and the assassination the less suspicion there would be, but once he knew for certain that Spider-Man wasn't going anywhere, and with the election rapidly approaching, why would he wait?

Any minute now, if Jonah happened to phone Osborn and mention that Peter had come in and given his decision, the orders for the mayor's death might go out.

So Spider-Man's duty was clear—protect the mayor, and when the assassination attempt came, stop it and work back up the hit man's chain of command. With luck the trail might even lead to Osborn—but he had probably covered his tracks too well to be caught so easily.

When Peter closed the door of Jameson's office behind him, he knew exactly where he was bound—Gracie Mansion, the mayor's official residence. City Hall was another possible site for an attack, but City Hall was always busy, full of cops, and just across Park Row and Centre Street from Police Plaza. Gracie Mansion seemed the easier target.

He rode the elevator down to the lobby, marched out

of the building, then detoured to an alley, where he changed into his costume.

The familiar smell of the mask covering his nose and mouth, the feel of the cloth over his ears, and the slight color distortion of his one-way eyepieces transformed his perception of the city. As Peter Parker he had the same view of New York as anyone else—the overwhelming size, the layered odors of asphalt, auto exhaust, and uncollected garbage, the constant din of traffic. As Spider-Man his mask filtered everything, made it seem somehow lighter and less oppressive. When he was in costume the city became his playground. Nothing was ever quite as serious when he was swinging from cornices in his red-and-blue longjohns—how could it be?

He wrapped his civilian clothes in webbing and slung the resulting bundle on his back, and then leaped upward, web shooter ready.

A moment later he was swinging his way up Third Avenue at the end of a sticky strand of goo. It was a strange way to travel, but he had come to love it. The rush of air as he swooped down in each long arc was exhilarating; his mask cut the wind and kept bugs and the city's grit out of his eyes and mouth, and he took delight not just in the sheer physical thrill of it, but in the knowledge that he could so easily do this thing no one else could. Even if someone else built web shooters to provide the lines, no one else had the speed, the strength, the agility, the ability to catch himself on any surface if he misjudged somewhere.

And some of the people on the sidewalks always stared and waved and shouted at him as he passed; even in New York, the sight of a super hero swinging overhead was generally worth a second look.

This was the *fun* part of the job.

He covered the two and a half miles to East 88th Street in less than ten minutes, then swung around the corner to the right and headed east, to Carl Schurz Park. One last long swoop across East End Avenue landed him in a treetop.

Trees were not really practical for serious webswinging—they usually weren't tall enough, and all those branches got in the way. On the other hand, he could simply leap from one to the next, catching himself with a strand of webbing if he misjudged the exact distance.

At this time of year this produced a great deal of rustling, and red and gold leaves went showering to the ground each time he launched himself into space, but it was still the quickest, easiest route to his destination. A few such leaps brought him to the rear of Gracie Mansion, and onto the roof.

He ran the length of the roof, looking for signs of illicit entry—other than his own, that is. He found nothing out of place; everything seemed quiet. The view of Hell Gate was splendid, but uninformative. He dropped down to the long porch and continued his inspection, but still found nothing.

He poked around for a while longer, growing steadily more frustrated. This was *not* the fun part of the job—searching for clues, waiting for something to happen. It was, in fact, tedious.

It was also necessary.

He wished he knew the mayor's schedule. He didn't even know when Hizzoner would be home. He was almost certainly somewhere else right now—in his office at City Hall, or at some function or event somewhere in the city.

It occurred to him, a little belatedly, that the mayor's schedule might be posted somewhere, but he had no idea where that might be.

The mansion and its environs were so quiet that he quickly became convinced the mayor was *not* home—which meant he was in the wrong place. He had thought he might find the Rat Pack skulking about, setting booby traps or choosing sniper positions, but there was no sign of anything of the sort. Add in the likelihood that the mayor wasn't here, and . . .

He checked to be sure his web shooters had plenty of fluid, re-wrapped the liquifying bundle that held his street clothes, then launched himself off the mansion's roof, toward the trees. A moment later he was swinging south on First Avenue, bound for City Hall.

He had been able to get atop Gracie Mansion without being noticed, so far as he knew, but City Hall was another matter. It stood in City Hall Park, in the heart of downtown rather than in a quiet residential area by the river, and people were coming and going constantly, on all sides; he couldn't sneak in the back here.

Instead, as he swung across the front of the Municipal Building and dropped to the top of a mailbox across the street from the park he tried his best to look as if he were just passing through, pausing in the vicinity to catch his breath, nothing more.

He sprang across to the top of one of the concrete barriers alongside the park and stood casually, looking about, as if he were an ordinary tourist.

He doubted it was a very convincing act; tourists didn't generally wear skintight red-and-blue suits and masks, and stand atop fences and walls. Still, after a few minutes the people who stared and pointed lost interest and moved on, and none of the cops patrolling the surrounding streets did anything about his presence. The fences and concrete barriers that appeared around City Hall any time there was a known terrorist threat were in place, to keep car bombs or the like from approaching the building, and in theory the police were on heightened alert because of the Rat Pack's raids, but none of them gave him more than a glance.

He could imagine their thoughts. "Oh, it's just Spider-Man. I know about him. He's one of the good guys; I can ignore him."

At least, he *hoped* they thought of him as one of the

good guys. He'd tried his best, ever since he was just a kid, to be one of the good guys. It hadn't always come across that way once he became Spider-Man; he'd been framed for, or accused of, an assortment of crimes over the years, but he'd always been able to clear his name in the end.

Osborn hadn't managed to change that yet—but he might. Those police officers treating their friendly neighborhood Spider-Man as just another part of the scenery might be reacting with drawn guns and panicky radio calls next time.

He worked his way around City Hall Park, first exploring the trees for snipers or surveillance devices, then scurrying up the side of City Hall itself, looking for any signs of Rat Pack activity—or any other assassins, for that matter, since he couldn't be sure Osborn would use the Rat Pack for this. He certainly had other resources available—after all, it hadn't been the Rat Pack that caught an intruder at Osborn's Astoria plant last night.

SecuriTeam appeared to be a legitimate outfit, though; they wouldn't assassinate the mayor. But Osborn had other, less savory connections. He had employed a wide assortment of thugs and super-villains over the years. Spidey had to be ready for anything, up to and including the Green Goblin himself—either Osborn or one of the hirelings he had used in that role over the years.

He scampered across the roof, from west to east, then doubled back and clambered up the cupola. He paused at the top to salute the statue of Justice, then headed back down—literally headed; he climbed head-down, like a spider, in a position that would make an ordinary man dizzy.

He proceeded to the walls, peering in the windows.

He found nothing out of place. His spider-sense never buzzed.

Frustrated, he bounded across the park to the Tweed Courthouse and did a similar search there. When that yielded nothing he returned to City Hall.

When he had completed a second search without result he paused, hanging head-down from a web-line over the front steps, thinking.

He couldn't stay on guard every second of every day until Osborn made his move; he had to eat and sleep, after all. He had done his best to forestall an attack—he was as certain as he could be that there were no traps set anywhere around City Hall, no snipers lurking around Gracie Mansion.

Knowing Osborn as he did, he thought it was likely that the attempt to kill the mayor would be as public as possible. The murder of Paul Charenton had been very quiet, but that had been because Osborn didn't want anyone thinking of it as anything more than, at worst, a continuation of the Rat Pack's ongoing reign of terror. Killing the mayor, though, was another matter. Just shooting him in his office or strangling him in his bed wouldn't cause the same sort of public outrage that gunning him down in the middle of a speech would, and Osborn would want to maximize public outrage to help him push through a demand for emergency powers . . .

At least, Spidey *thought* he would. It was all still just guesswork, really. He had no *proof* that Osborn wanted to be mayor, or meant the present mayor any harm.

The best course of action he could think of now was to go home, make a few phone calls, find out what public appearances the mayor would be making, and then make sure he was at all of them. As a newspaper photographer he could easily have a legitimate interest; there wouldn't be anything suspicious in getting the schedule.

He hated to leave the mayor unguarded. . . .

He stopped in mid-thought and looked out at Park Row, where no fewer than four cops were walking. Now, *there* was a display of spider-ego at work, he told himself. The mayor was always surrounded by guards and cops—he was the *mayor,* a major public official, a prominent figure on the national scene. He was *never* unguarded.

But still, ego or not, Spider-Man knew he'd be happier if *he* was guarding the mayor, as well as all those cops and security people.

But he couldn't. He hadn't eaten since breakfast, for one thing, and it was well after noon. He couldn't stay on guard forever. If he went home now, made that call, got the schedule, he could easily be back on watch at Gracie Mansion before the mayor retired for the night.

Or perhaps he'd come up with a better plan by then. One way or the other, it was time to go. A quick shot of webbing and he was off, swinging eastward across the south facade, headed for home.

Forty minutes later he climbed in the old familiar bedroom window in Forest Hills, reached up to pull off his mask with one hand—and froze.

Mary Jane was asleep in their bed, her red hair gleaming brilliantly in the slanting autumn sunlight.

But she should be in class, he told himself stupidly. *She should have been up and gone hours ago.*

Then he thought she might have laid down for a nap and overslept—but she was still lying on her side in the same position she had been in when he got up that morning, still wearing the same nightgown. If she had gotten up and dressed she wouldn't have undressed just for a nap.

He snatched off his mask and bounded to the bedside, leaning over her. "MJ?" he asked. "You okay?"

She didn't move, didn't answer. He grabbed her shoulder and shook her gently, but she still didn't stir.

At least she was warm, he thought, and he could see that she was breathing, but her breath seemed faint and shallow. He put an ear to her chest and listened for a heartbeat.

It was there, but it seemed weaker than it should be, weaker than he had ever heard it.

"Oh, no," he breathed.

He hesitated for a fraction of a second, considering calling 911, but then he yanked his mask back into place and snatched his unconscious wife up in his arms.

Sometimes there were delays. Sometimes the paramedics got caught in traffic, or made a wrong turn. Mostly, though, he couldn't bear to wait for them to arrive.

He slung Mary Jane over his shoulder and jumped out the window to the waiting tree, headed for Parkway Hospital, the nearest place he could find medical help.

Eleven

Peter Parker knew Parkway Hospital well; he had been there a hundred times with Aunt May. Spider-Man burst into the front entrance and turned sharp right into the emergency room, calling, "I need some help here!"

A nurse appeared at the admitting window, and a young doctor hurried over. At the sight of the unconscious woman in Spider-Man's arms he stepped aside. "This way," the doctor said, gesturing past the glass-block barrier into the emergency room proper. "We'll deal with the paperwork later."

Spider-Man nodded, carrying Mary Jane quickly to the nearest empty bed. "We found her unconscious," he said as he lowered her onto the thin mattress. "Shallow breathing, unresponsive. She . . . her husband says there's no history of anything like this."

"We'll take care of her," the doctor said as he peeled back an eyelid and shone a light into MJ's pupil. "D'you know who she is, anything about her?"

"Her name's Mary Jane Parker. She's a student at ESU. Married, no kids. Her husband's on the way. Let me go get him in here."

The doctor was tilting Mary Jane's head back and forth, studying her features. "Good idea," he said, without looking up from his patient. "We may need some consent forms signed. Muscle tone's still pretty good—no drooling. That's something. Doesn't look like a stroke."

A nurse had appeared on the other side of the bed and was holding MJ's wrist, feeling for a pulse.

"Right," Spider-Man said. "Right," he repeated. "Her husband is . . . I'll . . . I'll go get him."

He turned away and headed for the door, to "get" Peter

Parker. He hesitated, not wanting to leave Mary Jane alone for even a moment—but she wasn't alone; she was surrounded by doctors and nurses, and he could do far more good here as Peter Parker, loving husband and next of kin, than as Spider-Man, scourge of the underworld.

A stroke—he hadn't even thought of that. She was much too young for a stroke, wasn't she?

He cursed himself for being away from her so much. If he'd stayed home today, or come directly home from the *Bugle* after talking to Jameson, whatever had happened might not have happened. At the very least he would have discovered it sooner.

Maybe something one of his enemies had done, somehow. Maybe something *he'd* done, something he'd brought back somehow from one of his fights.

Not knowing what had happened, not knowing what *would* happen—that was the worst part. He hurried out of the building—the faster he left, the faster he could return.

Once outside he fired a web-line to the roof and swung around the corner to the left, then dropped down into the sloping driveway. Hidden by the concrete walls, he unwrapped the dissolving bundle that held his everyday clothes. He pulled on his slacks and shirt, then peeled away Spider-Man's mask to reveal Peter Parker's worried face.

A moment later he re-entered the emergency room in his new identity and looked around. Mary Jane was nowhere in sight, nor did he see the nurse or the doctor who had attended to her. He crossed to the admissions nurse and cleared his throat.

She looked up. "Can I help you?"

"I'm Peter Parker," he said, his voice hoarse with concern. "Spider-Man brought my wife in a few minutes ago— a redhead in a nightgown, unconscious?"

"Oh, yes, Mr. Packer," the nurse said, smiling. "If you could just fill out a few forms for us—it won't take a minute . . ."

It didn't take a minute; it took twenty-eight minutes and

repeatedly correcting "Packer" to "Parker" every time the nurse entered anything in her computer, but at last Peter was directed to the curtained cubicle at the far end of the emergency room where Mary Jane now lay.

He pushed aside a drape and stepped in to find the same young doctor standing by a still-unconscious Mary Jane. An IV had been inserted in one arm, and she looked pale in the fluorescent light, but otherwise she was unchanged from when he had first found her in their bed an hour or so before.

"Hi," he said.

"Hello," the doctor replied, looking up. "Are you the husband?"

"Yeah," Peter said. "Peter Parker. They made me fill out the paperwork, or I'd have been here sooner."

"Oh, you'd just have been in the way. I must say, Mr. Parker, it's an interesting case."

"Is she going to be all right?" Peter asked anxiously. "What happened? What's wrong with her?"

"Well, the short and not exactly accurate version is that it looks like she's been chloroformed," the doctor said, slipping into a lecturing tone. "If you take a close look right here"—he pointed at her nose—"you can see faint chemical burns right around the nostrils on both sides, and the symptoms are pretty much consistent with chloroform. There was a time, you know, not long ago, when people regularly used to use chloroform as a knock-out drug—there were cases of burglars using it to keep their victims from waking up while their homes were being robbed. But nobody with any sense has done anything like that in, oh, at least thirty or forty years. Chloroform's tricky stuff—too little and the victim wakes up, and too much and you've got a corpse on your hands, and burglars usually don't want to risk a murder rap. It's mostly the so-called super-villains or the outright crazies who use the stuff now." He shook his head. "I don't know why anyone would use something like chloroform on *her*. She wasn't guarding a vault or something, was she?"

Peter shook his head, unhappy at the mention of super-villains. More than ever he feared that his actions as Spider-Man had brought this on her. "She was at home, minding her own business."

"Was anything stolen?" the doctor asked. "Any signs of forced entry? Maybe burglars have gotten stupid again."

"Nothing that I could see," Peter said. "But I didn't exactly stop to take inventory once I realized she wasn't just sleeping."

"Of course you didn't." He looked back down at Mary Jane. "Well, I don't know why it happened—that's a job for the police, I suppose, not for me. It might even have been an accident of some sort."

Peter didn't think it had been an accident, but right now he didn't care. He wasn't concerned yet with how this had happened, or who was responsible; that was his *second* priority.

His first, far more urgent, was much simpler. He shuddered as he asked, "Will she be okay?"

"We think so," the doctor said, "but I'm not making any promises, because . . . well, I told you I wasn't being entirely accurate. That's because whatever was used on her, it wasn't chloroform."

"But you just said . . ." Peter began.

"I said it *looks* like she was chloroformed," the doctor said. "It does. But from the traces we've tested, it's not actually chloroform at all. It's a chlorinated hydrocarbon, all right, but it's *much* more complex than chloroform." He shook his head. "We haven't identified it yet. I don't think it's anything I've ever seen before, but maybe I'm just behind the times. Anyway, left alone, it . . . well, it wouldn't kill her, it's actually not as toxic as chloroform, but it's also harder for her system to handle. She's pretty much comatose, and without treatment she'd stay that way for days, maybe weeks—long enough that there might be some permanent nerve damage. I'm pretty sure we can flush the stuff out of her system, though, and have her back on her feet in a few days. We're getting the equipment ready to give that a try."

He turned and at last looked directly at Peter. "If this happened at home, do you have any idea where she might have gotten this stuff? Is she a chemist? When Spider-Man brought her in he said she's a student . . . in chemistry, perhaps? Or biochem?"

Peter shook his head. "Psychology," he said. "She isn't taking any lab courses."

"Then it's a mystery to me how she got this stuff. I can't imagine much of a use for it in psychology."

"She was home asleep," Peter said. "Look at her—she's in her nightgown. You said burglars used to use chloroform—maybe one *is* trying this new version, but panicked before he took anything."

The doctor frowned. "You should see whether anything's gone. Have you reported it to the police?"

"Not yet," Peter said.

"The facial burns seem to indicate that the poison was administered as a gas—if 'administered' is the right word. There's no sign that it was on a pad or cloth, which was the traditional method for chloroform; I suppose it could have been piped in somehow. An accident with some sort of plumbing, perhaps?"

"Maybe," Peter said.

He didn't believe it for an instant, though. He knew what had happened.

An exotic chemical, appropriate for a super-villain, applied not long after his visit to the Osborn Industries chemical plant—the connection wasn't too hard to make.

"You can't touch me, Spider-Man," Osborn had said, "but I can touch *you*."

This was meant as a demonstration, just in case Spider-Man had any lingering doubts. This was Osborn's way of showing Peter Parker just how completely in control he was.

And this was a warning to stay out of his way.

It might be more than that, of course. Osborn could be deep when he wanted to, could build layers of cruelty atop one another.

"There's just *one* poison, Doc?"

The doctor looked startled. "I don't know," he admitted. "We haven't found any sign of anything but this chlorinated hydrocarbon . . ."

"Look more closely," Peter suggested.

"Well, I . . . I'm not sure we *can*," he said. "We can check for all the obvious toxins, I suppose . . ."

"You do that," Peter said. He stared down at MJ's sleeping face.

Trusting the woman he loved to this emergency-room doctor wasn't good enough. The doctor seemed competent enough, but he had to be more familiar with burns or gunshot wounds than with exotic poisons. Peter knew enough chemistry to know that Osborn could have hidden almost anything in that gas—there could be a second, slower poison, a deadly one; there could be a hypnotic that would make Mary Jane susceptible to Osborn's control; there could be anything.

And even if this doctor—his name tag said "Huntington," Peter finally noticed—were capable of finding a subtle second poison, that didn't mean he *would*. He might well be in Osborn's pay—Osborn had infiltrated his people into institutions all over the city. He could be lying about everything, right down the line—how would Peter know?

He wanted a second opinion. He wanted a doctor he knew, a doctor he *trusted*, to look over Mary Jane, to see whether Dr. Huntington was telling the truth, whether there was anything Dr. Huntington had missed.

"Curt Connors," he said to himself.

Dr. Curt Connors was a biochemist, a genius herpetologist, and a former surgeon, and he owed Spider-Man a favor or three. His experiments with regeneration had transformed him to the monstrous Lizard, and it had been Spider-Man who brought his rampages under control and got him transformed back to his sane human self. Among other things, he was an expert on human blood chemistry—while there might be other people out there who knew more about detecting and neutralizing poisons, Peter didn't know them and couldn't trust them. Connors he had known for years, and trusted completely.

"Is there a phone I can use?" he asked.

"In the waiting room, just the other side of the entrance," Dr. Huntington said, pointing.

"Good. I'll be right back."

"You're welcome, but there's no need to hurry—she won't wake up for hours yet."

Peter nodded an acknowledgment, then slipped out through the curtains, left the emergency room and trotted down a corridor to the waiting room. The phones were in an alcove right by the entrance.

He had Dr. Connors's phone numbers in his wallet—creased and smudged, but still legible. He dialed the number for Connors's lab quickly.

The phone on the other end rang—and rang, and rang, and rang. No one answered, and after fourteen rings Peter slammed the receiver down.

He dialed again, just in case, but another thirteen rings still yielded no response.

He tried the Connors's home—maybe Doc Connors had gone home early, or if not, perhaps his wife would know where he was. Again, the phone rang endlessly, unanswered.

Giving up at last Peter stood for a moment, trying to think what his next move should be. There had to be some way he could reach Connors—why didn't the man at least have an answering machine?

Doc Connors was a frequent guest lecturer at Empire State University, Peter remembered; perhaps someone in the biology department there would know how to reach him. Peter didn't have that number written down or memorized, but he knew how to call directory assistance.

He worked his way through directory assistance to the university switchboard, and then to whoever answered the biology department's phone.

"To whom did you wish to speak?" she asked.

"I'm trying to reach Dr. Curt Connors . . ." Peter began.

"He's not on the faculty here," the voice said.

"I know that!" Peter shouted. "Don't hang up!"

"All right, there's no need to yell. I don't see how I can help you, though—I'm not allowed to give out his phone number. I don't even know if we still *have* it—he hasn't spoken here this semester."

"I have his home phone number," Peter explained, "but he's not answering."

"Well, then, what do you expect *me* to do?" She sounded genuinely offended.

"I was hoping someone there might have some idea where he's gone, where I might reach him . . ."

"Well, *I* don't. I never met the man."

"Could you ask around, maybe? I can hold . . ."

"I'm sorry, but I can't do that. What, just ask people at random whether they know where you can find him? I don't *think* so . . ."

"But it's an emergency!"

She hung up.

He stared at the receiver for a moment, then slammed it onto the hook. It cracked from the impact—just a little, just enough to remind him that he had to stay in control of himself.

Calling back wouldn't do any good, but if he went down there and talked to people, maybe he could find someone who could tell him where Connors was. He couldn't think of any other way to find him.

He hurried back down the corridor and ducked quickly

back into Mary Jane's cubicle. Dr. Huntington was going over a chart while a nurse did something with MJ's IV.

"I need to go find someone," Peter told the doctor. "I'll be back as soon as I can."

Dr. Huntington looked up. "Oh, that's fine. We'll take good care of her, I promise, and"—he glanced at the clock on the wall above Mary Jane's head— "she won't be conscious until at least eight o'clock, I'd say, at the very best. Probably not until midnight."

"Thanks, Doc," Peter said. He reached down and patted his wife's hand. It was reassuringly warm, but distressingly limp.

"I'll be back as quick as I can, MJ," Peter said. Then he turned and left.

From Parkway Hospital to the ESU campus was no great distance as the crow flies, but neither Peter Parker nor the amazing Spider-Man was a crow. Crows didn't have to fight traffic, or cross bridges. The afternoon rush hour was starting, but the main current of traffic would be flowing out from Manhattan into Queens; Peter decided he could probably make better time on the F train than he would by web-slinging. He wouldn't tire himself out, and wouldn't need to worry about finding places to change in and out of his costume, or about some old enemy spotting him and deciding it was time to settle an old grudge.

The subway ride was uneventful and he encountered no unusual delays, but all the same it was close to an hour later when he finally burst into the biology department offices at ESU, looking for anyone who might know where Curt Connors was.

The outer office was empty; from an inner room he could hear a TV chattering away.

That was almost certainly the unhelpful receptionist, or departmental secretary, or whatever she was; Peter decided to leave her to her television and look elsewhere. He headed down the corridor, toward the labs and the various professors' offices.

He didn't know exactly who or what he was looking for, so he took the direct approach, and grabbed the sleeve of the first person in a lab coat he saw. The gray-haired man he had chosen whirled, startled. His face was vaguely familiar—Peter had seen him around the campus before, but couldn't remember his name. He should remember Dr. Connors, Peter thought—he had definitely been around ESU at the time of Connors's lectures.

"I'm looking for Curt Connors," Peter said. "Do you know where he is?"

"Osaka," the man said.

"What?"

"Dr. Curtis Connors, right? Herpetology and serum biochem, spoke here last year? Good man—top-notch researcher. He's in Osaka for the IABR conference. Should be back home the middle of next week—but you know, he's not on the faculty, he's . . ."

"Osaka?" Peter interrupted. "He's in *Japan*?"

"For a two-week conference. I understand he took the whole family along, to let 'em see a bit of the world."

"But it's an *emergency*!"

The gray-haired man looked concerned. "I believe he's at the Osaka Hilton—one of the international chains, anyway. I don't remember exactly what the time difference is, but it must be the middle of the night there, or very early in the morning . . ."

Peter stared at him for a moment. "You're *sure* he went to Japan?"

"Quite sure, young man; I talked to him just last month about a grant application I was putting together, and he was, you might say, pumped about it. Wouldn't have missed it for anything."

"Thank you," Peter said, trying to contain his frustration.

"No problem," the man said. "Listen, if it's really an emergency and you need a biochemist, I do know something about the field . . ."

"Poisons?" Peter asked hopefully.

"Well, most of my work is with intracellular energy transfer systems, not toxins. Dr. Wang might be able to help, though—he's done some first-rate work on neurotransmitter imbalances, and that involved several neurotoxins."

"Thank you," Peter said, "but no." He turned away. He couldn't trust this man, whoever he was, nor Dr. Wang. Almost anyone might be in Osborn's pay.

In fact, how did he know this man was telling the truth? He paused—but just then a word on the departmental bulletin board caught his eye.

The word was "Conference." He stepped closer and read a notice—or rather, a call for papers for the annual conference of the International Association for Biochemical Research, to be held in Osaka. The notice was slightly faded, with a dog-eared corner and several thumbtack holes.

Even Norman Osborn could not possibly have been thorough enough to have put that notice in place, as well as the gray-haired man. Dr. Connors was really in Japan, too far away to help.

He would have to find someone else—but who? Reed Richards? Henry Pym? Hank McCoy? Stephen Strange?

He was having trouble thinking clearly; his worry about Mary Jane was making him frantic. He forced himself to stop and think about his choices.

Richards knew more about space-time physics than toxicology, and Stephen Strange had long ago abandoned science for magic, but Henry Pym or Hank McCoy—Giant-Man or the Beast—might be able to help.

If he could find them. And if they were needed. And if it wasn't too late. He had been on a wild goose chase for over an hour, trying to find Curt Connors, and anything might have happened back at the hospital in Forest Hills.

Before going any farther, he thought he should check on Mary Jane's condition. There wasn't any point in bothering people if she was really going to be fine. If she was awake—well, Dr. Huntington had said she wouldn't be, but he might have been wrong. And her condition might have deteriorated if a second poison was present.

Peter decided he would call the hospital and ask for an update, and then try to get a message to Avengers Mansion—even if neither Pym nor McCoy was an active Avenger at the moment, whoever was at the mansion would know where to reach them. Which was more than Peter knew.

He stepped into the department office. The TV was still on in the back room, talking about ways to whiten teeth, but he ignored that and found the Queens phone book.

He didn't have permission to make any calls, but he was in no mood to worry about it. He looked up the number for Parkway Hospital and dialed.

The phone on the other end rang—and rang, and rang . . .

"What *is* this?" Peter asked, slamming down the phone and double-checking the number in the book. "Aren't the phones working?" He dialed again, slowly, reading out the number digit by digit.

Again, no one answered.

"What kind of hospital *is* that?" he demanded of no one in particular. "What kind of incompetents have I entrusted my wife to? They can't even answer the phone!"

He hung up, and stared at the phone, trying to think what he should do next. Should he try to call the Avengers, or head back out to Queens to see what was going on at the hospital?

Could it be that the phone system *was* out? Had the Rat Pack done something to it?

In the background he could hear an announcer on the TV talking about some breaking news story, but he paid no attention until the words "Parkway Hospital" suddenly penetrated his consciousness. He whirled and almost ran to the door of the inner office.

A woman was seated in a desk chair, leaning back, a slice of pizza in her hand, her feet atop the desk. On the desk, next to her feet, a small TV was showing a news report. Peter instantly recognized the location.

". . . scene here in this quiet Forest Hills neighborhood as the Rat Pack holds Parkway Hospital hostage," the reporter said. "The terrorists are demanding that each and every doctor and patient be individually ransomed, and announced that they will start shutting off life support systems in the Intensive Care Unit if their demands are not met by eight o'clock. As yet neither the mayor nor . . ."

Peter did not stay to hear any more; he ran out of the office and out of the building.

It was rush hour—the Rat Pack had undoubtedly chosen their time deliberately, to make everything more difficult for cops and city officials, and any super heroes who might decide to get involved. The F train would be jammed.

But web-slinging would work. Peter looked for somewhere to change clothes.

"You did this on purpose, didn't you, Norman?" he muttered to himself as he tugged at his shirt buttons. "You picked Parkway because you *knew* that's where I'd take Mary Jane. You'd made your point by gassing her—you can touch me, but I can't touch you, right? That was the message. And you decided to rub it in a little, didn't you? You wanted to show me that nowhere is safe—not my own home, not the hospital, nowhere." He pulled off the shirt.

"Well, you've made your point, Norman," he said as he pulled up his mask. "And now you've pushed it too far. You never did know when enough was enough—I don't think the word is even in your vocabulary. Well, I'll *show* you when it's enough. When you go after my wife it's *more* than enough, and I'm going to show you the error of your ways."

He pulled on his gloves and checked his web shooters, sliding new cartridges of web-fluid into place in both. He had made up a fresh supply just recently, and his belt was generously stocked.

"You've made it *very* personal now," he said, "and you're

going to regret it. Because now I'm coming after you, Norman Osborn. I'm coming after you, and I'm not going to stop, not going to rest, until I have shown you just how big a mistake you made."

He pulled off his slacks, pulled on his boots, then rolled shirt, slacks, and shoes into a bundle. A quick shot of webbing wrapped the clothes securely, and another strand of webbing provided a strap that would hold the package on his back.

A moment later he was swinging crosstown, and not long after he was eastbound on the Williamsburg Bridge. He wasn't sure yet exactly what he was going to do, once he had reached the hospital and stopped the Rat Pack, but he knew he would do *something*. Osborn had gone too far this time.

If only he were up against the Green Goblin himself, in open battle, instead of fighting Osborn's schemes . . .

Behind him, glimpsed between the towers of Manhattan, the sun was sinking below the western horizon. Ahead of him the moon was rising, and shining full and round and bright over Queens.

Part Three

Ambrose Wiggins was terrified as he sat on the floor, his back against the wall, his face inches from the barrel of an AK-47.

The man holding the AK-47 wasn't even looking at Ambrose, but that didn't matter; Ambrose was staring at the gun barrel the way a mouse watches a snake that's preparing to strike.

Ambrose had come to the hospital to see his sister Angela; she'd been found curled up in a doorway on Queens Boulevard, covered with bruises. She hadn't said a word about how she got them, but neither Ambrose nor their mother had the slightest doubt—Angela's no-good punk boyfriend had beaten her, probably while drunk, stoned, or both. Mamma had sent Ambrose here to tell Angie once again to dump that good-for-nothing louse, once and for all.

He hadn't gotten that far. He had been waiting for the elevator when the men in olive-drab hoods and gray-green leather jackets had burst into the hospital and started waving guns around and shouting orders.

He had been herded around the corner, out of sight of the entrance. Now he was one of at least twenty people sitting lined up against the back corridor wall, waiting to see what the terrorists would do next—and one of their captors had chosen to stand right in front of Ambrose. If anyone started shooting, Ambrose knew he'd be one of the very first targets.

This wasn't how it was supposed to happen. He had always known the world was a dangerous place, that he might not live to grow old, but he had always assumed that if he was going to get shot it would be out on the streets, not in someplace like this. He'd thought he might piss off a local dealer, or get in the way of a shoot-out, or just misjudge a step when someone went charging down the street at sixty m.p.h. in a hot car. It had never occurred to him he might die for visiting his stupid sister in the hospital, in a quiet neighborhood a dozen times safer than his own.

He tried to look away from that gun barrel, but when he turned to one side he saw a middle-aged woman in a nurse's uniform weeping silently, obviously even more frightened than he was; when he turned the other way he saw a young black man with fists clenched tight and mouth pinched to a thin line. He wasn't sure if the black guy was scared and trying to hide it, or crazy mad and getting ready to try to grab the gun away from the terrorist. Either way, Ambrose knew he didn't want to be involved.

He lifted his head and looked at the ceiling, muttering a bit of prayer—he wasn't devout, hadn't set foot in a church since he was sixteen, but he figured that it couldn't possibly hurt.

He was sitting across from a stairway door—the terrorist standing guard over them had apparently been positioned there deliberately, maybe to relay commands up or down that stair if the walkie-talkies weren't working, or maybe to be ready to dash up to help the men on the second floor if the order came. His gaze slid across the ceiling to the little window in the stairwell door.

That was how he saw the shape in the shadows, crawling down the *underside* of the stairs.

Ambrose blinked. How could that thing stay there? What held it up? It was shaped more or less like a man, but moved strangely, with an odd, jerky rhythm. It clung to the stairs without any ropes or gadgets, just hung there, like a lizard on a windowpane. It wore red gloves and boots and mask, and a dark blue body-suit . . .

"Spider-Man," Ambrose said quietly to himself.

The terrorist had been staring down the corridor; at the sound of Ambrose's voice he looked down.

Ambrose quickly lowered his own gaze.

"What'd you say?" the terrorist said, pointing the AK-47 at Ambrose's chest.

"Nothing!" Ambrose said, struggling not to look up as the stairway door opened silently behind the guard. "I just said, y'know, 'oh, man.' "

The terrorist didn't have time to reply before a wad of webbing whacked him on the back of the head, knocking him forward.

Ambrose was too frightened to do anything but scramble aside; the guy next to him, though, was ready. He sprang up and grabbed the AK-47.

The terrorist was staggered, but not down; he held onto the weapon and tried to grab it away.

"Hey!" the terrorist stationed two dozen yards down the corridor shouted. "What's going on over there? Terry . . . I mean, Fourteen, you need some help?"

Then a red-and-blue blur struck, smacking the first terrorist against the concrete wall, wrenching the AK-47 from his hands and tossing it to the fighting hostage.

The stunned terrorist slumped to the ground, clearly out of action.

"Just cover those two—and leave the heroics to me," Spider-Man said quietly to the man he'd just given the gun. "Too many innocent bystanders around here." Then he bounded away down the corridor in a sort of twisted cartwheeling motion that sent him bouncing off the walls, first one side, then the other.

Ambrose was cowering in fear, but from under his hand he could see Spider-Man. He watched him in amazement. The wall-crawler moved so *fast*—Ambrose had never seen anything like it. And his crazy zigzag down the passage made him an impossible target even if the other terrorist had had time to aim his weapon.

"Forget that innocent bystander stuff," the black guy said, as he flicked off the safety and pointed the rifle—but then webbing splattered across the other terrorist's mask, another strand snatched away the other terrorist's AK-47, and before the former hostage could really take aim a hay-maker connected with a web-smeared chin, and the second terrorist went down.

"Blast," the black guy said, resetting the safety.

At the other end of the corridor another hostage jumped up, snatched up the fallen, web-encrusted AK-47, and in an instant was standing over his former captor.

Ambrose had curled into a ball, hands over his head, when the web-slinger first attacked, so he had missed most of the details. Now he uncurled to find there were still two men with guns standing in the corridor—but one was the black guy, the other a blond man in a doctor's white coat. The two terrorists both lay motionless on the floor, putting up no further resistance.

And Spider-Man was already gone, around a corner into the emergency room and out of sight—but somewhere in that direction Ambrose could hear the slap of fists against flesh, and the thud of bodies falling.

A single burst of three shots cut through the air, but then, after a particularly loud thump, silence fell.

"Wow," Ambrose said softly. "Spider-Man!"

"He could have got us all killed!" the weeping woman said, her terror turning to rage.

"Naah," the nearer guy with the gun said. "Spidey does this kind of stuff all the time. Y'know, I saw him take down the Rhino once."

"You did?" Ambrose asked.

"Yeah. Not up close like this—from my apartment win-dow. He was just bouncin' all over, dissin' the Rhino, driv-ing him nuts until the guy couldn't see straight. Then he just pounded on him till he fell over. And he was real care-ful to see that nobody else got hurt."

"He wasn't dissing anybody this time," someone said. The hostages were all getting to their feet, brushing them-selves off and looking around warily.

"Yeah," the man with the gun said. "This time he looked *mad*."

"How can you tell through that mask?"

The man with the gun just shrugged. He looked down as the terrorist at his feet stirred and moaned; then he pointed the AK-47 at the hooded head and said, "You just stay right where you are, buddy."

The terrorist rolled over far enough to see the rifle barrel pointed at him, then slumped back down to the tiles.

Just then something on the terrorist's belt said, "Check-in time, Fourteen. Everything okay there?"

Everyone froze for a moment. "Don't say a word," the man with the gun said.

Rat Pack Fourteen didn't say a word.

"Fourteen, this is Two—do you read me? Over."

"If no one answers they'll know something's wrong," someone said quietly.

"I'm getting out of here," said someone else.

"Fourteen! Last call! Report!"

"Someone's gonna come check on this," Ambrose whispered loudly.

"The lobby's clear," someone called from down the hall. "We can leave!"

"There are cops and reporters everywhere outside," someone else added.

The other downed terrorist's communicator then spoke up. "Sixteen, this is Two—check in *now!*"

"Where's Spider-Man?" a plaintive voice asked.

Ambrose got to his feet.

"Sixteen! Fourteen's not answering—if you're there, say something!"

Everyone was moving down the corridor except the downed terrorists and the two men who had taken their guns. "What do we do with *them*?" the blond doctor asked.

"I'll tell the cops," someone offered.

Then Ambrose was running down the passage, around the corner, past the elevators and the office to the front entrance, as both terrorist radios spoke at once, calling, "Rat Pack! Time to go—Operation Wasp!"

A moment later Ambrose was out on the sidewalk on 113th Street, surrounded by cops and reporters. SWAT team members in flak jackets were trotting in as Ambrose came out, and the first few hostages to emerge were surrounded by cameras and microphones.

"Wow," Ambrose said.

Now that he wasn't sitting on the floor with a rifle pointed at him his nerve was coming back, and what had been terrifying began to seem exciting.

"Excuse me, sir," an expensively coiffed and elaborately made-up woman said, thrusting a microphone toward Ambrose. He didn't recognize her, but she was unmistakably a television reporter. "Can you tell us what you saw happening inside the hospital?"

"I saw Spider-Man take down a couple of those leather boys," Ambrose said. "Bam! Just punched 'em right out, so fast they never knew what hit 'em!"

"Then it *was* Spider-Man who freed you? You're certain of that?"

"You got it. He was stickin' to the ceiling and shootin' webs around—who else does that?"

"And there we have it," the reporter said, taking back the microphone. "Despite reports of earlier sightings around City Hall, Spider-Man was seen *here*, freeing hostages from the Rat Pack inside Parkway Hospital here in this quiet neighborhood in Queens, at the very moment that the other Rat Pack team, in Manhattan, was taking the mayor himself hostage."

"The mayor?" Ambrose said, startled. "They got the *mayor*?" He turned and looked at the hospital, where the SWAT team was dragging out downed Rat Packers.

"Wow," he said.

Meanwhile, inside the building, Spider-Man was crawling along the ceiling, alert for the slightest sound, the slightest flicker of movement.

He had gotten into the hospital easily enough by prying open a third-floor window, then quickly taken out two Rat Packers—one at the elevators across from the nurses' station, one in the central corridor—and left them webbed for the police to collect. He had taken a moment to free the three nurses and two doctors the Rat Pack had locked in a storeroom by the stairs, and had turned the floor over to them.

Then he had had to choose a direction, up or down. There was a helicopter sitting on the roof—probably the Rat Pack's, as it bore no visible identification—but he had chosen down; there were three police copters circling overhead, and they would keep that mystery copter from going anywhere. His job was to stop the Rat Pack from hurting anyone, or getting out any other way, and that meant working fast. The best approach he could see was to get down to the ground floor quickly and open the way for the cops.

Besides, Mary Jane was probably still on the ground floor, in Emergency.

He had taken down two more Rat Packers on the second floor, then continued downward.

The ground floor had had twenty or thirty hostages lined up along the central corridor, and another dozen in the Emergency Room, where one of the Rat Pack, the one farthest back in the south end of the room, closest to Mary Jane, had actually gotten off a burst before Spidey's webbing clogged his weapon into uselessness.

All in all he had put another five Rat Packers out of action on the ground floor so far, for a total of nine—how many of these guys *were* there, he wondered.

More, he was certain—at the very least there would have been half a dozen more on the top three floors—but he didn't *see* any more.

The ones on the upper floors must know something had gone wrong; Spider-Man had heard the calls over the belt radios, including that final call for "Operation Wasp," whatever that was. He had snagged himself one of those spiffy little radios from the very first man he took down, so that he could listen in on their plans, but so far he hadn't heard a thing since that last announcement. They should be regrouping somewhere, collecting hostages, preparing to bargain—or maybe trying to escape, either in that big copter or . . .

A thought struck him. These guys wore those leather coats and face masks, with fancy equipment in belt pouches and backpacks—but what if they took them off? What did they wear underneath? Ordinary street clothes, probably.

They could probably just blend in with the fleeing hostages, then.

If he found abandoned uniforms or weapons, he would know that was what they were doing. And if they were, well . . .

He didn't intend to capture all of them. He wanted their boss, the current Number One or their employer or whoever was giving them their orders, and he wouldn't get that one by collecting everyone here. The radio messages had come from Number *Two,* not Number One.

The cops were coming in, now that the main entrance was unguarded. The Rat Pack should be retreating to some sort of fallback position—but instead they seemed to have melted away completely. *Had* they shed their uniforms and blended with the crowd?

Since he was in the Emergency Room he took just a second to look in on Mary Jane—she was still in the same bed, still unconscious, still breathing. He wanted to stay with her, to be there to comfort her if she awoke . . . but he couldn't. Half the Rat Pack was still loose in the building.

He leaped onto the wall, and then the ceiling, where he was out of the way of the surging traffic of cops, doctors, and freed hostages, and began prowling through the parts of the hospital he thought the cops might miss at first, places where he thought the Rat Pack might be holing up— linen rooms, ladies' rooms, kitchens, and so on.

He rounded a corner in the back of the coffee shop, and a faint whirring caught his attention.

A service elevator was running—and coming down, according to the indicator.

Would the Rat Pack be using the elevators? It seemed reckless, to say the least—it would be easy to corner them in there, or ambush them as they emerged.

In fact, Spider-Man decided that that was exactly what he would do. When whoever it was stepped out of the elevator he'd find himself facing a pair of loaded web shooters.

The whirring grew louder—and then faded again, as the elevator went past without stopping, still heading down.

The basement, Spidey realized. The Rat Pack was gathering in the basement.

There was at least one exit from the basement, at the north end, and for all Spider-Man knew there might be another at the back, facing the access road onto Grand Central Parkway, but those would all be surrounded by cops. Were they planning to shoot their way out? Did they have hostages they could use to buy their way out? Did they have an escape vehicle waiting for them down on the Parkway, perhaps?

He didn't know, and it didn't really matter—he intended to stop them, whatever their plans were. He didn't bother with the service elevator; instead he found the stairs and bounded downward.

The hospital basement was a maze of corridors, rooms, pipes, and ductwork, but Spider-Man could hear the Rat Pack and just followed the sound, scampering along the ceiling wherever his path wasn't blocked by exposed plumbing.

He came in sight of the last of the Rat Pack just as they vanished through a steel door. There was no sign of any hostages; apparently they weren't planning to try to bargain with the cops.

At least, Spidey realized as he saw the sign above the

door, not with *live* hostages. They were going into the hospital morgue.

Moving as silently as he could, he followed them.

They were hurrying, and were almost out of sight around a corner before he could slip safely through the door; he flung a spider-tracer at the last of them, and smiled grimly under his mask as it snagged on the back of that last man's belt.

The Rat Pack had gone straight past the one short row of tables and the wall of drawers without even slowing; apparently they weren't planning to do anything with the corpses. That was a relief.

He rounded the corner at the end of the room carefully, not wanting to let them slip around by another route and back out of the morgue.

They were hurrying through a door labeled "Heating & Refrigeration Plant."

Spider-Man was baffled—what could they want in there? Wasn't it a dead end?

How many of them were in there? How did they all *fit?* How big was that room? He dropped to the floor and ran to catch the door before it closed behind the last Rat Packer.

His spider-sense warned him just before he heard the burst of gunfire; he ducked behind the steel door, out of the line of fire. When the tingling began to fade he thrust his head out again.

The utility room was not quite so small as he had expected, but it *was* mostly full of massive equipment—a huge condenser was roaring steadily, and thick pipes were dripping with condensation. The concrete floor sloped toward a central drain . . .

A manhole-sized drain that was open, its protective grating tossed aside. And standing on the other side of that drain was one member of the Rat Pack, helping to lower another down the opening.

That was their escape route—the sewers. Just like real

rats. It was probably how they'd gotten so many of them into the hospital unnoticed in the first place.

The man standing over the drain was not the one Spider-Man had tagged with the spider-tracer—the weapon slung on his shoulder was different. That meant there was no reason at all not to take him down.

Spider-Man didn't bother with any sort of subtlety; he sprayed webbing generously across mask and chest, knocking the man back against a tangle of pipes. The webbing wrapped itself around him when he hit, tangling in the pipes and holding him there.

The man *in* the drain dropped out of sight with a splash. Spider-Man hurried forward and swung himself down over the edge, crawling headfirst into the opening . . . then stopped.

He had expected to see flashlights moving around, lights he could follow, but everything was dark. His own body was blocking most of the light from the refrigeration room. The Rat Pack presumably knew the way—for all he could see the pipe only ran one way. Or perhaps . . .

He pulled his head back up long enough to look at the man he'd webbed to the pipes. Sure enough, he wore a pair of high-tech goggles over his mask.

Night-vision equipment. The Rat Pack could see where they were going just fine, without using any light visible to anyone pursuing them.

Spidey stuck his head back down the hole. He could *hear* the fleeing terrorists—they were splashing through something, presumably sewage—but he couldn't see anything. Following them in the dark, completely blind, while they could see well enough to aim their weapons . . .

No. It would be suicide, even for him.

He had a sudden thought, and looked at the captured Rat Packer. If he took those goggles . . . but they were thickly plastered with webbing, and the man's impact with the pipe appeared to have cracked something on one side. By the time Spider-Man could get them cleaned off and functioning—assuming they still worked at all—the others would be long gone.

Besides, he told himself, he had to make sure Mary Jane was all right.

He climbed back out of the drain and looked at his captive; one gleaming plastic lens stared back through the gooey gray-black tangle of webbing. Ordinarily he would have patted the fellow on the cheek and made some sort of wisecrack, but right now he didn't feel like it. This wasn't fun, not when Mary Jane was endangered. Osborn was toying with him.

Osborn was going to learn that Spider-Man was no toy. He turned away and trotted out of the room, quickly making his way back to the stairs.

On the ground floor he found cops everywhere; he grabbed one by the sleeve and said, "There's one in the utility room behind the morgue."

The cop glanced at him, then said, "Right. Thanks."

That taken care of, he headed down the corridor toward Emergency. Doctors and nurses were hurrying back and forth or standing in the corridor talking to cops; cops were hurrying back and forth or standing in the corridor talking to doctors, nurses, and each other. Making his way through the crowd was more of a challenge than usual; he seriously considered climbing a wall, but he didn't want to frighten anyone.

Around him he heard snatches of conversation:

". . . figure out the overtime later—I want *everyone* . . ."

". . . Hostetler in 306, Hernandez in 308 . . ."

". . . a distraction? You think . . ."

". . . didn't see how he got in—might've been the back stair . . ."

". . . the mayor was the real . . ."

He stopped dead, and spun around to listen.

"So who do you think they were trying to decoy away?" the SWAT sergeant asked.

The plainclothes officer noticed Spider-Man listening,

and nodded in his direction. "Him," he said. "At least, that'd be my guess. He was seen around City Hall earlier today, but when the Rat Pack got the mayor, he was way the hell out here in Queens."

"The Rat Pack got to the mayor?" Spider-Man asked, feeling as if the bottom had just dropped out of his stomach. "He's dead?"

"We sure as hell *hope* he's not dead," the plainclothesman replied. "But he's been kidnapped by those guys, yeah. Right outside City Hall. They left a note asking for half a billion in ransom."

Spider-Man didn't answer; under the mask his brow furrowed and his jaw tightened in anger.

"So, wall-crawler—you *were* down at City Hall earlier today? You thought something was up, and you didn't tell us?" the cop asked.

"I didn't have any evidence," Spider-Man answered. "Just a suspicion from something someone said. But I was expecting an assassination attempt, not a Rat Pack kidnapping. And if I'd been at all *sure,* I wouldn't have come out here in the first place, I'd have stayed with the mayor."

"You think they staged all this"—the detective waved a hand at the hurrying chaos around them—"to get you out of the way?"

"Your guess is as good as mine," Spider-Man said. Which was a lie, unless this cop was sharper than he looked. "If you'll excuse me, though, I brought a woman in here earlier—I want to be sure she's all right."

"Sure, sure." The detective waved him on. "Good work on these guys, by the way—you probably saved some lives."

"Thanks," he said absently, as he turned away and headed on into the ER.

He might have saved lives here, he thought, but they were only endangered in the first place because Osborn had wanted to draw him here, away from the mayor; had wanted to taunt him with his own vulnerability.

And Osborn had lured him away from the mayor so *easily*. Osborn knew him much too well.

He no longer had even the slightest doubt that Norman Osborn was behind it all—the infrastructure raids, gassing Mary Jane, kidnapping the mayor, it all fit together too perfectly to be anything else but a scheme to elevate Osborn to the mayor's office. And he was sure that Osborn was letting him know deliberately, to rub his nose in his own helplessness. Osborn was playing with him, staying always one step ahead.

He hadn't *had* to set up a diversion to lure Spider-Man away; he could have just waited until he went home to eat or sleep. He could have snatched the mayor while Peter Parker was still filling out Mary Jane's admission forms— but he hadn't. He had waited, had done it this way deliberately, knowing that it would hurt more.

And it *did* hurt. He had reacted just as Osborn expected, dashing to his wife's rescue, thereby leaving the mayor at the Rat Pack's mercy.

But the mayor was still alive—so far.

And Spider-Man knew why.

The mayor was bait. Osborn wanted to tease him some more, lure him somewhere. Probably he intended to murder the mayor right in front of Spider-Man. In fact, as he thought about it, Spider-Man guessed that Osborn intended to somehow frame him for the mayor's murder.

That would be completely in character. It would let Osborn laugh at *everybody*. It would put him in the mayor's office and eliminate Spider-Man as a threat at the same time.

Spider-Man had been suspected of murder before—several times. It was an old, tired, tiresome routine for him, but still could be effective. Each time he was accused, there were a few more people who believed he was a killer— where there's smoke, there's fire, after all. He couldn't just shrug off a frame, no matter how often he had cleared his name in the past.

But Osborn wasn't going to get away with it. Spider-Man wouldn't let him.

Osborn thought Spider-Man couldn't touch him. Osborn was wrong. Spider-Man didn't know yet exactly *how* he would get to Osborn, but he would.

He found Mary Jane's curtained bed—she still hadn't been moved, and was still unconscious. Dr. Huntington was there at her bedside now, talking to a uniformed cop.

"Doctor," Spider-Man called. Huntington turned. "I'm sorry to interrupt, but I brought this patient in and I have a personal interest—is she okay?"

"Oh, she'll be fine," Huntington replied. "At least, we think so. The treatment was interrupted briefly during the excitement, but we should have her up and around some time tomorrow."

"Good," Spider-Man said. "So the Rat Pack didn't hurt her, then?"

"No, but they did make threats," Huntington said. "In fact . . ." He glanced at the cop.

The cop shrugged. "I don't see why you shouldn't tell him."

"Tell me what?"

"Well, three of those terrorists were in here, and they were particularly looking for her—'the hot redhead,' they called her. The one they called Three stood right here with her the whole time, and it sounded like he had orders to kill her, or maybe just take her with them, if anything went wrong."

"But you said they didn't hurt her."

"They *didn't*," Huntington agreed. "If he did have those orders, I guess he didn't follow them. Or maybe you were just too fast for him."

"Three was the one whose gun had been fired," the cop offered.

"Thanks, officer," Spider-Man said. He knew now exactly who they were talking about. The man had already been taken away by the police, but Spider-Man glanced over at where Three had been standing when Spider-Man webbed up his AK-47 and then pounded him into helplessness.

That had been much too close; he was glad he hadn't known at the time that the nearness to Mary Jane wasn't just a coincidence.

He took another look at his sleeping wife—she looked so peaceful, untouched by the madness around her!—then stepped back out through the curtain.

He didn't leave yet, though; instead he leaped to the ceiling, out of the way of the hurrying police and hospital staff. He clung there and waited.

He thought he knew why they hadn't killed Mary Jane, or taken her with them. Nothing had really gone wrong. Spider-Man had come, just as he was supposed to, to save his woman. Osborn wasn't ready to kill Mary Jane yet—she was too valuable as a hostage.

But if her husband *hadn't* come, then she'd be dead, to teach him a lesson, to smother him in guilt.

Dr. Huntington and the policeman emerged from the cubicle, and Spider-Man sidled across the ceiling, past the curtains, and dropped down inside. He pulled up his mask enough to expose his mouth, then bent down and kissed her gently on the cheek. He brushed her long red hair away from her ear and knelt down beside her.

"MJ," he whispered, "I have to go. I can't stay here with you. I don't want to leave you, but I have to." He let out a long, shuddering sigh.

"I have to stop Norman Osborn," he said. "He knows I'm coming, he *wants* me to, but it doesn't matter. I still have to go. I know you'd understand."

He kissed her again, then pulled down his mask and sprang for the ceiling.

Thirteen

The most obvious place to look for Norman Osborn and his captive was at the Osborn Industries plant in Astoria, but Spider-Man knew better than that. Osborn wouldn't dare have the mayor die there, or at the tower in Manhattan—it would be far too suspicious, would drag him into the mess when his role now was to stay above it all until the mayor was dead, when he could emerge as the hero of the hour. If Spider-Man went to the Astoria plant he would undoubtedly find SecuriTeam ready and waiting—but if he was right about Osborn's plan to frame him, there would be arrangements to ensure his escape, and some clue that would lead him to wherever Osborn had set his trap.

Spider-Man did not intend to make it that easy for Osborn. He intended to skip the preliminaries, and if at all possible to come at Osborn from an unexpected direction.

He had to work quickly, though. If Osborn realized that Spider-Man wasn't following the script he might decide to give up the sideshow of tormenting his old enemy and get on with the main feature, and kill the mayor on the spot.

Spider-Man imagined the mayor tied up somewhere, sweating with fear, wondering what would happen to him. He knew the city had a no-ransom policy—he himself had confirmed it repeatedly in dealing with the Rat Pack. He couldn't expect that to change; his only hope was rescue.

Well, Spider-Man hoped to provide that. He reloaded his web shooters as he headed for the door; this brought both wrist-reservoirs up to full capacity. As soon as he was outside the hospital he fired a strand at the cornice of the apartment building across the street and was off, headed west down 71st Avenue, toward Manhattan.

He had gone just a few blocks, not even as far as Queens Boulevard, when he sensed a faint tingle from somewhere below him—his spider-tracer at work. He homed in on it, adjusting his course, but the signal stayed faint; he dropped to the ground, trying to narrow it down, and finally realized why it was so weak—the Rat Pack was still underground.

He had half expected them to emerge from a storm drain somewhere on Grand Central Parkway, but instead here they were, headed the other way.

They were moving straight toward Queens Boulevard, he judged. He followed the signal, debating with himself whether this was the best course—would these guys be joining up with the group that snatched the mayor?

Probably not; they were just a diversion, after all, and Osborn knew that spider-tracers existed, that Spider-Man was bright enough to follow escaping enemies.

But they weren't obviously moving the wrong way, either. Maybe Osborn's instructions to the Rat Pack hadn't been that detailed.

He wondered whether they would come out in the Forest Hills subway station, where 71st met Queens Boulevard—but then the signal veered off to one side. Spider-Man turned aside himself to follow it.

A moment later, as he came within half a block of the Boulevard, the signal suddenly began to strengthen—the man with the tracer was emerging from the sewers. Spider-Man pulled the Rat Pack communicator from his belt and turned it on, hoping someone would say something into a live mike.

Someone did. "Anyone still out there, we're at Checkpoint Three, and heading home. Join up on your own."

Then the gadget fell silent again.

"Checkpoint Three," they called it. Spidey looked around. He was just yards from the entrance of a parking garage, and that seemed to be the direction of the tracer signal. That was almost certainly Checkpoint Three.

And he didn't want to be seen here; he jumped for the nearest wall and scampered straight up, then ducked around a corner, half-hidden between two buildings, and waited.

A moment later a nondescript blue van pulled out of the garage, the tracer signal moving with it. Spider-Man dropped, paying out web-line as he went, and swung out over the street long enough to fling another tracer at the vehicle's bumper, and to read the license number—New York plates, AAX-54E. Then he landed back on the wall of the garage and scurried upward, out of sight.

The van was heading straight up Queens Boulevard westbound—heading in the general direction of the Queensborough Bridge and Manhattan. That was also the best route toward Astoria, of course, and they might well be going to the chemical plant in an attempt to lure him there—if they thought he might be following them.

But he was not going to follow them. Not yet. Even if they weren't part of a diversion to Astoria, if they were taking Queens Boulevard at this time of night he could probably get to Manhattan faster than they could, and take a look around, maybe find something to help him locate the mayor.

He turned south, aiming for the Williamsburg Bridge, and set out for Manhattan at the best speed he could manage.

City Hall Park was still awash in cops, reporters, and yellow crime-scene tape when he arrived, especially just east of City Hall on the service driveway—obviously, that was where the Rat Pack had grabbed the mayor. He found himself a place in a convenient tree and listened to the reporters interviewing cops and the cops interviewing witnesses.

At least half a dozen members of the Rat Pack had appeared as if out of nowhere as the mayor left City Hall, and had immediately flung tear gas everywhere in the vicinity. A van had blocked the mayor's limo, and gas-masked men with pickaxes had then smashed in the limo's windows and gassed the mayor and his driver. They had pulled the gasping, choking mayor from the car, shoved him into the van, and taken off out of the park and headed up Centre Street.

The rest of the Rat Pack contingent had then scattered by several routes. None had been apprehended yet. The tear gas had kept anyone in the area from reporting coherently in time to get police pursuit out before the van disappeared in traffic. The vehicle had later been found parked, presumably abandoned, on East 24th Street.

That would be on the way to Astoria, of course—but Spider-Man didn't believe that. It was a decoy, he was sure. Probably the mayor was transferred to another vehicle while still somewhere in lower Manhattan, and *then* the van was driven up to 24th and ditched.

The Rat Pack might not have been clever enough to do that, but Spider-Man knew that Osborn was.

Where they really *had* taken him was a whole separate question. Eliminating Astoria left the rest of the world. Osborn wouldn't take him far—there was no point in shipping him to Katmandu—but he could be almost anywhere within a fifty-mile radius.

Well—anywhere the Rat Pack could get to unnoticed. Staten Island was out—even if they ditched their masks and leather coats, a bunch of armed men with a hostage would be noticed on the ferry. There was all of Manhattan—except East 24th Street, which would undoubtedly be swarming with New York's finest, and open places such as the parks. There were three bridges and a tunnel that led to Brooklyn, so anywhere in Brooklyn or Queens, or further out Long Island, would be possible.

And in the other direction . . .

"If I were kidnapping the Mayor of New York City," Spider-Man muttered to himself, "I'd want to get him out of New York." After all, in New York just about everyone knew his face. The police would be everywhere, searching for him.

But across the river, in New Jersey, he'd be much easier to hide. And if that van had headed up Lafayette and
turned west on Canal, it was a fast, straight run to the Holland Tunnel.

And that would be almost the opposite direction from
Astoria. That would give Osborn plenty of time to make
sure his trap was set, the frame ready to spring, by the time
Spider-Man got there—if Spider-Man had gone to Astoria,
and if SecuriTeam had told their boss when he left, and if
Spider-Man had had to work his way all the way across
town.

Of course, New Jersey was a big place. He still didn't
know where the mayor was—but he was pretty sure he
knew which direction to start looking.

And thinking about it, he even had an idea of how to
look. Osborn wouldn't want the Rat Pack in Astoria—it
would look bad, would ruin his story that he was just an
innocent businessman. He *would* want them at his chosen
site for the final trap, to provide some muscle. He might
want them stationed along the route, as well, to report that
Spider-Man was on the way.

That would take a lot of manpower, and the Rat Pack
wasn't an army; no one had ever seen more than maybe a
dozen of them at a time.

They must have more than that; they had lost at least
ten men at Parkway Hospital, a few had gotten away—
Spider-Man estimated at least five—and there had still been
enough of them for their other team to pick up the mayor.

All the same, they had to be stretched very thin. Osborn couldn't spare the ones who had gotten away through
the sewers out in Queens; that group had to be headed out
to join the others.

And that group had two spider-tracers attached. They
might find one—in fact, he'd be surprised if they didn't—
but would they find *both?*

He doubted it. His best guess was that they would find

the one on the man's belt, but that they would miss the one on the van.

So if he waited at the mouth of the Holland Tunnel, sooner or later they should pass underneath. He had to hurry, to be sure he would get there before they did—the traffic on Queens Boulevard wasn't *that* bad.

As soon as he'd thought it through he leapt from the tree and headed up Broadway toward Canal Street.

He had only been waiting in the shadows above the tunnel entrance a few moments when he felt a growing tingle; a familiar blue van was approaching.

And sure enough, he could only sense *one* spider-tracer—the one on the rear bumper. He couldn't be sure what had happened to the other—it might have been found and destroyed, or sent off to Astoria to lure him. He didn't worry about it; he dropped down on a web-line and transferred himself as gently as he could to the van's roof as it passed beneath.

He hoped that any bump would be attributed to the potholes—the entrance ramp, as usual, was not in the best of shape, which was hardly surprising given the staggering amount of traffic it carried every day.

The van proceeded steadily onward—if the occupants were aware of his presence, they were hiding it well. He clung easily to the roof with his feet and one hand, and pulled the Rat Pack radio from his belt with the other.

No one was transmitting, so far as he could tell—but then, they were in the tunnel; the signal would be blocked.

He looked around and noticed the driver of the car behind the van staring at him; he waved, then held a finger to his lips, hoping the woman would recognize him and remember that he was generally on the side of the angels.

Her mouth fell open, then she dropped her gaze to the van itself. Her mouth snapped shut again, and she kept her attention focused on her driving—mostly; she still stole occasional glances at the web-slinger.

He waved again, a jaunty signal of acknowledgment—she was trying, after all. Then he bent down and put an ear to the metal, hoping to overhear something.

He could make out men's voices, but it was hard to distinguish any of the words over the roar of tunnel traffic. He concentrated.

". . . might hear you!" That was loud enough to cut through the background noise, and helped him focus, so that he could understand what the man said next. "These radio gadgets we're using don't shut off completely, short of taking out the batteries, and he could have bugs in the car."

"We're in the Holland Tunnel, blast it! This may be the last chance we *have* to talk!"

That elicited a murmur of reluctant agreement—and considerable interest from the rooftop passenger. So these people weren't particularly happy with someone?

"When it was just Number One, we never lost *anyone*," the voice that had pointed out that the tunnel would block the radios said. "Even when Number One started us working for this Mr. Green, we never lost anyone. Now Mr. Green takes charge himself, and we lose, jeez, it's gotta be a dozen guys in one stupid raid!"

"It's like he's deliberately throwing us away," someone else complained. "Like he's done with us, and would just as soon let us rot in jail!"

"What, you think he's not gonna keep going?"

"He's kidnapped the *mayor!* Where do you go from there? I figure after this, either he's gonna take the money and retire, or he's gonna get taken down big time—the Avengers or the FF or somebody is gonna figure him out and punch his ticket."

"And where's that leave us?"

"Sitting in jail!"

"Number One won't take that," a new voice said. "He'll get us out of this somehow. Forget Mr. Green—maybe he *is* double-crossing us, but Number One would never do anything like that to us!"

"You sure? I mean, I haven't been with you guys that long—Number One's a stand-up guy? You trust him?"

"You bet we do."

"Look, we're gettin' near the end of the tunnel. You guys shut up about this stuff. I don't trust Green any more than the rest of you, but I trust Number One, and we do what he tells us to do. He tells us to rough up Spider-Man, we rough up Spider-Man."

"I *hate* fighting super-guys. What's he want us to mess with Spider-Man for?"

"I dunno. He just said to let him know when we got the bug-man down, and he'd take it from there."

There was more, but the rest of the conversation was unenlightening, and Spider-Man lost interest. Instead of listening, he was thinking.

This "Mr. Green" was obviously Norman Osborn—Green as in Green Goblin—keeping his identity a secret so that captured Rat Packers couldn't divulge too much. He expected the Rat Pack to soften Spider-Man up for him—heck, he probably assumed that SecuriTeam would start the softening, and that Spidey would already be tired by the time he found the Rat Pack.

And when Spider-Man was exhausted and beaten—then what?

Then Osborn or one of his henchmen would kill the mayor and leave Spider-Man holding the murder weapon, most likely. The whole reason to have the wall-crawler defeated first was to make sure he was in no shape to avoid the frame-up.

"It's not going to be that easy, Norman," Spider-Man muttered.

Mr. Green—so he hadn't completely ditched his Green Goblin identity.

In fact, if Spider-Man knew Osborn as well as he thought he did, he guessed that Osborn missed being the Green

Goblin. Osborn had always been a hands-on criminal, never eager to leave anything to his subordinates. He had been smart enough to give up his costumed identity, to play the role of the power behind the scenes, but surely, given his obvious delight in confronting his foes directly, some part of Osborn still *wanted* to be the Green Goblin.

That might be his fatal weakness.

They were in Jersey City now—unfamiliar territory to Spider-Man. He knew most of New York City reasonably well, but he almost never got over to Jersey. They were turning off onto local streets, not heading up onto the New Jersey Turnpike—that was a bit of a surprise.

The little radio crackled suddenly. "Team One, do you read? Over."

"We read you," someone replied. Spider-Man thought he recognized a voice from the van, the voice that had warned the others they were leaving the tunnel.

"Good to hear from you," the radio said. "You remember where Checkpoint Six is? Set up there, ambush formation. You've got maybe an hour, maybe two—we still haven't heard anything from Queens. We'll give you an update when we hear from Mr. Green. Over."

"Got it. Out."

Spider-Man smiled. They thought he was still on his way to Astoria. That was good; that was just what he wanted.

He remembered that the Rat Pack thought Mr. Green might be listening in over the radios; Spidey *hoped* Osborn was listening. Because he had to stop *Osborn*, not just the Rat Pack.

And he couldn't touch Norman Osborn, respectable businessman and public official.

But he could touch whoever was behind kidnapping the mayor. If he could show that it was Norman Osborn who masterminded the entire project, *then* he could touch Osborn.

But he doubted Osborn would be stupid enough to leave

any evidence. If he did intervene directly, rather than leaving everything to the Rat Pack, he'd do it as the Green Goblin. And Spider-Man could touch the Green Goblin. He could beat the daylights out of the Goblin, and the city of New York would applaud. He wouldn't need to worry about finding solid evidence tying Osborn to the mayor's kidnapping or murder.

If he could goad Osborn, play on his hunger for revenge, his ego . . .

And that was what he had to do. He had to force Osborn to show his hand, to become the Goblin. If he could *prove,* once and for all, that Osborn was the Green Goblin, and if he could defeat the Goblin and get him behind bars, then the whole long nightmare would be over. He would be safe; Mary Jane would be safe; all of New York would be safe.

But first he had to get Osborn to put on that costume once again and come out to fight.

Osborn would be crazy to do it, of course—but Osborn *was* crazy. Spidey just had to play on his insanity the right way, provoke him enough without scaring him off . . .

Scare him off—*ha!* Osborn was insane, but one part of that was that almost nothing scared him.

Angering him was easy. Angering him enough that he gave up his plans and came out to fight in person—that might not even be possible.

But Spider-Man intended to try. After all, what choice did he really have?

The van had been winding its way through unfamiliar streets, but now it pulled to a stop, and Spider-Man looked around.

They were on the Jersey City docks; the towers of Manhattan gleamed brightly on the opposite side of the Hudson, but near at hand he saw only empty pavement lit by the occasional streetlamp, darkened warehouses, the looming shadows of cargo cranes.

Cargo cranes would be perfect; there was no need to let

these goons know how he'd gotten there. He timed the "thwip" of his web-shooter to match the click of an opening door, and as the Rat Pack emerged from the van he yanked himself off the roof and swung up into the yellow-painted metal framework of the nearest crane.

"All right, Eighteen, you take the rocket launcher over on that ramp," one man said, pointing. "Nine, you and your grenades . . ."

"Go directly to jail," Spider-Man called from the crane. "Do not pass go, do not collect two hundred dollars."

He could see the men start at the sound of his voice. He didn't wait to see what else they might do; he swung down and slammed both feet into the man giving orders, sending him sprawling on the asphalt.

The man went down hard and didn't get up, but that left the others—Spider-Man had seen five men, but he wasn't sure there weren't one or two others still in the van. He let go of the web-line and did a midair somersault, making himself a less predictable target.

Gunfire rattled, but his spider-sense barely buzzed—the Rat Packer was shooting wild. Spider-Man landed, cartwheeled, and slammed into a second Rat Packer.

"Check your masks!" someone shouted.

Spider-Man had expected that—these boys had been using tear gas pretty often of late. He hadn't brought a gas mask of his own, but that was no problem; he grabbed the Rat Packer he had just rammed, picking him up one-handed by the lapel of his leather coat.

The man clutched at Spider-Man's arm, struggling futilely, as Spider-Man snatched the gas mask from the Rat Packer's face.

He thought of saying something, some light-hearted bit of banter—but he wasn't feeling light-hearted. His wife was lying in a hospital bed in Queens, and he was here in Jersey City instead of at her side, and that did not leave him inclined to make his usual wisecracks.

He heard the first rattle of canisters and hiss of escaping gas just as he slid the gas mask into place. He adjusted the filter, then dropped his captive.

"Don't get up," he warned the man. "Stay under the gas—or if it doesn't get you, I will."

The Rat Packer lifted a hand and tried to say something—but then the tear gas reached him and he started coughing uncontrollably.

Spider-sense screamed a warning, and Spider-Man bounded away as something shrieked through the space where he had been standing. An instant later a warehouse wall erupted in a ball of orange fire, and some of the tear gas caught and blazed up brightly for a second or two before being consumed.

Spider-Man had turned to see what had gone past him, and was looking directly at the flash; he was momentarily blinded by the glare. When he could see again he spotted the shoulder-mounted rocket launcher, just as its wielder locked another missile in firing position.

"I don't think so," he said into his gas mask—not trying to say anything to his opponents, but merely talking to himself. "Shoot me once, shame on you; shoot me twice, shame on me." He unleashed a stream of webbing.

Rocket met web in midair, a few feet from the launcher; the resulting blast sent launcher and man backward against the side of the van. Metal rang loudly, and the launcher bounced off, leaving a large dent; then the Rat Packer hit with an appalling thud, and bounced as well, though not as far. He slid to the ground and lay in a heap by the van's rear tire.

Spider-Man had been half-deafened by the explosions and had spots dancing in his vision, but his spider-sense was as good as new; he knew when the next threat came, and danced nimbly aside well before he realized just what sort of danger he was reacting to.

"Only bullets?" he said, as steel-jacketed lead passed inches from his head. "Is that all?" He spotted the shooters easily enough, three of them running into the open door of a warehouse loading dock; he began a zigzag approach, dodging back and forth, leaping impossibly high into the air every so often, so that they couldn't get a good bead on him.

The Rat Pack gas masks were strap-on affairs covering the nose and mouth, but not the ears, and his hearing was recovering from the two big detonations; the automatic rifles were loud, but not deafening. That was how, perhaps halfway to the warehouse, he could make out a sort of muttering that he realized was the Rat Pack radio on his belt. Someone was calling.

Osborn, perhaps?

He didn't worry about it right away; instead he attached himself to the warehouse ceiling and scampered in after the gunmen.

They were backing farther in warily, moving along one wall with their weapons ready—but as usual, they forgot to look up. Spider-Man had no trouble getting directly over them, then swinging down, fists flying.

Two of the men went down, but he only had two fists— the third ran back out the loading dock door, and dodged behind a Dumpster.

Spider-Man took a moment to snatch away the AK-47s from the two men he had downed, and to web them to the floor. Then he bounded out the door and swung himself up atop the Dumpster. He dropped the guns in.

Gunfire rattled again, but he dodged easily, dropping down on the other side of the Dumpster. He waited there until the firing stopped; then he sprang back up onto the edge of the big metal box.

The last gunman was ejecting an empty magazine; he undoubtedly had another, but it would take a moment before the next attack, and that muttering was back. Spider-Man snatched the radio from his belt.

". . . going on there? Is it Spider-Man, or someone else? Over."

Spider-Man pressed the "transmit" button. "It's Spider-

Man, all right," he said into the mike. "And I'm coming for you, all of you. You're not good enough to stop me, any of you—you're hardly even slowing me down." He released the button for a moment and glanced at the man with the gun.

He had the empty magazine out, but he was still trying to fumble a new one into place; he was obviously on the verge of panic. Spider-Man had a few more seconds before he had to respond.

He pushed the button again.

"This Mr. Green you're working for—that's green as in 'Green Goblin.' Did you know that? Did you realize just which big-time loser hired all you small-time losers? And he's not here to help you, is he? There's just me, and you."

Then the magazine was in place—but a stream of webbing shot out and filled the AK-47's barrel.

"Oh, no," the Rat Packer said, looking at the useless weapon. If he fired it now it would blow up in his face.

"Just me, and you," Spidey said as he launched himself off the Dumpster at the gunman.

A moment later he stood over him, and looked around at the others—all either unconscious, securely webbed in place, or still coughing and gagging uncontrollably. He lifted the radio again.

"And now, right here, there's just me," he said. "But I'm coming after the rest of you."

Then he tucked the radio away and hurried across to the coughing man. He hauled him upright and carried him easily away from the remaining cloud of gas.

He slammed the man up against a wall. "Where's the mayor?" he demanded.

"I don't know!" the Rat Packer gasped, between coughs. "Not my job!"

"Then what *do* you know?" Spider-Man shouted. "Where are the rest of your goons?"

"I don't know! I just . . . just follow orders." He wheezed

desperately, then gasped out, "Number Two's the team leader!"

"Which one is he?"

He pointed at the first man Spider-Man had taken down—the one who had been giving orders earlier. Still carrying the coughing man, the web-slinger walked over and prodded Number Two with the toe of one boot.

The fallen man didn't move.

Spidey dropped the man he was holding and crossed to the van; the driver's door was still standing open. He looked inside.

The van's interior was jammed with weapons and equipment. There were no more Rat Packers in there—he had hoped there would be—but he spotted a clipboard leaning against the passenger seat. He picked it up.

There was a single sheet of paper on it, a list of checkpoints—twelve in all. Numbers one through five, and numbers eight and nine, had all been crossed out with thick black marker. The others were just numbers, with no addresses.

That didn't help much.

He frowned under his double mask.

He knew Osborn wanted him to get closer than this—there had to be some way to take the next step. Or had he managed to get here so far ahead of schedule that the whole scheme collapsed? Were the mayor and the rest supposed to have been here?

He doubted it; this was Checkpoint Six, after all, and there were four more not yet crossed off on the list.

He looked at the equipment in the van, and a thought struck him. The Rat Pack was a bunch of scavengers, and this van held quite an accumulation of their acquisitions. There might well be something here he could use. He climbed in and began to look through the racks of gadgets.

He found what he was after quickly, and pulled it out—a radio direction finder.

He pulled the Rat Pack radio from his belt and pushed the "transmit" button; with that signal to work from he only needed a few seconds to set the RD finder to the right frequency. Now he just needed to get the rest of the Rat Pack to say something, and he would be able to track them down—or at least get an idea of which direction he should go.

He pushed the "transmit" button. "Number Two calling, over," he whispered hoarsely into the mike.

"Two, are you all right?" The voice on the other end sounded jubilant. "Where's Spider-Man? Over."

Spider-Man grinned grimly under his mask as the needle on the RDF swung; the signal was strong and clear, and coming from due north.

He lifted the microphone again. "Right here," he said. "Watch your backs."

illy Vanderlyn had joined the Rat Pack because the Army wouldn't take him—his rap sheet was too long for the feds. He'd started shoplifting as a kid because his step-father wouldn't give him enough money to buy the stuff he needed if he was going to get by on the street, and then after he'd been caught a few times and all the shopkeepers in Baychester knew to keep an eye on him, he'd started running errands for the corner pusher. He got caught at that a few times, too, and next thing he knew Uncle Sam was telling him he wasn't good enough to get shipped to Iraq or Bosnia or Somalia or somewhere else.

He'd been going around wearing an old Army jacket and telling all his buds that he was gonna be a soldier, and then the Army wouldn't take him—let alone the Marines, which is what he'd hoped for. He knew what getting turned down would do with his street cred, so he'd started looking for some other way to make himself a big man—and there was Number One, the first Number One, recruiting some guys for his plans to take advantage of the stuff that got busted up or knocked down when nature turned mean or the costume guys played rough.

It had sounded good to Billy; he'd signed up. And like that old song he heard once as a kid, they gave him a number and took away his name, and now instead of Billy Vanderlyn, punk kid from the Bronx, he was Number Six in the Rat Pack.

They'd had a few setbacks, but they'd done okay, even after that mess with the Super-Skrull. Number One, whoever it was at the moment, made their deals, set up their plans, worked out all the contingencies, and the rest of them learned their parts and their options and carried through.

Billy had had a pretty good time with it so far. He'd found his niche. He'd found something he was good at, something that made him special even in the Rat Pack. He could take orders like any of them, he was good with gadgets, he'd learned to spot what to grab and what to leave, he'd absorbed all the training on obeying commands and following plans—and on top of all that, he'd wound up the team's top sniper. He had a real inborn knack for it.

And he was happy with that role; he wasn't interested in trying for anything bigger. He'd done fine so far, just doing what Number One told him to.

But on *this* operation the guy who had hired them, this Mr. Green, was running the show. Green was giving Number One his orders and making the plans for the entire Rat Pack, instead of letting Number One run things his own way. Billy didn't like that.

He especially didn't like it because the current plan didn't seem to be working, and they didn't have the contingency plans Number One always gave them. There wasn't any "The plan's ruined, run for it," option, the way there should be. There wasn't any plan for what to do if the target, Spider-Man, didn't do what he was supposed to.

And that's what was happening. The plan had called for Spider-Man to hit the ambush at Checkpoint Six some time after midnight—but it wasn't even eleven o'clock and apparently he was already there. The word had just come over the team's radio link—and now Billy could hear the sounds of fighting, tinny little noises of distant explosions, like a war movie on a cheap TV.

He wasn't even in position yet, hadn't had time to set up, and if the team at Six didn't get their act together Spider-Man might be on the way past them any second.

There were three other patrols out there, between Checkpoint Six and his own location, but how could he be sure they'd be set up any better than he was? What if Spider-Man just slipped right past them?

Billy was on the roof, behind the parapet; he looked down at the deserted street below, judging lines of sight, lines of fire, and available cover. Then he chose his spot—he had made a preliminary choice during the practice run-through, and now confirmed it. He lowered his pack, unzipped it, and lifted out his two rifles.

Billy was not paying close attention to the sounds from the radio as he worked the action and dry-fired his own personal favorite rifle. He hadn't named it, he wasn't the kind of geek who named his tools, but he loved this weapon. He'd picked it up on an earlier job, and realized what he had the first time he used it.

He didn't even know what make it was, the name and number had been filed off, but it was the finest rifle he'd ever seen. He had never missed with it, not once. If he got a clear shot at Spider-Man with it, the web-slinger was as good as dead—but he wasn't supposed to use it for that. That wasn't what the plan called for. He had brought it along because *he* wanted it there, not because his orders required it.

He reluctantly put his own rifle aside and picked up the other.

He'd been given this one especially for tonight. It fired anesthetic darts. This mysterious Mr. Green didn't want Spider-Man's brains splattered on a wall; he wanted the wall-crawling freak down, but alive.

Billy thought this was nuts, that messing with Spider-Man was stupid but that if you had to do it you should go all out for a kill—but Number One had given him the order, and he didn't argue with Number One.

"Number Two, what's going on?" Number One's voice asked over the link as Billy sighted down the tranquilizer gun's barrel. "Is it Spider-Man, or someone else? Over."

Billy worked the action on the dart rifle; it seemed a

bit stiff, and he frowned. Then he froze as an unfamiliar voice spoke from the link.

"It's Spider-Man, all right," the voice said. "And I'm coming for you, all of you. You're not good enough to stop me, any of you—you're hardly even slowing me down."

"Not good enough?" Billy said. "We're the *best!*" He slid the dart magazine in place. "Just wait until you get this far, Bug-Man!"

He didn't much like the fact that Spider-Man had one of their radio links; that meant they couldn't make any changes in the plan without the enemy knowing it. If Number One had been doing this himself he'd probably have had an alternate frequency picked out beforehand—but he'd left it to Mr. Green, who hadn't been taking suggestions, and the only means of communication they had was the link.

Then the radio crackled, and Spider-Man—if that was really who it was—spoke again.

"This Mr. Green you're working for—that's green as in 'Green Goblin.' Did you know that? Did you realize just which big-time loser hired all you small-time losers? And he's not here to help you, is he? There's just me, and you."

Billy looked down at the radio, startled.

The Green Goblin?

People in the business talked, when they weren't working. Sometimes guys serving time had a few choice comments that got passed out. Word got around. There were guys out there who were pretty good to work for, like the Kingpin—guys who took care of their people, who shared the money fairly, who seemed to understand that the people they hired were human beings, and who didn't screw up big time and wind up behind bars. You had to know the rules, of course—arguing with the Kingpin could get you a quick ticket to the morgue—but in general, guys like that were just fine.

And there were guys who were okay, but not really good, like Hammerhead—they treated their guys okay, but they spent a lot of time in jail, and the odds were pretty good that working for them could put you in there with them.

And then there were the raving loonies, the people you did *not* want to work for under any circumstances, the guys who'd kill their own men just for the hell of it, or lose it completely and flatten the whole area, or who'd take off in the middle of a fight leaving their guys defenseless, or who just *always* lost. Hydra was a bunch of loonies like that. Doctor Octopus wasn't that bad, but he was a loony, too.

And the Green Goblin was a raving loony—not at Hydra's level, but it was about a toss-up between him and Doc Ock. The Goblin won more fights, on average, but he was more likely to screw over his own team.

Billy looked down at the two rifles.

He had orders to use the dart gun, but if those orders came from the Green Goblin . . .

But they didn't, he told himself. They'd come from Number One. Maybe Number One got them from Mr. Green, but *Billy* had gotten them from Number One. And he wasn't going to cross Number One.

That voice, the one that claimed to be Spider-Man, spoke again. "And now, right here, there's just me," it said. "But I'm coming after the rest of you."

Billy shuddered. Team Two was all down, then? All of them? That had been pretty quick work. Billy knew a lot of Team Two had been lost earlier, at that stupid diversion out in Queens—that was another of Mr. Green's hot ideas Billy hadn't liked—but Number Two was a smart guy, and he'd still been there, and he must have had some other good guys with him, and a lot of equipment.

So now Spider-Man should be headed toward the next checkpoint, where Nine and a new guy, Thirty-one, were supposed to go after him with a bunch of high-tech crap the Pack took out of an abandoned old Hydra base—mind-control gadgets, illusion projectors, stuff like that.

Billy patted his own rifle. *This* was all the tech *he* needed!

A moment later the radio crackled. "Number Two calling, over," a voice whispered. At first Billy smiled; good old Two must have hidden somewhere, and the wall-crawler hadn't spotted him.

But then the smile faded; that voice didn't really sound like Two. Billy hesitated, considering reaching for his own radio.

Nine's voice spoke before he could. "Two, are you all right? Where's Spider-Man? Over."

It definitely wasn't Two who answered; it was Spider-Man. "Right here. Watch your backs," he said.

"Blast it," Billy muttered. He hesitated, then picked up the dart gun. He crouched down by the roof's edge and waited. "You better know what you're doing," he said.

Time passed; the night air cooled. Autumn had been mild so far, but it was October, and the warm evenings weren't quite so warm any more.

Traffic hummed in the distance. The glow of Manhattan that lit the eastern sky seemed to have dimmed slightly—Billy wasn't sure if that was something to do with the weather, or because people were turning off lights as the hour grew late.

Somewhere out there was a guy in red-and-blue tights who could do all this amazing stuff, who could punch through walls and stick to ceilings and shoot sticky webs, and he was trashing Billy's friends.

Billy didn't understand that. If he had powers like that, he'd have robbed a few banks and retired to a Caribbean island or something; he wouldn't go around beating up guys who were just trying to get by without having to put up with all that boring crap the working stiffs lived through every day.

Why was Spider-Man after them? Why did he sound so mad on the radio? What had the Rat Pack done to *him?*

They were just trying to make a quick buck, earn themselves a little respect.

Billy thought he understood the Avengers—they were all rich guys, with that mansion of theirs. Captain America was practically a walking billboard for the bosses, Iron Man had a cushy corporate job—but why was Spider-Man out here?

Not that it mattered. Any minute now, when the wall-crawler ran up against all that Hydra stuff . . .

The radio crackled. "Do you really think you can stop me with *that* stuff?" Spider-Man's voice said from the link. "It's not the gun that's dangerous, kids—it's the man *behind* the gun. Which means I'm just as safe here as if I were home in my own bed."

So the bug-man had already spotted the old Hydra junk Nine and Thirty-one were using. Billy grimaced. That wasn't good; Nine must have been careless.

"Go!" Nine's voice barked.

There was a burst of static—interference from the gadgets, Billy guessed. When that cleared he could hear thumping, and then tearing metal.

Billy blinked. The sounds from the radio were of wrenching, crunching steel, like a car caught in a crusher—but there wasn't any crusher there; just Spider-Man.

He reached down and got his radio from his belt. As a team leader, even if his team was just him, he had one of the fancier models; at present the master switch was set to "Accept," meaning that he heard whatever went into a link with the "Transmit" button, and anything loud enough to trigger the emergency voice activation. Most of the links only had three choices, "Off," "Accept," and "Transmit," but team leaders had a fourth—"Monitor."

He slid the switch to "Monitor," then used the tiny keypad to enter the codes 09 and 31. That forced those two links to permanent "transmit" status, but on the separate command frequency that only team leaders received.

". . . how's he *do*—look out!" Thirty-one said. Then metal crunched again.

"Oh, my God!" Thirty-one said. "He ain't human!"

"Of course not," Nine responded. "He's a freak, like—"

Then Nine's voice cut off in a choking sound, followed by spitting.

"Loser," Spider-Man's voice said—even through the tiny radio, Billy could hear how cold and hard that voice was. "You think these toys make you tough? You aren't tough. You're *nothing*. You think you can stop me with this stuff? You're not good enough to stop me with an entire *arsenal*. You Rat Packers are all a bunch of losers; all of you put together aren't up to the job of stopping me."

"That's what *you* think," Billy muttered to himself. He stroked the polished wood of the dart rifle.

"And that boss of yours, Mr. Green, a.k.a. the Green Goblin, is the biggest loser of you all," Spider-Man said. "At least you punks are out here trying. The Goblin's not even up to doing *that* much any more. He's not man enough to come out here and do his own dirty work."

"You got *that* part right," Billy muttered.

"Now, are you going to tell me where I can find the mayor?" Spider-Man said.

"I don't know!" Thirty-one wailed. "They didn't tell us, I swear! Said we couldn't tell what we didn't know!"

"Wimp," Billy growled.

"What about the Goblin? Your Mr. Green?"

"I don't know!"

"What *do* you know?"

"Ah! Ah!"

"What do you know?"

"Where the next checkpoint is!"

"Blast it," Billy said. "I knew we were getting sloppy with these new recruits. He should've held out longer than *that!*" He hit the "Transmit" button. "Seven, Twenty-three, Twenty-six, he's coming your way. Over."

That bunch didn't have any fancy Hydra weapons, but

they were holed up inside one of the warehouses on the Hoboken waterfront, and the whole place was booby-trapped. The Rat Pack had spent a lot of time over the past few weeks preparing it, during the lull after their raid on the old IRT power plant—everyone had made suggestions, talked over what worked and what didn't, helped set it all up, and half a dozen of the guys had trained for days in leading into traps without getting caught themselves.

Nets, pitfalls, tripwires, cages . . .

"Ready and waiting, boys," Seven's voice said.

"You think you're ready?" Spider-Man broke in. "You have no idea what you're up against. You're in this one *way* over your heads. That's why the Goblin's not out here—he at least has *some* idea what I can do."

"I know everything about you, Spider-Man," a new, oddly distorted voice replied. "I know what you're capable of, and what my men are capable of. *You're* the one who's in trouble here!" Billy started; that was Mr. Green, speaking through that gadget he wore over his mouth.

So he *was* the Goblin. That was bad.

"Seven, I see him," Twenty-six said. "He's coming up on the right, out on . . . blast! I lost him!"

"We're ready for him, Al . . . I mean, Twenty-six," Twenty-three said. "You just let us know when you see him again. Over."

Billy waited for the reply, for the report that Spider-Man had been spotted again, that he was entering the building, that he was walking blindly into the traps that had been set for him there.

It didn't come. Instead, after a wait, Seven asked, "What's that I'm hearing? Twenty-six, report! Over."

If Billy held the radio to his ear he could just barely make out an irregular thumping noise somewhere in the background; he supposed it was traps going off.

"Twenty-six! Blast it! Twenty-three, can you see where that idiot brother of yours went?"

"I don't see him, Seven. Wait a minute—something's moving over there . . ."

"Twenty-three, wait a minute, don't go after him alone—you hear me?"

Billy heard a sound like a spring snapping, and then a thud—a trap, had to be one of the traps. There was an odd little wet sound.

Twenty-three didn't reply.

"Number One, this is Seven," Seven said. "We've got trouble here. I've lost all contact with both the other members of my team, can't find them. Spider-Man's inside, and half the traps have gone off, but I can't see him anywhere. I could use some help here. . . ."

"You won't get it," Spider-Man's voice cut in. "It's too late for that."

"He's right. . . ."

Seven's voice cut off.

Billy frowned. Seven was good at his job. He had probably just taken his finger off the "transmit" button while he did something to stop that wall-crawling menace.

But then Billy remembered his radio was set to "Monitor." He typed in 07.

For a long moment he waited silently, hoping to hear Seven return and report victory—but expecting, dreading, Spider-Man's voice.

He heard neither; instead Eight, team leader for the last squad left out there between Billy and Spider-Man, said, "Seven, you okay?"

Seven didn't answer—but Spider-Man did.

"He's not okay," he said. "He's a loser. He lost. And you're next."

Billy looked down at his two weapons.

His orders were to use the dart gun, but he didn't care any more what Mr. Green wanted, not even if Number One had agreed to it. He pushed the dart gun aside, picked up his sniper rifle, and began methodically readying it for use.

Eight's team—himself and Eleven, their explosives expert—was just two blocks away from the booby-trapped warehouse Seven's team had used. At the rate Spider-Man was moving he could be there in seconds.

The rifle was ready. Billy pressed "transmit."

"Eight, is he there? Over," he asked.

Eight and Eleven had the simplest setup of them all; they'd mined a building, and were going to drop it on the web-slinger's head. All they had to do was lure Spider-Man in, run for it, and hit the switch the instant they were clear.

"I see him coming, Sp . . . I mean, Eight," Eleven's voice said. "He's heading straight for . . . blast! He turned! He's up on the roof next door!"

Billy waited.

"I know you're listening," Eight said at last. "You want us, Spider-Man? You'll have to come in and get us. We're not coming out."

"Oh, yes, you are," Spider-Man replied.

Billy frowned. What was *that* about? How did he expect to get them outside?

"Oh, my God," Eleven said. "He's tearing out the entire *wall*!"

"Move!" Eight barked. "Move, J.J., move!"

"But he's not in . . ."

"*Move,* blast it! This is the best we're gonna get!"

Billy heard running feet on concrete as Eight and Eleven fled—and then the radio speaker fuzzed out as the flash of the explosion lit the sky to the southeast.

A second later the sound of the blast reached him, bouncing down Hoboken's empty streets like a strange amplified echo of the squawk from the radio.

"Oh, man! There's gonna be cops all over *that* one," Billy muttered.

Sure enough, a police siren began calling almost immediately, as echoes of the explosion—real echoes—rattled down the streets. The crunch of settling debris came from the radio.

Then, faintly, Billy heard a voice ask, "Eight? Spud? Are you okay?"

"He'll live," Spider-Man said, clear and strong, "but I don't think he can talk right now through the webbing."

Billy pressed "transmit" and barked, "Eleven, run for it! Get out of there!"

"I'd be worrying about *you,* not Eleven," Spider-Man answered. "He's running. I'm giving him half a block head start, just to make it interesting."

"Blast it!" Billy frowned. This was not going well. He was supposed to put anesthetic darts in a frantic, confused Spider-Man, but the guy coming his way didn't sound the least bit frantic or confused. He sounded seriously angry, and close to unstoppable.

And if Eleven was following the escape route he was supposed to use, Spider-Man was on his way right into Billy's sights. Billy settled the rifle against his shoulder.

Forget the dart gun, for sure; he wasn't going to try that against someone who took out everyone else on four teams in less than forty minutes, travel time between their ambush sites included. He was going to take Spider-Man down for good, two shots, one to the chest to slow him down and one to the head to finish him. If Mr. Green Goblin didn't like it, that was just too bad.

"Six, I don't see him," Eleven said. "I thought he said he'd be coming after me. I'm heading your way, but I don't know if he's following."

"Oh, right, *tell* him there's another trap!" Billy grumbled. Eleven knew better than that; he was rattled, getting panicky. Billy pushed "transmit."

"He's after you, all right—shut up and run."

He could hear Eleven's running footsteps now; he slid his eye down to the scope and focused on the street.

There was Eleven, coming closer at an all-out run; he scanned backward, looking for Spider-Man.

He thought he saw a glimpse of red and blue, but then it was gone. He frowned, and scanned back toward Eleven.

Nothing. No sign of any pursuit—just the one man running headlong down the streets of Hoboken.

Eleven was at the corner; he'd be past Billy's position in just a minute.

"Where *is* he?" Billy mumbled, staring intently into the scope.

"Behind you," Spider-Man said.

Billy yelped, quite unprofessionally, as he whirled to find the wall-crawler crouched atop an air conditioning unit fifteen feet away. He had landed sitting with his back to the parapet; now he swung the sniper rifle around, trying to bring it to bear, but something dark sprang from Spider-Man's hand and splashed against the sight and along the barrel, something *sticky,* that hardened almost instantly into a sort of dark plastic string.

And then the stuff was hitting *him,* splattering across his chest and mask, getting in his eyes—and now he screamed, a scream of fear and rage and disgust, and tried to fling the useless rifle aside, only to find it was stuck to his hands. He couldn't get them free to wipe his face; his eyes were stinging and watering, and his vision was clouded, as if he were looking at everything through black cloth.

He tried to kick himself away from the parapet and get to his feet, but now fresh webbing was wrapping itself around his legs, tying him down, sticking him to the tarred surface of the roof.

"Now," Spider-Man said, "where's the mayor?"

"I don't know!" Billy choked out—his mask had kept the webbing out of his mouth, anyway.

"That's not what I want to hear," Spider-Man said. He stalked closer—Billy could see him as a looming blur of color. Billy cowered back against the parapet; he'd have slid sideways if he could, but the webbing wouldn't let him.

Spider-Man reached down and grabbed the rifle, then snatched it out of Billy's hands—webbing tore, but most of the removal was accomplished by yanking Billy's leather gloves off. The web-slinger took the gun in both hands and snapped it like a dry twig, then tossed aside the pieces, with Billy's gloves still clinging to them. The fragments of Billy's precious rifle bounced and rattled across the roof.

Even through the webbing Billy could see it happen, and at the sight he felt as if someone had torn out his heart. That beautiful, beautiful rifle . . . !

Then Spider-Man reached down again, and Billy struggled desperately to pull free of the webbing, without success. Red-gloved hands closed on the lapels of Billy's leather coat, and heaved.

The webbing snapped and tore as if it were grass being ripped from a lawn, and a moment later Billy hung in Spider-Man's grip, his legs dangling helplessly, still bound to each other by webbing. He tried to kick, but only managed to squirm.

Then Spider-Man took two steps forward, and Billy's feet brushed against the parapet. He tried to catch himself, to stand atop that thin row of bricks, but Spider-Man pushed him relentlessly outward, past the edge, until he dangled helplessly over the street.

The bug-man was holding all his 180 pounds forty feet above the pavement as easily as Billy might have held a bag of kitchen trash. In fact, Spider-Man was balancing on the parapet, holding Billy at arm's length as if the Rat Packer were a kitten that might try to scratch.

"Now," Spider-Man said again, "where's the mayor?"

"Forget it!" Billy managed, but his voice cracked.

Spider-Man took away one hand; Billy hung from just one side of his own coat, just four fingers and a thumb keeping him from a four-story drop onto concrete.

"You think I won't drop you?" Spider-Man said. "You think I'm a super hero, and we're the good guys, we don't kill?" The grip loosened, and Billy thrashed slightly, trying desperately to get some sort of purchase without pulling free of the wallcrawler's grip. "Heroes don't kill, huh? Ever hear of the Punisher? And as for me being a good guy, ever read any of Jameson's editorials about me in the *Daily Bugle,* and think he might be right? Ever wonder if maybe I'm just better at covering it up than some guys are?"

"You won't . . ." Billy began, but then he stopped. Spider-Man had just said he *would* kill, and how did Billy know otherwise? Sure, Spider-Man had always been cleared when he was accused of killing someone, but so were a lot of fellas who really *had* whacked people.

And then Spider-Man's hand opened, and Billy dropped a foot before a strand of webbing caught him. He dangled, swaying back and forth.

"If you don't talk, there's always your buddy Eleven," Spider-Man said, in a hard, flat voice that reminded Billy of a couple of guys he'd known who were seriously bad news. "I can catch him in five minutes—and if I have to do that, you'll have been dead for four of them."

"Okay!" Billy said. "Okay, okay!"

"Where is he?" To Billy the voice from beneath the webbed red mask sounded like death itself.

"I don't know for sure," Billy said quickly, "but we've been working out of an old chemical plant, Torpey Chemical, six blocks from here! If he's not there I swear I don't know! It's Mr. Green's place, he set us up there!"

"Good," Spider-Man said. Billy found himself suddenly yanked upward and tossed aside, onto the roof. He landed hard, knocking the wind out of him—but he knew he'd have landed a lot harder if he'd fallen those four stories. "You get to live," Spider-Man said.

Then he sprayed a fresh tangle of webbing, gluing Billy to the roof.

"Hey! Lemme go!" Billy yelled—but he realized he was shouting at an empty rooftop.

Spider-Man was gone.

Billy stared at a chimney for a long moment, then tried to wiggle free of the webbing.

He couldn't move.

He'd broken, he'd told Spider-Man what he wanted to know. And he hadn't even gotten off a shot before the web-slinger took him down. He'd blown it completely.

Of course, so had all his buddies, but right now that wasn't much comfort. He didn't think the Green Goblin, if that was really who they were working for, was likely to be reasonable about it.

But then again, he might not have to worry about the Goblin. In the streets below those police sirens were coming closer.

Fifteen

Spider-Man didn't bother looking for a gate; he vaulted over the fence, ignoring the coils of razor wire. And once inside the grounds he didn't bother looking for a door; instead he simply climbed up past the bricked-up ground level and dove head-first through the nearest window, landing in a shower of glass on a darkened factory floor, surrounded by massive, dusty machinery, huge dark vats, and tangles of plumbing.

He was inside; now he just had to find Osborn and the mayor. And when he did, he desperately hoped that he could provoke Osborn into putting on his costume and becoming the Green Goblin—he could punch out the Goblin, or at least try to, while hitting Osborn would make him a criminal.

If the cops got here, and he told them the Green Goblin had been behind the mayor's kidnapping, they would believe him.

If the cops got here, and he told them Norman Osborn had been behind the mayor's kidnapping, they wouldn't admit to believing a word. Norman Osborn was a city official, with money and power and lawyers.

He wasn't too worried yet that Osborn would kill the mayor; Hizzoner was still worth too much as bait. If Osborn had a chance to frame Spider-Man for the mayor's murder, Spidey knew he'd grab it.

But if he saw things going wrong, saw Spider-Man winning, then the mayor would die. That was another reason to get Osborn out here fighting—he couldn't give the order to kill the mayor while he was busy brawling.

"Yoo hoo, Norm," he called. "Come out and play!"

Light sprang up on all sides, revealing a vast area, fifty

feet high and a hundred yards long, cluttered with rusting chemical equipment.

The tingle of his spider-sense, his reflexive dodge, his leaping to a nearby vertical surface while he looked for the danger—all that happened almost automatically, after all these years of practice. The rattle of gunfire and the spray of bullets seemed almost an afterthought; he was well out of the line of fire, clinging to a steel pillar and climbing, by the time the Rat Packer squeezed the trigger. A strand of webbing shot out, and the AK-47 was snatched out of the attacker's hands and sent flying. It smacked against the side of a long-empty vat.

At first Spider-Man didn't look at the vat, or at the rest of his surroundings; he was concentrating on the single Rat Packer, webbing him up securely. He was just finishing when a fresh warning tingle made him whirl.

The energy cannon the Rat Packers were wheeling into the factory aisle had clearly been salvaged from some super-villain's arsenal; who else would have built the forward mount in the shape of a chrome-plated skull?

For that matter, who else built energy cannons in the first place?

Spider-Man didn't know whether this one had been built by Hydra, or Dr. Doom, or who, and he didn't much care as he dived out of the way.

The cannon fired, and an intensely bright blue-white beam flashed through the factory; heavy machinery crumpled and melted as the beam blasted through it.

Spider-Man did not crumple or melt; he had already rolled aside and bounced back to his feet, and before the glare faded he was dodging between pipes and pillars, working his way around behind the cannoneers.

The cannon fired again as the crew serving it swung it around, trying to locate their target.

The energy cannon was certainly powerful—its beam was tearing easily through cranes, walls, and vats, reducing them to puddles and shredded scrap and showering the area with sparks and molten droplets. The blast filled the air with the stench of ozone and hot metal, with hissing and roaring and the rattle of falling wreckage. It was powerful—but it wasn't particularly maneuverable; Spider-Man had no trouble staying out of its way as he circled around.

He had started out bouncing and running, but once he was well clear of the blast zone he took a second to fire a web-line into the cobwebbed steel girders high overhead and pulled himself up, swinging through the air faster than the cannon's crew could possibly keep up with.

Once he was up there he took a quick look around.

The factory was pretty much one big room, fifty feet high, sixty feet wide, a hundred yards long, with huge expanses of dusty glass panes down both the long sides. Many of the windows had been painted white; through the others he could glimpse the towers of Manhattan in the distance, and the full moon hanging high overhead.

At one end were two big overhead doors, both rusty and closed tight. He could see chains holding them shut. At that end most of the floor was empty; paths in the dirt showed that the energy cannon had been stored there before being wheeled to its present position a few yards up the central aisle.

Most of the rest of the floor, save for a broad central passage, narrower aisles to either side, and several short connecting paths, was filled with old equipment—tanks the size of delivery vans, vats the size of houses, valves like steering wheels, pipes as thick as trees, winding and twisting around each other. Heavy chains dangled here and there; motors and furnaces were appended to some of the vessels where chemicals had required stirring, mixing, or heating. Gauges, too covered with filth to be read, were banked on every side—or had been, before the energy cannon sliced through much of this ancient machinery.

At the far end three doors led off the factory floor, presumably to offices, break rooms, and the like. Above them, at third-floor level, a dusty mirror reflected dully the whole interior of the factory; Spider-Man could see himself hanging from his web-line, dwarfed by the room and its contents.

There was no sign of the mayor or Norman Osborn anywhere, so far as he could see, but there were olive-drab masks peering out here and there amid the machinery.

And below him was the gleaming chrome-and-crystal energy cannon, with its five crewmen. That was obviously what he needed to deal with first.

He fired another web-line, caught it, and swung through the open air above the clutter, moving in for the attack.

"You know," he called out as he swooped toward the cannon's crew, "if your boss were here, with his spiffy little goblin glider and all those other toys, he could come up here after me. You guys, though—you're all ground-bound. Look at this place—I mean it, just look around you at all this space. Now, think about how much of it is more than six feet off the floor. All that space is *mine,* boys."

Then he slammed both feet into one man's chest, flinging him backward against an electrical box.

"Auugh!" the Rat Packer cried, as he crumpled, clutching his chest. "I think you maybe broke one of my ribs!"

"And I think you fired a honking big raygun at me," Spider-Man retorted, as he punched another crew member on the jaw, sending him sprawling.

The others were already running. Spider-Man tripped one with a tangle of webbing, then turned to the cannon. He tore open the control panel, yanked a handful of wires and circuit boards out, and flung them aside.

That ought to disable the thing, he thought. With that taken care of, he sprang into the air, looking for the rest of the Rat Pack.

The others were fleeing through the maze of machinery and plumbing—but it was a maze that Spider-Man could travel *over*. He could look down from above, locate his prey, and swoop down, picking them off as he pleased.

Besides the other two who had manned the cannon, there

were eight or ten more—probably all that was left of the Rat Pack after their losses at the hospital and the various botched ambushes.

These remaining members of the Rat Pack were armed with an assortment of weapons—everything from .45 automatics to flamethrowers to lasers—and several of them opened fire once Spider-Man was visible. It did no good; guided by his spider-sense, Spider-Man kept moving, leaping from web-line to web-line, from girder to chain, twisting and turning through the air over their heads, making himself an impossible target.

And he kept up a constant banter as he webbed one foe after another. He had noticed that large, dusty mirror at one end of the factory, at third-floor level, and noticed as well that when he got close to it his spider-sense itched slightly; he was now sure that Norman Osborn was behind that mirror, watching the fight through one-way glass.

If he wanted, he could smash his way in—but he didn't want to fight Norman Osborn.

He wanted to fight the Green Goblin. He could *beat* the Green Goblin.

Besides, he knew that he had to do the unexpected. Smashing in there would be what Osborn expected, and would therefore almost certainly be stepping into a trap, setting him up to be blamed for the mayor's murder. Perhaps the one-way window was rigged to drive a shard of glass through the mayor's heart if shattered, or something similarly diabolical; whatever the exact nature of the trap, Spider-Man had no intention of falling into it.

He wasn't going in there; he was going to make the Goblin come out.

"Hey, Normie," he called, "you should've given all these bozos jetpacks or something. I'm shooting fish in a barrel out here!"

He matched action to words, spearing a Rat Packer with a stream of webbing, snatching him up and hanging him, securely wrapped, from one of the steel beams overhead.

"Not much fun this way, is it, Norm? These guys can't do anything—if you want something done right, do it yourself. Except *you* can't do it, either, can you? You never *could* beat me, even-up."

He yanked a laser out of the hands of another Rat Packer and landed atop a huge glass cylinder. For a moment a dozen pairs of eyes were focused on him, on the laser, expecting him to turn it on them.

Instead he grabbed it in both hands and bent, and the laser snapped. Bits of metal and glass scattered, raining down across a bank of instruments, rattling and bouncing.

"There's no *challenge* to any of this, Norm," he called. "At least you could give me a real fight! Maybe you should've given all these guys goblin gliders or rocket brooms—but no, you keep the *fun* stuff for yourself, right? You never could delegate very well. You always picked such *losers* as henchmen." He fired a web-line and launched himself into the air again.

"I mean, just *look* at these guys," he said. "Sure, they've got some fancy weapons, but they're all just leftovers, you know? I go up against stuff like this all the time! And all that olive drab is just butt-ugly. How'd you find these guys? Why'd you hire them? Is it just because they wear green? I mean, what is it with you and green? Did you pick that because it alliterates, or just because it was the ugliest color you could find for that fright-mask of yours? You couldn't just be the Goblin; no, you had to be the *Green* Goblin, and you probably picked these losers just so their outfits wouldn't clash with yours."

He blocked a door with a webbed-in-place upended workbench, cutting off an escape route for the Rat Packers remaining on the factory floor.

"Oh, but I *forgot*," Spider-Man said, slapping his cheek in feigned astonishment. "You don't *wear* the costume any more! You leave all the nasty fighting to your hirelings! *They* get to have all the fun. What a *shame* none of them are good enough to stop me! It's just *such* a shame none of them can fly, when there's all this open space up here. In a few minutes I'll have them all mopped up, and then . . . and then *what,* Norm? Think I'm going to come smashing in there after you?" He dodged a spray of bullets, then swung down and sent one of the Rat Packers flying with a boot to the head.

"Rat Pack or Green Goblin, you're all just two-bit losers!" he called, over the echo of gunfire.

In the old manager's office Norman Osborn stood, hands behind his back, watching Spider-Man beat up his men. Every gunshot, every thud as a fist or boot landed, every taunt came loud and clear over the P.A. speaker on the wall above the window.

"Blast you," Osborn muttered into the electronic voice distorter he wore over his mouth—a precaution against the possibility of recordings and voiceprints that could identify "Mr. Green" as Norman Osborn. His fingers flexed against each other. "Show some brains, you fools! Don't let him exploit his command of the air like that—get *under* something! Make him dig you out! You're supposed to be the *Rat* Pack—whoever saw rats scurrying around in the open like that?" His hands separated and swung forward, clenched into fists.

"Why?" he said. "Why am I always surrounded by incompetents?" He turned and looked at the other occupants of the office.

There were only two members of the Rat Pack in the factory who weren't down there fighting Spider-Man, and they were both right here—Number One, the Pack's leader, and Number Thirty-seven, a huge man, a recent recruit who had showed some sign of wit and initiative and who had the size and strength Osborn had needed for one part of his scheme. They were standing against one wall; Thirty-seven held a pistol, and One held the remote control of the security cameras mounted in the corners of the room.

And there was one more person in the room—the Mayor

of New York, tied to a chair, securely gagged and thoroughly blindfolded.

Osborn had no intention of letting the mayor leave this place alive, but plans could go wrong, and he hadn't wanted Hizzoner to have a chance to recognize his captor's face; hence the blindfold, and another reason for the voice distorter. He didn't want to risk the distraction of the mayor making attempts to beg his old friend and campaign contributor for his life; it would be easier if the mayor never saw his face or heard his real voice, never knew who was behind the kidnapping.

But Osborn couldn't have stayed away entirely. That would have been safer, but there had been something in his plans he *had* to see in person.

The chair had been carefully placed, the camera angles calculated—if Spider-Man had come smashing through the center of the one-way glass, as he should have, the cameras would have shown his feet plunging directly toward the mayor's head. Osborn would be nowhere in sight on the videotapes—he was being very careful to stay out of camera range—but he would be here, watching the whole thing, gloating over the ruination of his greatest foe.

He would videotape Spider-Man's boots flying at the mayor's head. And once that was safely recorded, Thirty-seven would snap the mayor's neck with his bare hands.

Osborn knew better than to try to frame Spider-Man for premeditated murder; that had been attempted, and it never worked. No, he had intended to make it look as if Spidey had killed the mayor by accident while trying to save him. That would let him, as the new mayor, declare super heroes in general, and Spider-Man in particular, to be public menaces, no longer welcome in his city.

And if everything had gone just right, *Spider-Man himself* might have believed he was guilty!

But Spider-Man wasn't playing his part; he hadn't come anywhere near the glass. Instead he was swinging about on his webs, chattering away as he polished off those useless fools Number One had promised could handle anything. He *must* know the mayor was in here. . . .

He knew. And he wasn't coming.

It seemed the boy was learning.

Osborn frowned. It appeared he had misjudged his old enemy. That wouldn't change the final outcome, really— he would still win—but it seemed he would have to take a more direct role than he had intended.

"All right, get him out of here," Osborn said, pointing at the mayor.

"Kill him?" Thirty-seven asked.

"No," Osborn said. "Not yet. He's worth more as a live hostage at this point."

"You planning to bargain?" Number One asked. "Didn't think that was your style."

"It's *not*," Osborn growled. "You just get him out of here and leave Spider-Man to me!"

"Yessir," Number One replied. He gestured to Thirty-seven. "Come on, you take under the arms, I'll get his feet."

"He's tied to the chair," Thirty-seven objected.

"Then you get one side of the chair, I'll get the other. Come on; I don't think Mr. Green wants us around."

Thirty-seven grunted agreement, and the two of them lifted the mayor and carried him away.

The moment they were gone, Osborn turned back to the glass. Spider-Man was toying with the last of the Rat Pack, dodging about and calling, "Over here! No, whoops, I'm over here! You need to be faster, Mr. Rat Pack person!"

Osborn tore off the voice distorter. He had no more use for "Mr. Green."

"You want a challenge, Parker?" he growled. "You want a *real* fight? You'll have one. And you'll regret it!"

Spider-Man had caught the last of his opponents and hung the man fifteen feet above the factory floor, securely wrapped in a cocoon of webbing. Now he was idly pushing the captured terrorist, making him swing back and forth like an immense pendulum.

"So," he said, "do *you* know where the mayor is? I'll bet he's around here somewhere. But the mean ol' Goblin probably didn't tell you anything about that. He knew you guys weren't good enough to stop me. I mean, I don't know why he bothered with this whole thing—he knows *he* isn't good enough to stop me, any more than you were. He . . ."

Then Spider-Man heard a loud crash from the other end of the factory; his spider-sense went berserk. He whirled.

The Green Goblin, astride his batwinged goblin glider, was swooping down from the shattered remains of the one-way mirror, coming straight for him.

"I know what you're trying to do," the Green Goblin called. "You want me to fight you on your own simple-minded terms, face to face, didn't you? But you're a *fool,* Spider-Man! This is the *last* thing you should have wanted—for me to take a direct hand! Because despite all your bluster, we both know you're no match for me. You've lived these last few years on my sufferance, because I enjoyed the knowledge that you were out there—but the fun is over, Spider-Man." He reached in his shoulder bag for a weapon.

"It's time for you to die," he called.

Sixteen

pider-Man fired a web-line at a handy girder and swung out of the Goblin's path—but the Goblin swerved, leaning his weight to one side and sending the jet-powered glider into a graceful curve. His hand came out of his bag of tricks holding a clutch of miniature pumpkins—or rather, pumpkin bombs.

"You thought you had mastery of the air here," the Goblin called, "but all you do is leap about on those ludicrous webs of yours, while I can actually fly."

Then he flung three bombs—but Spider-Man's web shooter was already firing. The projectiles ran into a mesh of webbing, and exploded far short of their target—closer to the Goblin than to Spider-Man, in fact. The hard, flat sound of the triple explosion echoed from the concrete floor and the corrugated steel roof high overhead, and the concussion wave hit both antagonists, knocking them from their intended courses.

The Goblin struggled for a few seconds, steadying his glider, and then, when he had regained control, swooped around a rising curve, back toward Spider-Man.

Spider-Man had recovered more quickly; the Goblin found himself heading directly into a spreading tangle of webbing. He raised a finger, and goblin sparks cut through the clinging gray strands.

The glare of the sparks, which were intended as much to dazzle opponents as to cut at them, partially blinded the Goblin for a moment, and left Spider-Man an opening; he took it. Both his boots slammed into the Goblin's head.

The Goblin swayed; his glider tipped up on one wing for a moment, and his feet strained against the straps securing them to the glider's wings, but he stayed astride. His steadying weight and the glider's own built-in gyros leveled it out quickly.

The blow to the head would have stunned an ordinary man, at the very least—but the Green Goblin was no ordinary man. The weird serum Norman Osborn had ingested years before gave him superhuman strength and stamina, and near-miraculous healing ability.

Spider-Man and the other so-called heroes claimed that the serum had also driven him mad, but the Goblin knew better. Any change in his thinking after drinking that potion had merely been an improved understanding of the truth he had known all along—the truth that the world was all about *power*, power and competition, and a man's duty—a *real* man's—was to beat down anything in his way, bend the rest of the world to his will.

Norman Osborn had done that, had trampled everyone who dared to oppose him—everyone except Spider-Man. Peter Parker and Spider-Man continued to defy him, no matter what he did. He had tried to show Parker his own powerlessness, tried to teach him what it meant to oppose Norman Osborn, tried to drive him from the city, and still Spider-Man resisted.

It was time to pound the truth into that webbed head, time to show Spider-Man once and for all that he was no match for the Green Goblin.

"Is that the best you can do, Spider-Man?" he called. "A kick in the face?" He turned, expecting to see Spider-Man a dozen yards away, where the end of his swing would have taken him.

"No," Spider-Man said, as both boots smashed into the Goblin's head again. "I'm just warming up. We'll get to the *good* stuff later."

The Goblin bellowed wordless anger, and sprayed goblin sparks at his attacker.

Spider-Man dodged easily.

"You know," he said, "we're both chemists—maybe we should trade a few secrets. You know my webbing's a fast-setting polymer, and I can see that those sparks are some sort of burning metal flakes, but I've gotta ask, just what *is* that metal? Magnesium? Actinium?"

"You'll never know, bug," the Goblin said, as he flipped the glider sideways for a moment and landed a solid blow of his fist on Spider-Man's shoulder.

He had thought that would be enough to loosen the wall-crawler's hold on his web-line and send him crashing to the concrete floor, but he was wrong; Spider-Man didn't so much as wince. Instead he kicked back, connecting with the Goblin's belly.

The impact sent the two fighters reeling away in opposite directions, Spider-Man spinning on his web-line, the Goblin's glider veering wildly through space. Spider-Man fired another web to catch and steady himself, while the Goblin teetered, gradually using his weight to steady the glider.

He turned, spotted Spider-Man, and pulled a pumpkin-shaped gas grenade from his bag of tricks. He tried to calculate where it would be most effective, chose his spot, then pulled the pin and let fly.

Spider-Man intercepted it in midair with a hard wad of web, knocking it aside; it went off as it sailed harmlessly aside, trailing a streamer of thick white smoke.

"Gas again," Spider-Man said, and there was something different in his voice now, something cold and hard that the Goblin didn't recognize at first. Spider-Man let go of his web-line and dropped lightly to the top of a massive pump, then sprang from there to the floor and vanished between two steel vats.

A moment later he emerged with a Rat Pack gas mask in his hand. The Goblin wheeled about, preparing to swoop to the attack.

"You've been using gas a lot lately, Osborn," Spider-Man called as the Goblin approached. "You and your flunkies. You've used it against me, and the cops, and the mayor—and on my *wife*." He ducked as the Goblin's jet-glider roared overhead. "Except against *her*, it wasn't just tear gas. On a defenseless woman you used something stronger, didn't you?" He fired webbing at the glider, snagging a wingtip—and one of the Goblin's ankles. "You used some weird chloroform derivative. That had better be *all* you used, Osborn, or . . ."

The Goblin didn't hear the rest of the threat as Spider-Man yanked at his ankle, pulling it from the foot-strap; the sudden shift in weight sent the glider wheeling out of control. The Goblin struggled to regain his footing and right the machine, but before he could his right shoulder slammed into a pillar. The remaining foot-strap snapped; he tumbled off the machine, which, suddenly free of his weight, jetted crazily upward, looped back upside down, then nosed straight toward the floor.

At the last moment the gyros kicked in, and it started to complete the loop and level off—but then Spider-Man's webbing snagged it.

The jet had more than enough power to pull free or tear through that web ordinarily, but it needed the Goblin to guide it, to keep it pointed in the right direction—without its rider Spider-Man was able to swing it around, flying it in a circle around his head.

And he was reeling the web-line in, hand over hand, shrinking the size of the circle, pulling the glider in, closer and closer to his hand.

The Goblin, meanwhile, had landed rolling on the concrete factory floor and slammed into the base of a huge glass-and-steel tank. He turned and got to his feet just as Spider-Man brought the goblin glider within arm's reach and snatched it out of the sky.

The Goblin grinned broadly. Only *he* could ride that glider effectively—he had designed and built it, had practiced for hours learning to fly it. If Spider-Man tried he might well break his neck—which would be regrettable only in that it would mean Osborn could no longer torment his foe, and wouldn't have had the pleasure of snapping the wall-crawler's neck in his own two hands. He watched, expecting Spider-Man to climb onto the glider's wings.

Instead, Spider-Man took the glider firmly in both hands and snapped one steel wing across his knee.

The Goblin's jaw dropped. "You *broke* it!" he said.

Spider-Man didn't bother answering as he flung the ruined machine aside and started stalking toward the Goblin, fists clenched and head down.

The Goblin stared for a moment, then recovered his wits and reached into his bag of tricks.

"Oh, no, you don't," Spider-Man said. "It's just you and me, Osborn—no more of your tricks." Webbing spurted from his wrist.

The Goblin snatched the bag out of the path of the sticky stream with one hand, and pulled out a pumpkin bomb with the other. He took a look to see which variety he had grabbed, and, satisfied with his choice, he pushed the timer button and raised it to throw.

Just as he released it, a fresh shot of webbing caught it—not a hard, narrow strand, but a spreading, sticky mesh. It caught the bomb just as it left his hand, and smacked it back into his palm.

The Goblin's eyes widened in horror as he realized he had *three seconds* to get that thing away before it went off in his hand. It wouldn't kill him—these particular pumpkin bombs were low-yield explosives, meant more to frighten and stun than to kill—but it would probably seriously injure his hand, leaving him unable to fight effectively.

That it would be extremely painful did not trouble him; Norman Osborn was not bothered by such unimportant things as pain.

He snatched at it with his other hand, tearing at the webbing, and pulled pumpkin and mesh away at the last instant, flinging it aside just in time. It went off no more than three feet away, dazing him slightly.

And while he was dazed, Spider-Man's web snatched at the bag of tricks, pulling it from the Goblin's shoulder.

He bent his elbow and caught it, then grabbed the strap in his hand, clutching it tight. He grabbed at it with both hands, ripping it free of the webbing.

But while he did that, Spider-Man was closing the distance between them; as the webbing came free in the Goblin's left hand and the bag in his right, Spider-Man's fist hit the Goblin's jaw, hard.

The Goblin staggered slightly, and tried to fling away the webbing in his left hand—but it stuck, of course, tangling in his fingers. "Blast you," he said, as he struck an ineffective backhand blow at his foe.

Spider-Man ducked under it, and snatched at the bag of tricks with both hands. The Goblin tried to yank it away, but Spider-Man got one hand inside for a second.

Then the Goblin pulled it free, triumphant—until he heard the faint hiss from somewhere inside the bag. He stared at it, horrified.

Spider-Man had triggered one of the bombs—the Goblin couldn't tell which, or what kind—and had then sprayed a mass of frothy, tangled webbing into the bag, so that the Goblin couldn't possibly get anything out in time.

"*Blast* you!" the Goblin bellowed, flinging the bag aside. It sailed over a row of machines and vanished into the depths of the factory.

"I told you, no more tricks," Spider-Man said, as he crouched a few feet away.

Then the bag exploded, the initial bomb setting off others—a bang leading to a rolling thunderclap. The entire building shook. The multicolored flashes were blinding, leaving spots swimming in the Goblin's vision.

Debris rained down over both men, and a crackle of sparks mixed with the echoes of the blasts.

"You want it just the two of us?" the Goblin shouted. "Then that's what you'll get, Parker! Just the two of us, until only one is left standing!" He charged forward.

Spider-Man met him head-on, hands locked together for a combined blow.

The two fought furiously, trading punches that would have killed ordinary men, there in the concrete-floored aisle of the deserted factory. Both moved with superhuman speed, dodging and weaving, looking for any opening in the other's defenses, any momentary advantage.

Finally, after a few minutes that seemed like hours, the Goblin landed a blow to the head that staggered Spider-Man, and followed it up with a kidney punch. The red-and-blue-garbed adventurer folded double and staggered back.

"You can't beat me, Parker!" the Goblin gloated. "You never could, and you never will." He landed another blow, then stepped back to watch his foe crumple.

"Yes, I will," Spider-Man said through gritted teeth. He didn't crumple; instead he straightened up, and swung at the Goblin's jaw, catching him off guard.

As the fight continued, the gas mask was knocked from Spider-Man's face, but neither man cared—the gas grenades had all gone up with the bag of tricks.

Again, the Goblin landed what he thought was a decisive blow, knocking his enemy back against a vat. "Give it up, Spider-Man!" he said.

"Never," Spider-Man said through bruised, swollen lips, as he counterattacked more furiously than ever.

And yet a third time, the Goblin smashed Spider-Man off his feet—but by this time he was sufficiently battered and shaken himself that there was no braggadoccio left. "Stay down, you fool!" he growled.

"No," Spider-Man growled in reply, launching himself back into the fray.

The Goblin staggered back under this renewed assault, too busy defending himself, and too tired, to counterattack effectively.

He had fought Spider-Man at least a dozen times over the years, and knew he was a tenacious opponent, but he had never before seen him this determined. He wished he could see the man's eyes behind those white plastic eyepieces, to read just what he was facing—was this determination born of rage or despair? Was Spider-Man on the verge of surrender, or in a berserk fury?

But then he asked himself whether it really mattered. The point was to show this insolent little punk who was the master here, to show him that Norman Osborn, the Green Goblin, was the better man, the rightful lord of all he surveyed, whom all lesser men must fear.

And if Spider-Man would not fear him, then Spider-Man must die. He would have preferred to see Spider-Man on his knees, begging for mercy—which he would have denied, of course; only the weak ever showed mercy—but if he had to kill the blasted wall-crawler to end this, he would.

If he had finally pushed Spider-Man too far, so that he could only win this by killing him, it wasn't what he wanted, but if it was his only chance, he would take it.

He fought harder, trying to break through Spider-Man's defenses—and found he couldn't. The more he beat on the man, the more fiercely Spider-Man responded. Gradually, the Goblin realized that he had driven Spider-Man to a level of unchained ferocity he had never imagined the web-slinger could achieve—and a level he, the Green Goblin, couldn't match.

It began to sink in that he wasn't going to win this fight. He had pounded on Spider-Man until every movement must be agony, until there couldn't be an unbruised inch of skin on his body, but the web-slinger was *still coming,* madder than ever, stronger than ever.

The Goblin knew now that he couldn't win—but, he reminded himself, that didn't mean he would lose. He could still escape, to fight again another day, when the adrenaline that kept the wall-crawler going had faded away, when that absurd wife of his had recovered and his anger was spent.

The Goblin's glider was gone, broken and useless, and most of the factory doors were chained shut; if he fled through the doors that weren't, or out through the windows, Spider-Man would just follow him, and he wouldn't be able to get enough of a lead to do him any good.

He glanced up, and saw the shattered remains of the one-way mirror high above the factory floor. If he could get up there somehow, he had a hidden doorway leading from one of the offices into a secret passageway—he had used that so no one would see him coming and going, so no one would connect the Rat Pack's "Mr. Green" with respectable businessman and public official Norman Osborn. And there were weapons stashed away up there.

And the mayor . . .

The Goblin didn't know where Number One, Thirty-seven, and the mayor were, but they were probably up there somewhere, and might be enough of a distraction to keep Spider-Man from following him through the hidden door.

If he could get through that door, and give One and Thirty-seven the order to kill the mayor—well, it wouldn't stop Spider-Man, that part of his plan was ruined, but once he got home and took off his mask, becoming Norman Osborn again, he would be acting mayor of New York. That would pull *something* out of the ashes, at least.

But how could he get up there?

If he could somehow get up to the framework of steel girders supporting the roof, he could cross to just above the broken window and simply *jump* from there. That would put him where he wanted to go.

And getting up to the girders wouldn't be so very difficult—his foe had provided the means. There were abandoned web-lines, not yet dissolving, dangling a dozen places.

He took one more swing at his enemy, then broke away, turned, and ran.

It took the slightly dazed Spider-Man a second or two to realize what had happened, so the Goblin got a healthy head start. He had leaped atop a workbench and was climbing up a tangle of pipes before Spider-Man started after him.

Spider-Man was fast, though—the Goblin sometimes forgot just *how* fast. By the time he clambered atop the highest pipe Spider-Man was directly below him, reaching for his heels—but a strand of web dangled just a few feet away.

· He gathered himself and jumped, grabbing for the web-line. He caught it, and began scrambling upward.

Spider-Man didn't say anything; he simply raised one hand and fired a new web-line of his own, then began climbing.

Spider-Man was the more experienced at this sort of thing, but he was also on the verge of exhaustion; he closed the distance, but only slowly.

And then both men vaulted up onto the girder, fifty feet above the concrete floor. The Goblin began running toward that enticing broken window—and webbing wrapped around his legs, sending him sprawling. He caught himself easily before he could tumble off the beam and fall, but before he could tear free of the webbing or get to his feet, Spider-Man was on him.

The Goblin fought back, but in vain; his struggles grew gradually weaker. Up here, with no glider and no bag of tricks to help him, he had no room to maneuver, and was constantly aware that a wrong move could send him plummeting; Spider-Man, on the other hand, was at home in this environment. He was able to cling to any surface, able to catch himself with his webbing if he *did* fall—this place held no terrors for him. It wasn't even seriously inconvenient.

The last thing the Goblin saw clearly was that hated webbed, white-eyed red mask, hovering over him as blow after blow rained down on him.

And finally Spider-Man picked up the Green Goblin by the throat with one hand, the other hand drawn back in a fist. The Goblin was no longer resisting; he was still twitching feebly, but no longer putting up any sort of fight.

"Up there!" someone shouted.

Spider-Man stopped, and an instant later he was unsure what he had been about to do, whether he had intended to beat Osborn senseless or even kill him. He had been operating on automatic, running on fury and adrenalin, without any conscious thought, for some time.

Now, though, the unexpected voice from below cut through the fog and brought him back to reality. Still holding the Goblin, he peered down at the factory floor.

Two men in Rat Pack uniforms were down there, near a door at one end of the vast room, one wearing a mask, one not; the unmasked man was handsome and brown-haired, the masked man huge and heavily muscled. Between them a third man sat tied to a chair, gagged and blindfolded.

The mayor.

He was tied to a chair, bound and gagged and sweating, just as Spider-Man had imagined him, and for a moment Spider-Man, battered as he was, was unsure whether this was real or a sort of flashback.

"Yo, Spider-Man!" the unmasked man called out. "Put him down!"

That really was the mayor, Spider-Man realized, and both Rat Packers were pointing pistols at his head, one on either side, at point-blank range.

It occurred to him, despite his muzzy confusion—or perhaps because of it—that if they both fired, the bullets would go right through the mayor's head and they'd hit each other, as well. For a fraction of a second he thought this might even be a good idea, since it would eliminate both of them and leave him free to finish off the Green Goblin, but then he came to his senses—the mayor would be *dead* if that happened, and he would be responsible.

And if he let Norman Osborn live, Osborn would then be mayor—and he couldn't bring himself to kill even the Goblin in cold blood.

Reluctantly, he lowered the Goblin onto the steel beam, settling him against a strut so he wouldn't fall.

"Now, get lost, Spider-Man, or we blow Hizzoner's brains out!" the unmasked man called.

Spider-Man stared down at them.

They were out of web range, and even if he had been

closer, they would have time to pull the triggers before he could snatch the guns away with webs.

He could leave, of course—he had beaten the Goblin and thrashed almost the entire Rat Pack—but then the mayor might still die, Osborn might still become mayor.

He hadn't come this far to allow *that*.

He glanced at the fluid cartridges on his web shooters—they were low, and he had no more spares, but neither was quite empty. He looked down at the tableau again—Rat Pack, mayor, Rat Pack, two guns aimed.

Then he stepped off the girder, and fired a web-line to catch himself. He didn't try to swing toward the kidnappers; instead he simply lowered himself to the factory floor, dropping the last few feet.

He had carefully placed himself in a long, broad aisle that ran down the center of the factory, unimpeded by vats, machinery, plumbing, or pillars. At the farther end were the three men, the mayor and the two Rats.

He straightened up and stared at them.

They stared back.

"Go on, Spider-Man, get out of here!" the unmasked one called.

Spider-Man didn't reply; instead he began walking.

Directly toward them.

He didn't run, didn't hurry at all; he strode forward slowly, one measured step after another. He made no threatening gestures, said not a word—but he advanced relentlessly toward him.

"Stay back, you freak!" the masked one shouted suddenly. "I swear I'll shoot!"

"Don't shoot!" the unmasked one said, quietly and urgently, apparently thinking, incorrectly, that Spider-Man couldn't hear him. "Are you crazy? He can't touch us as long as we have the mayor, but if you shoot our hostage he'll kill us!"

Spider-Man continued his implacable march, step by slow step.

"But what good is a hostage if we *don't* shoot him? C'mon, One . . ."

"Shut up! Shut up!"

They were within web range now—though Spider-Man doubted *they* knew that. He kept his hands at his sides, but tucked his middle fingers up onto the web-shooter firing studs.

"Stop *right there,* Spider-Man, or I swear I'll shoot!" Number One called.

"No, you won't," Spider-Man said coldly, without breaking stride.

"Blast it, One, if I can't shoot the mayor, I can still shoot *him!*" The masked one turned his gun from the mayor's head toward Spider-Man.

The other one threw his companion a panicky glance, then turned his own weapon, as well.

The masked one got off one shot that tore through the air so close to his ear that Spider-Man thought he could hear it; then the bullet spanged off machinery somewhere behind him—Spider-Man had waited this long to be sure both guns were turned away from the mayor.

But now they *were* both turned toward him, instead of the mayor, and his hands flashed up, fingers pressing the buttons. Webbing flashed out and wrapped itself around the two guns and the hands that held them.

Then Spidey did a forward handspring and landed directly in front of the mayor. "Thanks," he said to Thirty-seven. "If you hadn't turned the gun when you did, I don't know what I'd have done."

Then his fists lashed out, and both Rat Packers fell.

He webbed them quickly, tore away the mayor's gag and blindfold, then bounded away to collect the Goblin.

At first he thought he might have landed on the wrong girder, but then he saw that the dust had mostly been wiped away by the fight; this was, indeed, where he had left the Green Goblin.

He was gone.

Spider-Man couldn't see how—even while he was busy with the mayor and the Rats, he thought he would have noticed the Goblin climbing down a web-line or dashing across the floor toward one of the unchained doors. There were no open windows except the one Spidey himself had smashed through on the way in, and that was nowhere near the girder where he had left the Goblin.

All the same, the Goblin was gone. There were pointy-toed footprints on the girder, leading toward one end, but Spider-Man couldn't see any way down from there.

Still, he somehow couldn't really manage to be surprised by the Goblin's escape. He dropped back to the floor and hurried to the mayor, to make sure that at least that portion of Osborn's plan was finished once and for all.

He snapped the ropes that held the mayor, and Hizzoner immediately reached into his jacket. Spider-Man stepped back, startled—he had expected a thank you, or a comment of some sort, not to see the mayor pulling a gun. Did Hizzoner think that Spider-Man was a criminal? Had he read too many of Jonah's editorials?

But it wasn't a gun; instead the mayor pulled out a cell phone.

"Thanks, Spider-Man," he said as he dialed. "Nice piece of work, there."

Ten minutes later, when the cops broke in, Spider-Man launched himself back out through the same window he had smashed to get in. His job here was done.

And Mary Jane was waiting for him at the hospital. She might even be awake by now.

"Take it easy, Tiger," Mary Jane said, as her wheelchair bumped over a crack in the sidewalk. "I know you're in a hurry to get me home, but take your time. I'll make it worth the wait."

"Sorry, MJ," Peter said, pushing the chair a little more carefully as they came alongside the cab he had waiting at the curb.

"Don't be," she said, smiling up at him. "From what I saw on the news while you were filling out my release papers, you done good, kid."

"Not *that* good," he said.

"You . . . I mean, Spider-Man cleaned up the Rat Pack," she said, as she got to her feet, leaning heavily on Peter's shoulder. "Whoo, I'm still a bit dizzy after being horizontal so long."

"Yeah," Peter agreed. "The Rat Pack's pretty much finished, I guess."

"And they said that Osborn Industries owns that old factory, right? So Norman's got egg on his face."

"Not enough," Peter said, as he steadied her while she settled into the cab. He closed the door and went around to the other side.

"I thought I'd nailed him," he said as he climbed in. "I thought I really had him this time, even after he got away; I thought there'd be some kind of solid trail, proving he was the Rat Pack's Mr. Green."

"There wasn't?"

Peter shook his head. He leaned forward and gave the cabby the address, then sat back and said, "He had it covered. Everything led back to some corporate vice president named Lewiston; Osborn's getting off clean."

"They said on the news that he'd resigned as public advocate, though."

"Well, yeah, there's that," Peter conceded. "I mean, even if *he* wasn't officially involved, one of his companies was, and that's enough of a scandal that he couldn't very well stay in office."

"So he's out of the line of succession."

"And the mayor's safe for the moment," Peter agreed.

"The whole *city* is safe for the moment," Mary Jane said. Then she giggled. "But we'll never have Paris."

Peter smiled back. "Here's looking at *you,* kid," he replied. "No, we'll never have Paris, but we've got each other. I like that better."

The cab pulled out into traffic. The two of them were silent for a moment, Mary Jane enjoying the sight of something other than hospital walls, while Peter was lost in his own thoughts.

"I'm sorry I didn't stay with you," Peter said at last, serious again. "I *wanted* to . . ."

Mary Jane turned and stared at him for a second, then burst out laughing. "Why?" she asked.

"To protect you!" he said. "You were out cold, you didn't know what was going on . . ."

She put a finger on his lips to shush him.

"Peter," she said, "I only had seventy-five cops guarding me, while you went after the *cause* of the problem. I think I can handle that sort of desertion."

"Well . . . but I didn't *get* the real cause," he said. "He's still out there."

"So? That doesn't matter. I'm safe from him for now, you're safe, the whole *city* is safe, and he knows you beat him again."

Peter considered that, then acknowledged, "You're right. Of course, you're right." He leaned over and kissed her.

She responded enthusiastically. "I *did* miss you, Tiger," she said.

He winced at first—he was still bruised, his lips still

swollen, from the fight with the Goblin. Then he forgot that at the touch of Mary Jane's mouth.

He had taken a beating, all right, but Osborn had taken worse.

Norman Osborn had said earlier that Spider-Man couldn't touch him, but even if Osborn had escaped, he hadn't escaped unscathed.

Spider-Man had shown Osborn—and himself—that he could, indeed, touch Osborn. And wherever he was now, Osborn knew it—and would know it forever. That would give him pause before he tried something new.

Oh, it might not stop him—probably wouldn't, in fact. But it would make him think, and for a while, at least, the city would be safe.

And right here, right now, that was enough.

In the back of the cab Peter put his arms around his wife and kissed her again.

KURT BUSIEK has been writing comic books professionally since 1982, for such series as *Power Man and Iron Fist, Red Tornado, Avengers, Thunderbolts,* and even *The Adventures of Jell-O Man.* In recent years, Kurt has won rave reviews and industry awards for his work on such projects as *Marvels, Untold Tales of Spider-Man,* and his own *Kurt Busiek's Astro City,* which has won multiple Harvey and Eisner Awards since its inception, including Best Writer and Best Series. With Stan Lee, he co-edited the *Untold Tales of Spider-Man* prose anthology.

Kurt lives in Washington State with his wife, Ann, his new daughter, Sydney, and their faithful corgi, Hector.

NATHAN ARCHER was born and raised in New York City, and discovered comic books as a boy. After college he worked for a branch of the government he declines to specify, though he will say his job wasn't anything exciting. Budget cuts left him unemployed in 1992, and he decided to try his hand at writing.

So far he's been lucky. He's the author of *Star Trek: Deep Space Nine #10: Valhalla, Star Trek: Voyager #3: Ragnarok, Mars Attacks: Martian Deathtrap, Predator: Concrete Jungle,* and *Predator: Cold War.* He hopes to someday soon sell a novel that doesn't have a colon in the title. He also reports that collaborating has turned out to be fun and he may do it again someday.

Archer has no children, pets, or permanent address—now that he's not tied down by a job he prefers to travel, lap-top in hand, rather than stay in one place. Other details are still classified.

CHRONOLOGY TO THE MARVEL NOVELS AND ANTHOLOGIES

What follows is a guide to the order in which the Marvel novels and short stories published by BP Books, Inc., and Berkley Boulevard Books take place in relation to each other. Please note that this is not a hard and fast chronology, but a guideline that is subject to change at authorial or editorial whim. This list covers all the novels and anthologies published from October 1994–October 2000.

The short stories are each given an abbreviation to indicate which anthology the story appeared in. USM=*The Ultimate Spider-Man*, USS=*The Ultimate Silver Surfer*, USV=*The Ultimate Super-Villains*, UXM=*The Ultimate X-Men*, UTS=*Untold Tales of Spider-Man*, UH=*The Ultimate Hulk*, and XML=*X-Men Legends*.

X-Men & Spider-Man: Time's Arrow Book 1: **The Past [portions]**
by Tom DeFalco & Jason Henderson
   Parts of this novel take place in prehistoric times, the sixth century, 1867, and 1944.

"The Silver Surfer" [flashback]
by Tom DeFalco & Stan Lee [USS]

The Silver Surfer's origin. The early parts of this flashback start several decades, possibly several centuries, ago, and continue to a point just prior to "To See Heaven in a Wild Flower."

"In the Line of Banner"
by Danny Fingeroth [UH]
This takes place over the course of several years, ending approximately nine months before the birth of Robert Bruce Banner.

X-Men: Codename Wolverine ["then" portions]
by Christopher Golden

"Every Time a Bell Rings"
by Brian K. Vaughan [XML]
These take place while Team X was still in operation, while the Black Widow was still a Russian spy, while Banshee was still with Interpol, and a couple of years before the X-Men were formed.

"Spider-Man"
by Stan Lee & Peter David [USM]
A retelling of Spider-Man's origin.

"Transformations"
by Will Murray [UH]
"Side by Side with the Astonishing Ant-Man!"
by Will Murray [UTS]
"Assault on Avengers Mansion"
by Richard C. White & Steven A. Roman [UH]
"Suits"
by Tom De Haven & Dean Wesley Smith [USM]
"After the First Death . . ."
by Tom DeFalco [UTS]
"Celebrity"
by Christopher Golden & José R. Nieto [UTS]

CHRONOLOGY

"Pitfall"
by Pierce Askegren [UH]
"Better Looting Through Modern Chemistry"
by John Garcia & Pierce Askegren [UTS]
  These stories take place very early in the careers of Spider-Man and the Hulk.

"To the Victor"
by Richard Lee Byers [USV]
  Most of this story takes place in an alternate timeline, but the jumping-off point is here.

"To See Heaven in a Wild Flower"
by Ann Tonsor Zeddies [USS]
"Point of View"
by Len Wein [USS]
  These stories take place shortly after the end of the flashback portion of "The Silver Surfer."

"Identity Crisis"
by Michael Jan Friedman [UTS]
"The Doctor's Dilemma"
by Danny Fingeroth [UTS]
"Moving Day"
by John S. Drew [UTS]
"Out of the Darkness"
by Glenn Greenberg [UH]
"The Liar"
by Ann Nocenti [UTS]
"Diary of a False Man"
by Keith R.A. DeCandido [XML]
"Deadly Force"
by Richard Lee Byers [UTS]
"Truck Stop"
by Jo Duffy [UH]
"Hiding"
by Nancy Holder & Christopher Golden [UH]

"Improper Procedure"
by Keith R.A. DeCandido [USS]
"The Ballad of Fancy Dan"
by Ken Grobe & Steven A. Roman [UTS]
"Welcome to the X-Men, Madrox..."
by Steve Lyons [XML]

These stories take place early in the careers of Spider-Man, the Silver Surfer, the Hulk, and the X-Men, after their origins and before the formation of the "new" X-Men.

"Here There Be Dragons"
by Sholly Fisch [UH]
"Peace Offering"
by Michael Stewart [XML]
"The Worst Prison of All"
by C.J. Henderson [XML]
"Poison in the Soul"
by Glenn Greenberg [UTS]
"Do You Dream in Silver?"
by James Dawson [USS]
"A Quiet, Normal Life"
by Thomas Deja [UH]
"Chasing Hairy"
by Glenn Hauman [XML]
"Livewires"
by Steve Lyons [UTS]
"Arms and the Man"
by Keith R.A. DeCandido [UTS]
"Incident on a Skyscraper"
by Dave Smeds [USS]
"One Night Only"
by Sholly Fisch [XML]
"A Green Snake in Paradise"
by Steve Lyons [UH]

These all take place after the formation of the "new" X-Men and before Spider-Man got married, the Silver Surfer ended his exile on Earth, and the reemergence of the gray Hulk.

"Cool"
by Lawrence Watt-Evans [USM]
"Blindspot"
by Ann Nocenti [USM]
"Tinker, Tailor, Soldier, Courier"
by Robert L. Washington III [USM]
"Thunder on the Mountain"
by Richard Lee Byers [USM]
"The Stalking of John Doe"
by Adam-Troy Castro [UTS]
"On the Beach"
by John J. Ordover [USS]
   These all take place just prior to Peter Parker's marriage to Mary Jane Watson and the Silver Surfer's release from imprisonment on Earth.

Daredevil: Predator's Smile
by Christopher Golden
"Disturb Not Her Dream"
by Steve Rasnic Tem [USS]
"My Enemy, My Savior"
by Eric Fein [UTS]
"Kraven the Hunter Is Dead, Alas"
by Craig Shaw Gardner [USM]
"The Broken Land"
by Pierce Askegren [USS]
"Radically Both"
by Christopher Golden [USM]
"Godhood's End"
by Sharman DiVono [USS]
"Scoop!"
by David Michelinie [USM]
"The Beast with Nine Bands"
by James A. Wolf [UH]

"Sambatyon"
by David M. Honigsberg [USS]
"A Fine Line"
by Dan Koogler [XML]
"Cold Blood"
by Greg Cox [USM]
"The Tarnished Soul"
by Katherine Lawrence [USS]
"Leveling Las Vegas"
by Stan Timmons [UH]
"Steel Dogs and Englishmen"
by Thomas Deja [XML]
"If Wishes Were Horses"
by Tony Isabella & Bob Ingersoll [USV]
"The Stranger Inside"
by Jennifer Heddle [XML]
"The Silver Surfer" [framing sequence]
by Tom DeFalco & Stan Lee [USS]
"The Samson Journals"
by Ken Grobe [UH]

These all take place after Peter Parker's marriage to Mary Jane Watson, after the Silver Surfer attained freedom from imprisonment on Earth, before the Hulk's personalities were merged, and before the formation of the X-Men "blue" and "gold" teams.

"The Deviant Ones"
by Glenn Greenberg [USV]
"An Evening in the Bronx with Venom"
by John Gregory Betancourt & Keith R.A. DeCandido [USM]

These two stories take place one after the other, and a few months prior to The Venom Factor.

The Incredible Hulk: What Savage Beast
by Peter David

CHRONOLOGY

This novel takes place over a one-year period, starting here and ending just prior to Rampage.

"Once a Thief"
by Ashley McConnell [XML]
"On the Air"
by Glenn Hauman [UXM]
"Connect the Dots"
by Adam-Troy Castro [USV]
"Ice Prince"
by K.A. Kindya [XML]
"Summer Breeze"
by Jenn Saint-John & Tammy Lynne Dunn [UXM]
"Out of Place"
by Dave Smeds [UXM]
   These stories all take place prior to the Mutant Empire *trilogy.*

X-Men: Mutant Empire Book 1: **Siege**
by Christopher Golden
X-Men: Mutant Empire Book 2: **Sanctuary**
by Christopher Golden
X-Men: Mutant Empire Book 3: **Salvation**
by Christopher Golden
   These three novels take place within a three-day period.

Fantastic Four: To Free Atlantis
by Nancy A. Collins
"The Love of Death or the Death of Love"
by Craig Shaw Gardner [USS]
"Firetrap"
by Michael Jan Friedman [USV]
"What's Yer Poison?"
by Christopher Golden & José R. Nieto [USS]

"Sins of the Flesh"
by Steve Lyons [USV]
"Doom²"
by Joey Cavalieri [USV]
"Child's Play"
by Robert L. Washington III [USV]
"A Game of the Apocalypse"
by Dan Persons [USS]
"All Creatures Great and Skrull"
by Greg Cox [USV]
"Ripples"
by José R. Nieto [USV]
"Who Do You Want Me to Be?"
by Ann Nocenti [USV]
"One for the Road"
by James Dawson [USV]

These are more or less simultaneous, with "Doom²" taking place after To Free Atlantis, *"Child's Play" taking place shortly after "What's Yer Poison?" and "A Game of the Apocalypse" taking place shortly after "The Love of Death or the Death of Love."*

"Five Minutes"
by Peter David [USM]

This takes place on Peter Parker and Mary Jane Watson-Parker's first anniversary.

Spider-Man: The Venom Factor
by Diane Duane
Spider-Man: The Lizard Sanction
by Diane Duane
Spider-Man: The Octopus Agenda
by Diane Duane

These three novels take place within a six-week period.

CHRONOLOGY

"The Night I Almost Saved Silver Sable"
by Tom DeFalco [USV]
"Traps"
by Ken Grobe [USV]
These stories take place one right after the other.

Iron Man: The Armor Trap
by Greg Cox
Iron Man: Operation A.I.M.
by Greg Cox
"Private Exhibition"
by Pierce Askegren [USV]
Fantastic Four: Redemption of the Silver Surfer
by Michael Jan Friedman
Spider-Man & The Incredible Hulk: Rampage (Doom's Day Book 1)
by Danny Fingeroth & Eric Fein
Spider-Man & Iron Man: Sabotage (Doom's Day Book 2)
by Pierce Askegren & Danny Fingeroth
Spider-Man & Fantastic Four: Wreckage (Doom's Day Book 3)
by Eric Fein & Pierce Askegren
   Operation A.I.M. *takes place about two weeks after* The Armor Trap. *The "Doom's Day" trilogy takes place within a three-month period. The events of* Operation A.I.M., *"Private Exhibition,"* Redemption of the Silver Surfer, *and* Rampage *happen more or less simultaneously.* Wreckage *is only a few months after* The Octopus Agenda.

"Such Stuff as Dreams Are Made Of"
by Robin Wayne Bailey [XML]
"It's a Wonderful Life"
by eluki bes shahar [UXM]
"Gift of the Silver Fox"
by Ashley McConnell [UXM]

"Stillborn in the Mist"
by Dean Wesley Smith [UXM]
"Order from Chaos"
by Evan Skolnick [UXM]
These stories take place more or less simultaneously, with "Such Stuff as Dreams Are Made Of" taking place just prior to the others.

"X-Presso"
by Ken Grobe [UXM]
"Life Is But a Dream"
by Stan Timmons [UXM]
"Four Angry Mutants"
by Andy Lane & Rebecca Levene [UXM]
"Hostages"
by J. Steven York [UXM]
These stories take place one right after the other.

Spider-Man: Carnage in New York
by David Michelinie & Dean Wesley Smith
Spider-Man: Goblin's Revenge
by Dean Wesley Smith
These novels take place one right after the other.

X-Men: Smoke and Mirrors
by eluki bes shahar
This novel takes place three-and-a-half months after "It's a Wonderful Life."

Generation X
by Scott Lobdell & Elliot S! Maggin
X-Men: The Jewels of Cyttorak
by Dean Wesley Smith
X-Men: Empire's End
by Diane Duane
X-Men: Law of the Jungle
by Dave Smeds

X-Men: Prisoner X
by Ann Nocenti
These novels take place one right after the other.

The Incredible Hulk: Abominations
by Jason Henderson
Fantastic Four: Countdown to Chaos
by Pierce Askegren
"Playing It SAFE"
by Keith R.A. DeCandido [UH]
These take place one right after the other, with Abominations *taking place a couple of weeks after* Wreckage.

"Mayhem Party"
by Robert Sheckley [USV]
This story takes place after Goblin's Revenge.

X-Men & Spider-Man: Time's Arrow Book 1:
The Past
by Tom DeFalco & Jason Henderson
X-Men & Spider-Man: Time's Arrow Book 2:
The Present
by Tom DeFalco & Adam-Troy Castro
X-Men & Spider-Man: Time's Arrow Book 3:
The Future
by Tom DeFalco & eluki bes shahar
These novels take place within a twenty-four-hour period in the present, though it also involves traveling to four points in the past, to an alternate present, and to five different alternate futures.

X-Men: Soul Killer
by Richard Lee Byers
Spider-Man: Valley of the Lizard
by John Vornholt

Spider-Man: Venom's Wrath
by Keith R.A. DeCandido & José R. Nieto
Captain America: Liberty's Torch
by Tony Isabella & Bob Ingersoll
Daredevil: The Cutting Edge
by Madeleine E. Robins
Spider-Man: Wanted: Dead or Alive
by Craig Shaw Gardner
Spider-Man: Emerald Mystery
by Dean Wesley Smith
"Sidekick"
by Dennis Brabham [UH]
   These take place one after the other, with Soul Killer
taking place right after the Time's Arrow *trilogy,* Venom's
Wrath *taking place a month after* Valley of the Lizard, *and*
Wanted Dead or Alive *a couple of months after* Venom's
Wrath.

Spider-Man: The Gathering of the Sinister Six
by Adam-Troy Castro
Generation X: Crossroads
by J. Steven York
X-Men: Codename Wolverine ["now" portions]
by Christopher Golden
   *These novels take place one right after the other, with
the "now" portions of* Codename Wolverine *taking place
less than a week after* Crossroads.

The Avengers & the Thunderbolts
by Pierce Askegren
Spider-Man: Goblin Moon
by Kurt Busiek & Nathan Archer
Nick Fury, Agent of S.H.I.E.L.D.: Empyre
by Will Murray
Generation X: Genogoths
by J. Steven York

CHRONOLOGY

These novels take place at approximately the same time and several months after "Playing It SAFE."

Spider-Man & the Silver Surfer: Skrull War
by Steven A. Roman & Ken Grobe
X-Men & the Avengers: Gamma Quest Book 1: **Lost and Found**
by Greg Cox
X-Men & the Avengers: Gamma Quest Book 2: **Search and Rescue**
by Greg Cox
X-Men & the Avengers: Gamma Quest Book 3: **Friend or Foe?**
by Greg Cox
These books take place one right after the other.

X-Men & Spider-Man: Time's Arrow Book 3:
The Future [portions]
by Tom DeFalco & eluki bes shahar
Parts of this novel take place in five different alternate futures in 2020, 2035, 2099, 3000, and the fortieth century.

"The Last Titan"
by Peter David [UH]
This takes place in a possible future.

MARVEL® Comics X-MEN®

star in their own original series!

BP Books, Inc.

☐ **X-MEN: MUTANT EMPIRE: BOOK 1: SIEGE**
   by Christopher Golden   0-425-17275-9/$6.99
When Magneto takes over a top-secret government installation containing mutant-hunting robots, the X-Men must battle against their oldest foe. But the X-Men are held responsible for the takeover by a more ruthless enemy...the U.S. government.

☐ **X-MEN: MUTANT EMPIRE: BOOK 2: SANCTUARY**
   by Christopher Golden   1-57297-180-0/$5.99
Magneto has occupied The Big Apple, and the X-Men must penetrate the enslaved city and stop him before he advances his mad plan to conquer the entire world!

☐ **X-MEN: MUTANT EMPIRE: BOOK 3: SALVATION**
   by Christopher Golden   0-425-16640-6/$6.99
Magneto's Mutant Empire has already taken Manhattan, and now he's setting his sights on the rest of the world. The only thing that stands between Magneto and his conquest is the X-Men.

®, ™ and © 2000 Marvel Characters, Inc. All Rights Reserved.

Prices slightly higher in Canada

Payable by Visa, MC or AMEX only ($10.00 min.), No cash, checks or COD. Shipping & handling:
US/Can. $2.75 for one book, $1.00 for each add'l book; Int'l $5.00 for one book, $1.00 for each
add'l. Call (800) 783-6262 or (201) 933-9292, fax (201) 896-8569 or mail your orders to:

Penguin Putnam Inc.   Bill my: ☐ Visa ☐ MasterCard ☐ Amex _____ (expires)
P.O. Box 12289, Dept. B   Card# _____
Newark, NJ 07101-5289   Signature _____
Please allow 4-6 weeks for delivery.
Foreign and Canadian delivery 6-8 weeks.

Bill to:
Name _____
Address _____ City _____
State/ZIP _____ Daytime Phone # _____

Ship to:
Name _____ Book Total $ _____
Address _____ Applicable Sales Tax $ _____
City _____ Postage & Handling $ _____
State/ZIP _____ Total Amount Due $ _____

This offer subject to change without notice.   Ad # 722 (3/00)